I've travelled the world twice over,
Met the famous: saints and sinners,
Poets and artists, kings and queens,
Old stars and hopeful beginners,
I've been where no-one's been before,
Learned secrets from writers and cooks
All with one library ticket
To the wonderful world of books.

© JANICE JAMES.

MASK OF TREASON

Lovely, independent Fiona Grant, a costume designer in the London opera world, returns for a holiday to her parents' home in the Scottish Highlands. On the way she meets imperturbable Max Wyndham, a naval officer on an investigative mission regarding leaks of military information from a naval base near Fiona's home. At some point everyone is a likely suspect—Fiona, her parents, even a star of the opera. Roles are constantly changing in a diverting way, until the final chapters bring a deadly game to a satisfying halt.

ANNE STEVENSON

MASK
OF TREASON

Complete and Unabridged

ULVERSCROFT
Leicester

First published in Great Britain in 1981 by
Judy Piatkus (Publishers) Limited
Loughton, Essex

First Large Print Edition
published November 1982
by arrangement with
Judy Piatkus (Publishers) Limited
Loughton, Essex
and
G. P. Putnam's Sons, New York

British Library CIP Data

Stevenson, Anne
    Mask of treason.—Large print ed.
(Ulverscroft large print series: romance)
I. Title
823'.914 [F]   PR6069.T449

ISBN 0-7089-0875-6

Published by
F. A. Thorpe (Publishing) Ltd.
Anstey, Leicestershire

Printed and Bound in Great Britain by
T. J. Press (Padstow) Ltd., Padstow, Cornwall

Love is
a time of enchantment:
in it all days are fair and all fields
green. Youth is blest by it,
old age made benign: the eyes of love see
roses blooming in December,
and sunshine through rain. Verily
is the time of true-love
a time of enchantment—and
Oh! how eager is woman
to be bewitched!

1

THE car had stopped. First it had driven past as far as the bridge. There was a house by the bridge. They had gone into it. And now returned. Had someone seen her as she crossed the stream further down? The house had seemed deserted, half hidden in its clump of trees. But she had avoided it anyway. She had learned some sense in the past few days.

The car had driven back and now it had stopped.

Four men got out. From that distance they looked like toy soldiers. Action men with rifles at the ready. No uniforms, though. They hadn't got around to uniforms. Not yet. One of the men raised binoculars to his eyes and began a sweep of the countryside. She dropped back behind the outcrop of rock that sheltered her and let her head rest on her arms. In spite of that blazing summer, the ground beneath her was damp. It was all bog, that moorland, strewn with rocks, lumpy and tussocky with sudden treacherous variations of the ground. She was lucky to have got this far without breaking an ankle. It had seemed to go on forever, mile after mile, with no sign of life, as desolate and lonely as the moon. She had thought she might find help when she reached the road. But they had thought of that too. Now she felt stupid and inept, as well as hot, miserable and frightened. Max had said she was no good at this and he was right. She swiped viciously at the midges, which as she rested, collected in a tormenting cloud about her. She wished she smoked; cigarette smoke might have kept them away. Though the flash of a lighter might have been the very thing an alert observer was watching for.

She risked another glance down at the car. The men were clustered together, looking at something spread out on the hood. A map, probably. The moment they moved away from her, she must move. And if they didn't move away? If they spread out and came up the hill toward her? She lay back and closed her eyes, trying to think, trying to make a plan. But at once the waltz tune was there again, swinging round and round in her tired brain, confusing, bewildering her. Ochs's waltz. Boris's waltz . . .

When it had come to her in that first desperate hour alone on the moor, it had been like a shot of alcohol in the blood, a joyous rush of sound to uplift the spirit, bring the courage back, to remind her that it was only days not weeks since she had left the theater with that music in her ears, that there was still time, if she could only get to a phone, get to a village. But she had not reached a village, had not found a phone, and now she wanted to be rid of that insistent driving sound, to be clearheaded, to be single-minded. She was going to have to be single-minded to survive, to ensure that any of them survived who had become caught up in this dangerous mess. And the *Rosenkavalier* waltz music was not, after all, suitable for funerals.

Five days before, in the chill of early morning, she had driven away from Inverness station, lighthearted and carefree, without a serious thought in her head. She had been away from home too long. She loved her life in London and the exotic, extraordinary world she moved in, full of crises and tensions, but as soon as she had stepped onto the train the evening before she had begun to relax in a way not possible at the theater. No more Fred, demanding, erratic, unpredictable. No more Boris descending on her for one of his little chats, kind, amusing, as equally demanding in his own way. One could have too much of overwhelming personalities, brilliant and talented as they might be. A little Scottish calm was what she needed, a few snatched days of pottering about in her father's boats, eating her mother's cooking, gazing at mountains and water instead of backcloths and materials, surrounded by silence instead of the creative hubbub of voices, music, hammering, knocking, shouts and laughter she had been absorbed in for so many months. Even the weather, the gray drizzle that greeted the passengers as they had descended pale and sleepy-eyed from the London train, could not depress her. It was almost a relief from a city struck by a summer heat wave and anyway she knew her native climate. It would probably clear by lunchtime.

As she turned out of the station yard, the fine mist of rain closed about her. It softened the edges of the buildings, blurred the sweep of the river as she crossed over the Ness and turned toward the west. She was conscious, as she drove, of the sea so near to her, the road edging the Firth so that at times the wall to her right was the seawall and the seaweed-strewn wastes of tidal estuary could be glimpsed, empty and mysterious, for brief moments through the veils of mist. To her left, beyond the trees standing motionless, tall, gleaming ghosts, beyond the farmlands and the settlements, she was aware of the old deer forests, patterned with small lochs and running streams that stretched west and north as far as the Western Islands and the northern edge of the land. London was another world away.

She wasn't yet used to her uncle's car and she took it steadily along a road whose twists and bends were not so familiar to her that she could afford to take chances. George had done her a good turn for once. If he hadn't asked her, once he knew she was coming north, to bring his Mercedes up to Scotland for him, Fred might yet have backtracked on his agreement to let her have a few days off before the Festival opening.

She had been working as Fred's assistant for almost three years. Newly graduated from college, she had thought herself lucky to be accepted by him with his international reputation for the brilliance and originality of his stage designs. She still thought so in spite of his often highly critical tongue and despairing rages. Once she realized the enjoyment he got out of his creative sufferings, she found little difficulty in dealing with him. He had tackled his latest commission to work on an entirely new production of Richard Strauss's *Rosenkavalier* with deepening gloom.

"It's going to look like a wedding cake," he had observed of his first-act set. "I knew I'd overdone it. I shall have to tell them to knock off a cherub or two.' The problem is how to get that wry Viennese melancholy into sets that, because of the necessity of informing the audience we are in eighteenth-century Austrian court circles, have an unfortunate tendency to look like the transformation scene in Cinderella." He sighed. "All those wigs. Still, the wigs and so on are your problem now."

For the first time in any important production, he had handed complete responsibility for the costumes to Fiona. She had appreciated the opportunity and had told him so. He had waved her thanks away. "What is the point of keeping a well-trained dog if you never let it bark? Anyway, if the costumes are successful, I shall let it be understood they

6

were basically my designs and I was kindly letting you take the credit, so don't expect much praise."

The directors of the opera company were throwing all its resources into this production. After the first night in London, the company was, a week later, to have the honor of opening the Edinburgh Festival. Determined to show that they could do things as well, if not better, than Covent Garden, they had engaged singers whose names alone were practically a guarantee of commercial success. Most prized and certainly the most famous of these, singing the part of the Marschallin's lecherous cousin Baron Ochs von Lerchenau, was the amiable and, in much the same way as Ochs, equally notorious Boris Askarian.

The first time she saw him Fiona had understood his reputation. Whatever name you cared to call it, magnetism, charm, sex appeal, he possessed it. Only charm was too weak, sex appeal too limited. It was power you sensed, power held in check, disciplined, that made you watch him rather than anyone else on stage. Of course, he was a difficult man to ignore, over six foot, broad of shoulder and thick of muscle, with the chest and diaphragm development of the well-trained singer. There was the magnificent head with the fine eyes, the imperious nose, the thick curling hair. And then there was the voice; the voice that had made him a fortune, that enabled him to go anywhere he wanted in the world, to choose any company he wished to sing with. And combined with all this there was his temperament, always pleasant, always friendly, a blessing to conductors and fellow singers alike. Askarian the imperturbable, the Merry Monarch of the opera stage.

He in his turn had not failed to notice Fiona, tall, slim, with chestnut hair and cool green eyes and an enviable serenity in the face of backstage crises. He had almost immediately contrived to adopt her as his guide through the intricacies of his temporary life in London, from the renting of a car to the hiring of a Bechstein. She still didn't quite know how she happened to have become involved. He probably, she reflected, found a Fiona Grant in every opera company he worked with. He was a man who liked comfort and women in that order and saw no reason why the one should not have a part in providing the other. She knew bets were being laid in the orchestra on the precise nature of her relationship with Boris but no one had had the nerve to ask her outright.

Just before she had left the theater to drive to the motorial terminal, Boris had called her into his dressing room. He had plied her with tea and his favorite Dundee cake, exuberant after the success of the final dress rehearsal, talking ceaselessly while he cleaned off his makeup. He had been full of praise for everyone, his fellow singers, the producer, the conductor.

"It was the performance we should be giving tomorrow night," he said. "We were all superb. Tomorrow, who knows? You are probably right to miss it. But still, to miss the London first night! By the way, did I tell you your father has written inviting me to go up there anytime to discuss the designs for my new boat?"

"And are you going?"

"I hope to. Perhaps at the weekend. I would go from there direct to Edinburgh. I could give you a lift."

"I'll look forward to it," Fiona said. "I still can't see you skippering a boat."

"I am an excellent sailor," Boris said. "Wait and see, my dear, wait and see. And don't forget, I shall expect a large discount on the price as a friend of the family!"

"From a Scotsman?"

Boris laughed. "I shall miss you this week, Fiona. Take care in those wild Highlands. Don't drive off any mountains, will you?"

She wasn't likely to drive off a mountain, Fiona thought, but in this mist she mustn't forget the danger of wandering sheep on the moorland road or a parked car on a single-lane stretch. The mist seemed to be thickening rather than clearing. The road had turned northward now and she was meeting the early morning traffic, tankers looming up out of the murk, yellow-eyed and threatening, a local bus grinding its gears, a farm truck.

At Bonar Bridge she left the A9, curling its way up the east coast to Thurso and the Orkneys, and went inland on a road which led to the empty heart of the Highlands. It was a good road but narrow, one of those designated as a primary route with passing places. There were plenty of places to pass but the traveler did well to be wary. Fiona did not fancy meeting one of those tankers, or a convoy of coaches, on the other side of a blind corner. She began to run into denser patches of fog. She sighed and switched on her headlights.

She was about eight miles from the village of Lairg, crossing a stretch of rocky moorland, when it happened. At a dip in the road she entered suddenly a thick white wall of vapor which enveloped the car like damp cotton wool, blotting out all visibility. As she broke through it into clearer air she saw two cars dead ahead, slewed across the road in collision. She stood on the brakes and brought the Mercedes to a stop only yards away from them.

It was hard to see how the accident had happened, for it had not been a head-on collision, both cars had been traveling in the same direction. Her direction. The second car seemed to have tried to avoid the first by going up on the verge. Or perhaps he had been trying to pass and had fatally misjudged it. Fiona ran forward. She could see a figure slumped forward against the steering wheel of the first car. The nearside door was open and a man was leaning in. It looked, for a moment, almost as if he were searching the unconscious driver. As he straightened up and turned to Fiona, she recognized him.

"I'm glad you've got good brakes," he said. "I thought you were going to hit us."

She had seen him twice before. Last night

on the train, and earlier yesterday, oddly enough, at the final dress rehearsal. This was a semipublic performance open to students, friends, relatives, fellow musicians. There were about fifty people scattered about the stalls when Fiona came into the auditorium to take a last critical view of her costumes in action. Wandering round the back of the stalls, she had come upon a solitary man standing near one of the exits to the foyer. He was leaning back against the wall, arms folded. He was dressed in a dark suit, white shirt and dark tie. His hair was dark, short, well cut. His complexion in the gloom of the dimmed houselights was pale. He gave Fiona one glance and then no more as if that had been enough to decide that she was of no interest or importance to him. It was difficult to place him among that audience: not a singer, or an actor. Nor did he look like anyone's agent, nor a musician or student.

When she left some five minutes later, he had neither moved nor made any further acknowledgment of her presence. He had not acknowledged her last night either, but now it appeared he had at least noticed her.

"You were on the London train, weren't you?" he said. "I saw you in the dining car."

He seemed perfectly calm, not even shaken by the accident. He made no mention of their encounter in the theater.

"What happened?" Fiona said. She felt shaken enough by the accident without even having been involved in it. She glanced nervously at the silent figure in the car; so still, so ominously still. There was something familiar about him. The gray hair, the tweed jacket. She said: "Is he badly hurt?"

"He's dead. I think he was dead before I got here. The car was in that position when I came out of the fog bank, at an angle right across the road. It wasn't the impact that killed him. I think he had a heart attack."

She stared at him. "How can you tell that?"

"I can't for certain. But it's obvious he'd slowed down, tried to stop the car safely. He must have felt ill."

Fiona made herself go forward until she could see the profile of the dead man's face, pressed against the wheel. She hadn't been mistaken. Poor man, she thought. Poor man.

"He was ill in the night," she said. "Don't you remember? His name is Eliot. He was on the train too."

He didn't answer her directly. He said:

13

"Look, we've got to get these cars off the road somehow, before there's a monumental pile-up. And we shall have to get him out to do so. Can you help?"

"Yes," Fiona said. "Yes, of course."

She brought the Mercedes closer and between them they manhandled the dead man out of the driving seat and half-carried, half-dragged him the short distance, finally lifting him onto the back seat. Fiona had known him as a tall, military, upright figure. He looked shriveled in death, a fragile old man whose clothes hung loosely.

It was very quiet on the road, an unreal, almost sinister silence with the shifting mists and no sounds but the settling of broken metal, the hiss of a cracked radiator, their own labored breathing. Fiona had never seen a dead body before, let alone handled one. She leaned against the car, resting, her arms wrapped around herself. She was beginning to shiver.

The man stood watching her. "He was a friend of yours, wasn't he? This must be a great shock to you."

She looked up, surprised. "No, I didn't know him. I happened to sit at his table in the dining car, that's all."

14

"I'm sorry. I saw you talking at Inverness while we were waiting for the cars to be unloaded and having seen you dining together—"

"He was apologizing for disturbing me in the night. He had the compartment next to mine. You were awoken too, weren't you? I thought I saw you in the corridor, talking to the attendant. Mr. Eliot said it was a bout of indigestion, but now—" She shivered again. She couldn't yet accept this fact of sudden death. Her mind couldn't make the jump from the vigorous man who had talked to her so enthusiastically about the fishing holiday he was embarking on, who had even offered to buy her a lunch at Lairg by way of apology for interrupting her sleep, and the gray-faced deadweight of flesh she had just been helping a total stranger to haul about a deserted road.

"Would you like to sit down for a moment?" he said.

She shook her head.

"Well, then, if you feel able to give me a hand. Something's going to come along this road sooner or later and we've no way of warning them."

He got an iron bar, like a crowbar, out of the trunk of his car and with it they managed to lever apart the tangled, crumpled bumpers and wings.

"Fortunately, I wasn't going fast," the man commented. "The fog had its uses."

"If it hadn't been for the fog, there wouldn't have been an accident," Fiona remarked.

He had squatted down on his haunches to rest. He glanced up at her with the slightest flicker of a smile. "How very true."

He had cut his hands on the sharp metal. His dark hair was beaded with moisture. His impeccable suit was impeccable no longer and where he had wiped his arm across his face to clear the rain from his eyes he had left long streaks of dirt. It had the effect of humanizing him. She began to look at him as a person, rather than a puzzling enigma.

"By the way," he said, "my name is Wyndham."

"I'm Fiona Grant."

"Well, Miss Grant,"—he got to his feet—"if you would be so good as to apply your elegant shoulders to the back of my car and give it a good old shove, I think we can get it off the road."

Once Wyndham's car was safely out of the way, they tackled Eliot's. They managed to steer it onto the verge facing oncoming traffic. Wyndham locked it and pocketed the keys. He took a grip from his own car and locked that. He said: "You still look very shaken. Would you like me to drive?"

"It is not my car," Fiona said. "I think I'd better stay in charge of it."

"As you wish. Shall we go?" He held open the door of the Mercedes for her.

They moved off down the road. The mist ahead seemed to be drifting. There were clear patches.

"This business is going to hold us up, you know," Wyndham said. "I'm sorry you've got involved."

"I'm not involved," Fiona said.

"You're a witness."

"I didn't witness the accident."

"You're a witness to the position of the car and the state of Eliot when you arrived. I'm afraid the police will want to talk to you as well as me."

She glanced at his face, calm, expressionless. Who was he? she wondered. What was he doing here? He didn't look like a tourist. An engineer, perhaps? Or something to do with North Sea oil? His hands looked squarely capable, well-kept. His face was attractive, strong features

17

marked by experience, the mouth well-shaped and unexpectedly sensitive, a face that looked as if it were used to imposing authority. His age, at a guess, was mid-thirties and his clothes, which she could not help judging with a professional eye, expensive.

His behavior throughout had been perfectly reasonable. They couldn't have left the cars like that. It had been far too dangerous. Nor could they have left Eliot slumped over his wheel or left him lying by the side of the road for the time it would take an ambulance to reach him. That would have seemed inhuman. Yet, in some odd way, she felt Wyndham had trapped her.

"There's a turnoff along here to the right," he said. "There it is, by the gate."

"I thought we were going to Lairg," Fiona said.

"There's a fishing hotel about a mile down the track. It's much nearer. We can ring for police and ambulance from there."

Fiona turned the car where he indicated. The road they were now on was, as he said, little more than a track.

"You must know this country very well," Fiona said. "I didn't even know there was a hotel down here."

"I like my fishing now and again."

"Is that what you're doing in Scotland, Mr. Wyndham, fishing?"

"Not this time. There we are, you can see it now."

It was a white-painted, pleasantly situated building with a gravel forecourt and to the side a small fenced-in garden. A gate led to a paddock at the far end of which, Wyndham told her, the river ran, leading into a chain of small lochs, guarded by high hills.

"It's quite impressive when you can see it," he said. "You've never been here?"

"No."

"You ought to come and stay sometime, if you like fishing."

The hotel entrance led through a wide glass porch, full of fishing gear and discarded wet weather clothing, into a square, tiled hallway with a broad staircase to one side and doors opening off the other. From one of these doors came a plump, dark-haired woman, investigating the new arrivals.

"Why, Commander Wyndham, we weren't expecting you!"

"Mrs. MacNeil, I'm afraid there has been an accident. A man is dead. Could you get on to the police for us?"

"Dear me, dear me! What a terrible thing. You're not hurt, either of you?" She gave Fiona a sympathetic glance.

"No, we're not hurt. My car is out of action, which is why Miss Grant kindly gave me a lift here. The body is in the back of her car, by the way. If you could—"

"Oh, I'll get the men to bring him in. Come along, Commander, you'd better talk to the police yourself. Come into the office. You know the way, don't you? Dear me, what a terrible thing!"

Commander, thought Fiona. Well, well. That would explain the short hair, the authoritative manner. Clearly a very trustworthy character. So why didn't she trust him? She wandered round the hall, looking at the pale watercolors, in their gold frames, of pearl-washed beaches in the Western Isles. She opened a couple of the doors; one led into a chintz-strewn sitting room, another into a bar. She looked at her watch, ten past two. It felt later.

Wyndham came back alone and asked for her car keys. "I haven't locked it," Fiona said. "You're bringing Eliot in?"

"Yes. Why don't you wait in the sitting

20

room? I've rung the police. They shouldn't be too long."

The police and the ambulance arrived together at three o'clock. In the interval, Wyndham had appeared in the sitting room carrying a tray with a bottle of whisky, a jug of water, two glasses and a vast plate of sandwiches.

"Mrs. MacNeil thought we might be in need of a wee drop of refreshment," he explained. He had washed the grease off his face and hands and changed his wet jacket for a sweater. His manner was friendly, his presence watchful. She almost got the impression that he trusted her as little as she did him. Yet what on earth had trust got to do with this situation?

"I'd like to wash before I eat," she said.

"There's a bathroom at the top of the stairs, second right."

She met Mrs. MacNeil in the hall. "Oh, Miss Grant, Commander Wyndham says you might be here sometime, so I've opened up one of the empty guest rooms in case you want somewhere to rest. You were on the night train, I understand. One never really sleeps on those trains, I find."

"Thank you," Fiona said, "I don't think it

will be necessary. As soon as I've talked to the police, I shall be off."

"Very well, but if you change your mind, it's number twelve."

In the end, because it was so much more convenient, she went to the guest room. As she washed and renewed her makeup she tried to analyze her sense of impatience. In some strange way ever since she had come out of the fog to find the crashed cars, everything seemed to have gone too smoothly. She had the sensation of having been led, or guided, down paths she didn't particularly want to follow. All the initiative was being taken away from her. It was irritating, to say the least.

"It is just," she told her reflection, "that I don't like being organized, by the navy, by the army, by anyone."

When she went back downstairs, Wyndham, was standing by the window, a glass of whisky in his hand. He turned to greet her. "One of the men has gone to stay with the cars until the police get here. By the way, I brought in your small case. It's in the hall."

The irritation surged up again. "It wasn't necessary for you to do that. I hardly think I'll be needing it."

"No, well . . . Eliot's feet were resting on it; it was in the way."

"Oh, I see."

"Would you like a drink? It's very good whisky."

She accepted the drink. It was very good whisky. She sat down and ate a couple of sandwiches and began to feel more human.

"It's nice to see you looking more relaxed," Wyndham said. "It hasn't been a pleasant experience for you. I want to thank you for your help."

"That's nice of you. I must confess I have been feeling a little like a not very efficient junior officer."

"Oh . . ." He pulled a face. "I'm sorry."

"Don't worry about it. I'm used to it. I have a boss who has the same effect. Are you stationed up here, Commander?"

"Temporarily attached. I'm on my way to the west coast."

"So am I," Fiona said.

"Indeed." He put down his glass. "Here are the police."

The police car which swept into the forecourt with a flurry of gravel was followed closely by an ambulance. Wyndham went out to meet the men, a uniformed sergeant and constable who got out of the car. They came into the hotel and disappeared through the door leading to the office. The ambulance men brought in a stretcher and carried it upstairs. After a while Fiona heard them returning, subdued voices, the sounds of feet on the tiles of the hall, the slammed doors of the ambulance. It drove off. Eliot had been quietly and efficiently removed.

Fiona wandered restlessly about the room. No one came near her, not even to see if she was still there. She could simply get in the car and drive away. If only one didn't have this deeply ingrained conviction that one should always be patient, helpful and law-abiding on such occasions. If only she had the temperament of the average opera singer. Would Boris passively sit around, hour after hour, waiting on other people's pleasure? She couldn't visualize it. And he had been in this position himself recently, so he would appreciate the situation. The police had been to see him about the death of a young singer in the company.

Elena Greer had been engaged to sing the part of Annina in *Rosenkavalier*, her first big role, a great opportunity for her. But in the middle of rehearsals she had been found dead in her flat from an overdose of drugs. An unhappy love affair, rumor within the company had had it. There had been a note. No one knew who the man had been.

"It wasn't me, thank God," Boris said. "No woman ever committed suicide because of me. If she had spoken to me about it I could have helped her, but as I told the police, I hardly knew her. Foolish girl. What a waste. Good contraltos are not all that common. A good part and the chance to sing with me—" he broke off. "She wasn't English, you know. She was a Czech, I believe. She'd changed her name. The police seemed to think that because we were both foreigners, both refugees, I suppose, from the same political bloc that she might have taken me into her confidence. Their very words, 'taken into her confidence.' They meant a great deal more than that. But she was not my type. Too quiet. She never spoke unless spoken to, did you notice that?" He sighed. "A broken love affair, an exile in another country, separated from her family. I suppose such desperation is understandable. If she'd been able to go back home, she would probably have been all right."

"Do you ever go back?" Fiona had asked him.

He shook his head. "No. I might if I was invited. I am still invited to embassy functions in most capital cities I find myself in. I was never a defector, you know. I never leapt frontier barriers to freedom. I just stayed away. It took them quite a while to realize I was never going back. I don't think they quite knew what to do about me. If they had made me the right offer, guaranteed me freedom of movement, I suppose I might have accepted even then. But no little bureaucrat was going to run my life, suddenly cancel a performance as a punishment for so-called insolent behavior, tell me what and where I should sing . . ."

No, Fiona thought, Boris would never allow himself to be ignored. For it was the neglect of her that was insulting. It meant they expected her to be not only obliging, delaying her journey, making statements, but to be submissive with it as well.

She opened the door to the quiet hall and went through it to the porch and the open air. Perhaps she was overreacting. She was tired. Mrs. MacNeil was right about the train, she hadn't had very much sleep. And it had been a long, wearing day's travel, even apart from the Eliot affair.

The air felt fresher. The drizzle had stopped. She could see the river and the waters of the first loch. The cloud was lifting from the hills. She could feel the warmth of the sun. She walked forward. The police car was parked to one side of the forecourt, the Mercedes on the other. The young constable was leaning against the gate into the paddock, midway between. Keeping guard? Fiona wondered. The thought cheered her up. Perhaps they weren't taking her for granted after all. As a small gesture of independence, she went to the car and locked it up.

There was a hiker coming down the track. Heavy walking boots, thick socks rolled down, shorts, anorak, rucksack on his back. When he got close to them he stopped, swung the rucksack off his back and looked inquiringly from one to the other.

"Any chance of a room here for the night, d'you think?" he asked. The policeman shrugged. Fiona said that she had no idea. Then she relented. He looked so young and vulnerable with his open sunburned face and tousled hair, and too slight to be weighed down with all the paraphernalia, the impossible boots, the sleeping bag strapped to a rucksack already crammed with gear.

"They don't seem to be full," she said. "Why don't you go in and ask?"

She turned to go in and the boy followed her. He left his rucksack in the porch.

"What's going on here?" he asked. "I mean, the police car—"

"There's been an accident further up the road," Fiona said. "That's all they're here for."

The door at the other end of the hall opened and the sergeant came out.

"Miss Grant," he called politely. "If you could spare a moment?"

She smiled at the hiker. "I have to go. But there's a bell somewhere. Ring it. Someone will come."

The hotel office was a small room with a large desk, a switchboard, filing cabinets, and a window through to the kitchen. While she talked to the sergeant Fiona could see two women in overalls preparing vegetables. The sergeant seemed most interested in her relationship with Eliot. She told him the simple facts of their brief acquaintance, how she had been put at his table in the crowded dining car, how he had introduced himself and chatted throughout the dinner in the noncommittal way one does with strangers, how they had discovered they had adjoining sleeping compartments, and how she had been awakened in the night by the noise of the attendant coming and going from Eliot's compartment.

"What sort of man was he?"

"Pleasant, courteous. I suppose you might call him old-fashioned. I got the impression he might be a retired army man."

"You didn't see him at breakfast this morning?"

"No, I didn't feel like eating. It was too early for me. I had a cup of coffee at the station buffet. There is no breakfast served on the train."

He nodded. "I am aware of that. Most people from the overnight train take breakfast at the Station Hotel. I merely wondered if you had seen Mr. Eliot there."

"The last time I saw him was in the station yard waiting for the cars to be unloaded. Look, is all this necessary? It's got nothing to do with the accident."

"We thought you might be able to help us establish exactly who the gentleman is, where he comes from and so on."

"I don't know where he comes from, but I know where he was going. Altnahara. He told me he was going there for a fishing holiday."

The sergeant made a note. "There you are, Miss Grant, you see you are helping us already."

"There must have been some identification on him surely," Fiona said. "His driving license or credit cards or something?"

"Unfortunately not. His wallet appears to have been mislaid. There will probably be something in his cases when we examine them. In the meantime . . ." He nodded to the constable who had followed Fiona in. "Could we borrow your car keys, Miss Grant."

"Why?" she asked.

"The body was on the back seat of your car. Something may have fallen out of his suit onto the floor. It is a possibility. I'd like to check it."

He held out his hand. Fiona took the car keys from her bag and gave them to him. He handed them to the constable.

"Don't forget to lock up when you've finished," he told him. It came across as the gentlest kind of rebuke to Fiona. It implied that she had behaved childishly in locking it in the first place.

"The wallet may have fallen out on the road when we moved him. Or outside the hotel, or on the stairs, or in the room they put him in," she remarked helpfully. Or the doughty Commander Wyndham might have taken it. When she first came up to him in the road she had thought that he looked as if he were searching Eliot. Did anyone really know if he was a genuine naval officer? It would be amusing if he turned out to be a con man. He was not entirely what he seemed, she felt sure. There was his appearance at the opera house, for instance. She must ask him about that. What was a naval officer doing at the dress rehearsal? She wondered how the company was feeling with the first night looming up. She must try and get hold of a paper tomorrow. She had a sudden desire to be back there, in the middle of the melee, with all the tension and excitement. It had seemed an excellent idea at the time but now she thought she should have told George to get someone else to bring his car to Scotland.

The sergeant slid a piece of paper across the desk to her. "Would you draw the positions of the cars as you saw them first."

She took the pen he offered and drew a rough sketch. "Is there any doubt," she

31

asked, "that Mr. Eliot was dead before the accident? Could it have been the accident that killed him?"

"We'll leave all that to the proper authorities, shall we?" the sergeant chided gently. "He was ill on the train, you told me."

"He thought it was indigestion. I suppose it was more than that."

"It could have been the forerunner of a heart attack. There will be no problem about finding that out. The evidence will be quite clear. Don't worry, Miss Grant, I don't think you will be needed to give evidence at any formal inquiry. We shall be interviewing the train attendants, the dead man's doctor when we trace him, and so on. We shall be in touch if we need you. Now my constable is going to type out your statement and I'd like you to read it carefully and sign it. Normally I'd ask you to do that at the police station, but in view of the unusual circumstances . . . I don't want to hold you up any longer than is necessary. Did you plan to go on with your journey this evening?"

"If I can."

"The weather is clearing rather slowly from the east. There's still quite a lot of fog

32

about. Might be better to wait till morning."

"I want to get on if I can," Fiona repeated.

"Quite so." He rose politely to his feet. "My constable will call you when the statement is ready. Would you like some tea while you're waiting? I'll ask Mrs. MacNeil if she can provide some."

Abandoned once more to the chintz sofas and the slightly dog-eared copies of *Country Life* and tourist magazines, Fiona felt as if she were drowning in a sea of tedium. When Mrs. MacNeil appeared bearing a tray of tea and cake, Fiona asked if there was a current newspaper available. "No London ones have come today. The fog, you know."

It was Dundee cake. It seemed incredible that only a day had passed since she sat in Boris's dressing room watching him dispose of slices of Dundee cake. She ate two slices out of boredom. It was fortunate George was not depending on getting the Mercedes by a certain time. As it was, he was hardly likely to put any other cars of his in her care. That emergency stop when she came out of the fog couldn't have done his tires much good, and she doubted if he'd approve of his property being used as a temporary ambulance to ferry bodies about the countryside. At least Eliot would have been the right class. George would have had strong feelings about that.

George Grant was in his way quite as outsize a figure as Boris Askarian. His brother, Fiona's father, called him a professional Scotsman but Fiona thought that a little unfair. Admittedly he did open up the private apartments of his ancient and gloomy castle to selected visitors, chiefly wealthy Americans and Germans, who were prepared to pay handsomely for the privilege of staying in an historical monument, complete with resident ghost, fishing its private waters and both shooting and dining with its esteemed owner. The laird put on a good show for them. But then he had a large estate, a decaying house and a flock of retainers to support, so who could blame him? At dinner he always dressed in full Highland rig, not forgetting the dirk in the stocking; pipers marched round the table; silver and china that would fetch some much needed dollars at Sotheby's or Christie's gleamed in soft candlelight; and since the guests came only in the warmer months of the year, the erratic nature of the central heating system went largely unremarked.

He was a large, awkward man, not noted

for the brilliance of his conversation, thin almost to the point of gauntness and with a manner some found daunting and others impressive. When he did talk it was more of a monologue than a dialogue, brooking no disagreement, but since this insensitivity and arrogance fitted exactly most of his guests' conception of a British aristocrat, this only intensified his appeal. But he appeared to get on well with his tenants and his servants in spite of his surface foreignness—an English public school and university education having eradicated any trace of Scotland from his accent—and Fiona was one of the few people with whom he seemed to unbend. Like Boris he was a bachelor, though no doubt for quite different reasons, and according to her father he had never been very close to any woman. It was not so much that he was a misogynist, he simply did not hold a very high opinion of their intelligence. Fiona could, by a stretch of the imagination, see him relaxing with a chorus girl, or whatever was the present-day equivalent of setting up a mistress in a house in Saint John's Wood. She could not visualize him with a wife and family.

There was not much love lost between the

brothers. They were so completely different, Fiona often wondered how they could have had the same parents. As a young man, with no prospect of an inherited property to help or hinder him, Murdo Grant had taken time off to hitchhike round the world. To cross the oceans he crewed on private yachts, spent some months in the Caribbean and finally returned to study naval architecture at Glasgow University. When, on his parents' death, he was left a certain amount of capital, he bought a small boatyard on the west coast of Scotland and settled there with his wife and young daughter. It was there he began to put into practice his ideas on boat design. For several years the business scraped by on the routine work of the boatyard, but now two of his early designs were in constant factory production and clients paid over the odds for a Grant boat, designed for them and built under his supervision in his own yard.

His brother George sometimes expressed envy of the way in which Murdo had managed to achieve wealth without responsibility. At one stage he tried to buy into the place himself but Murdo told him the time to invest had been in the early struggling years.

"You give me a couple of farms and a

few hundred acres of deer forest and I'll see about letting you into my business."

"Your father was always jealous of me, Fiona. I am sorry to have to say it, but it is true. It is natural enough, but it must always be taken into account in any reference he may make to me."

"Oh, he doesn't make many references to you, George," Fiona remarked. She had taken time off from the dress rehearsal to pick up the car from George's hotel. "You are flying up tonight?"

"Yes. It is very kind of you, Fiona, to look after the car for me. It was useful getting me around Germany but I'm getting too old to relish driving from one end of the country to the other in a night and I abhor sleeping on trains. This way I shall sleep in my own bed tonight and be ready to greet my guests in the morning."

"How many are coming this time?"

"I've no idea. I let others make the arrangements."

"And how was the German trip?"

"Quite satisfactory."

"Was it business or pleasure?" Fiona asked.

"Business. I have little appetite for

traveling for pleasure these days. Now, remember, you are not to worry about the car once you are home. Presumably your father will not object to garaging it for a day or so until I send someone to pick it up."

"No, I don't think he'll object to that," Fiona remarked dryly.

"I might even come myself," George said. He gave a thin smile. "Have a family reunion."

The constable, when he eventually appeared, bore what seemed a typescript of incredible length.

"Did I say all that?" Fiona asked.

He looked worried. "It's as it was in the notes."

She read it through. It was flat and banal but she couldn't see anything wrong with it. She remarked as she signed the copies under the constable's direction: "Your sergeant seemed very interested in the fact that the car I'm driving doesn't belong to me. I suppose he's going to check that I really have my uncle's permission, and that he is my uncle and I his niece." She was beginning to sound like something out of *The Comedy of Errors*.

The constable gathered up the papers. "Oh, he's already done that."

"Rung my uncle?"

"I don't know if he spoke personally to your uncle, miss, but I know he got confirmation."

"I hope he made it plain the car wasn't in any way involved in the accident. And since it wasn't, by the way, why the interest in its ownership?"

"Procedure, miss," said the contable. "A matter of routine. Your keys, miss." He handed her the car keys.

"Did you find anything?"

"No. May I ask if you are staying here at the hotel?"

"No. I'm going on as soon as you've finished with me. I shall be at the address in the statement. Will you need me again? Can I go now?"

"If you wouldn't mind waiting, the sergeant would like another word. He's on the phone at the moment."

Fiona stood up. "I'll be upstairs. Mrs. MacNeil has given me the use of a room."

"Very well, miss." He opened the door for her. He was a very polite young constable.

She met Wyndham on the stairs.

"All finished with the police?" he said.

"They want another word with me," Fiona

said. "And then I'm going. Would you like a lift? You said you were heading for the west coast."

"That's very kind of you. In other circumstances I'd take you up on it but I've got to organize repairs to my car." He glanced at his watch. "It's half-past five, you know. Isn't it a bit late to go on? It's quite a long way."

"I don't mind that. I'd rather go on."

"I get the impression you'll be glad to see the back of us," Wyndham remarked.

"Well, it wasn't the way I planned this journey."

"I'll be in the office. Come and say good-bye before you go."

In room number twelve, Fiona kicked off her shoes, punched the pillows into shape and made herself comfortable on the bed. She would close her eyes for five minutes. She had a long way to go and her interrupted night was catching up with her. Just five minutes' rest . . .

She was awoken by a sound like an express train. It shattered her. For a moment she could not recollect where she was and when she did the noise, in such a quiet place, seemed the more alarming. She leapt off the bed and ran to the window. Her room overlooked the forecourt and the paddock and in the paddock, settling down sedately like a broody bird settling on the nest, was a helicopter. The cessation of sound when the engine was cut and the blades stopped whirling was like peace at the end of the world.

The light had changed. And falling asleep had left her cold. She looked at her watch. Gone seven. Well, she could be furious with herself, but there wasn't much point in that. She'd be furious with the police instead. Why hadn't they wakened her? What were they doing keeping her waiting for that final word the constable spoke of? And what was a helicopter doing at a remote fishing inn? That landing would have scared off any fish for miles. She picked up her bag and went downstairs.

At the front door of the hotel, the hiker, now changed into jeans, sneakers, and a white Arran sweater, was standing watching the helicopter. Mrs. MacNeil, looking rather flustered, was beside him.

"More police?" Fiona inquired mildly. "Or more fishermen?"

"Something to do with the television," Mrs. MacNeil said. "I was only told an hour ago they were coming."

"To televise you, Mrs. MacNeil?"

"No, no, nothing like that, backgrounds for a film or such like. I'm not too clear myself. They are lucky we have the room. What with you and the Commander and then this young man arriving, we are practically full."

"Do you know where the sergeant is?" Fiona asked her.

"Oh, they've gone. Been gone this past hour."

"And Commander Wyndham?"

"He went with them. They were giving him a lift. He was going to see about getting his car taken in for repair. He'll be back soon. The bar's open,why don't you have a drink before dinner? You are staying the night, aren't you?"

Fiona acknowledged defeat. "Yes, I'm staying."

The place had livened up a bit. There were faces at the sitting room windows. A station wagon had arrived disgorging four jovial gentlemen back from their days's fishing, and another car could be seen lumbering down the track.

Three men were climbing out of the helicopter, heavily built, tough-looking characters. Fiona and the hiker stood aside to let them pass into the hotel.

"Good evening," Fiona said. They seemed surprised to be spoken to. The last one gave her a delayed "Good evening" as they vanished inside.

"Rather a surly trio," the hiker remarked.

Fiona turned to look at him. He gazed back at her with ingenuous blue eyes.

"You managed to get a room here?"

"Yes, thank God."

"Isn't that cheating?" Fiona asked. "Aren't you supposed to be sleeping out under the great canopy of stars?"

"Not if there's a pub nearby," he said. "I've been frozen and sodden and eaten alive by insects quite enough."

"Why do you do it then?"

"I can't afford to see the country any other way. There are quite a lot of enjoyable factors involved as well as disagreeable ones. Can I buy you a drink?"

"Can you afford to?"

"I can if you buy the second round."

"You're a student on vacation?"

"That's right."

"A student of philosophy, no doubt."

He grinned. "Theology, actually."

She ended up by sharing a table in the dining room with him. His name was David

Kenton and he was, as he put it, simply wandering round the Highlands without any fixed plan in mind.

"Since you've got this far north you ought to go on to John O'Groat's," Fiona suggested.

"I find there's never anything there at these overpublicized sites. A hotel, souvenir shop, a letter box to ensure your postcard arrives home with that evocative postmark on it, and a lot of people standing round rather aimlessly wondering what to do now they've got there. No, I think I'll go west tomorrow."

"I'm going west. Would you like a lift?"

"Thanks all the same. It's only at night the flesh grows weak. I shall be striding off like a two-year-old in the morning."

After the meal they went back to the bar. The three men from the helicopter were there, dourly putting away the whisky. Kenton asked them what television program they were working on. It was not a program, they told him, it was still in the stage of a project. They had been sent to survey possible backgrounds from the air. They consisted of a pilot, a mechanic and a cameraman. They'd already spent several days on it but the mists had held them up.

Now the weather was clearing, they could get on.

"So you're off again tomorrow?" Fiona asked.

"That's so," the pilot agreed. "Bright and early. Wake you all up from your beauty sleep." He nodded dismissively and turned back to his companions.

"What sort of project?" Kenton persisted. "Geographical, historical, sociological? The coming ice age, the Highland Clearances, or the antisocial tendencies of aging sheepdogs?"

They looked at him in complete bewilderment. "I think he's asking if it's going to be documentary or fiction," Fiona explained.

"Well, it's not going to be Walter Scott," the pilot said.

The others laughed. The pilot appeared to be the leader. The other two deferred to him. Even their gestures, their abrupt speech, seemed to be patterned on his. They lounged against the bar, looking in their uniform checkered shirts, their cords and boots, like a bunch of extras kitted out for *The Girl of the Golden West*. There was, Fiona thought, in spite of the workman's build and manner, a certain theatricality about them. The aura of television maybe. Or of helicopter flight. The glamour of the permanent *deus ex machina* constantly descending in clouds of noise and dust to amaze and alarm the peasants below.

She didn't stay long. As the bar filled, noise and cigarette smoke rose round her. Her head ached. Kenton had become caught up with a fishing group telling him the best route to follow west. The helicopter team had departed clutching a fresh bottle of whisky. There was no sign of Wyndham though she looked for him and half-unconsciously waited for him. When she realized that this was what she was doing, she got up and left. He was outside in the hall, talking to Mrs. MacNeil. Conspirators, Fiona thought tiredly. Why do they always look such conspirators?

Mrs. MacNeil nodded toward her. Wyndham turned. "I'm glad you're still here."

He came toward her and she felt with an inward sigh that the manipulation was about to begin again. Nothing that Commander Wyndham did, she felt, would ever be anything but planned. No seemingly spontaneous action but would have its root in some obscure policy.

She said: "I'm still waiting for that other little word the sergeant wanted to have with me."

"They've gone."

"Yes, I know." She watched the green baize door swing to behind Mrs. MacNeil.

"Mrs. MacNeil told them you were asleep. They didn't want to disturb you."

"Very civil of them. How did Mrs. MacNeil know I was asleep?"

"She looked in when you didn't answer her knock."

"Do you happen to know what the sergeant wanted?" Fiona asked.

"Nothing very important. He wanted to know how long you were going to be in Edinburgh and where you were staying there." Wyndham paused. "I told him he could always get in touch with you at the theater."

He waited. Waiting for her reaction, Fiona thought. It suddenly occurred to her that perhaps Wyndham wasn't absolutely sure that she remembered him from the London theater, that this was his way of seeing if she had noticed him there. Now why should that matter, one way or the other?

"You are interested in opera, Commander?" she asked coolly.

He smiled. "One of my passions."

"How did you happen to know I was connected with an opera company?"

Then as he began to reply, she joined in, echoing his words: "The sergeant told me . . ."

He broke off. She went on. "And because opera is one of your passions you happened to know which theater we would be performing in at Edinburgh."

"Exactly."

"Well, I'm glad we've got that straight."

Weren't naval officers allowed passions for opera? Was he supposed to have been somewhere else when he was at the theater? Did commanders really get involved in petty restrictions on their time?

"I wanted to see you," Wyndham said, "because I wanted to ask you a favor. I shan't be getting my car back for a week. Is the offer still open? Of giving me a lift west? I'll share the cost of the petrol, of course. I should be most grateful."

"You're very welcome," Fiona said. She walked past him to the stairs. "I'll see you at breakfast."

She noticed that he watched her all the way up the stairs. When she reached the top she turned back and looked over the rails. He gave her a mock salute. "*A demain.*" As she turned away, he was going into the bar.

Later that night, before going to sleep, she opened the window of her bedroom and leaned out, savoring the silence and the soft breath of moorland air. The mists had vanished. The moon was riding high. By its light she could see two men standing by the paddock gate. Wyndham and Kenton. They were looking at the helicopter and talking quietly together as cozily as old friends. The biting midges, she presumed, had retired for the night.

2

THEY left around eleven. They could have left earlier, but Fiona found herself overcome by an unexpected lethargy. She awoke at eight and promptly went back to sleep. She emerged an hour or so later to find the hotel almost deserted. She ate her breakfast in an empty dining room. She regretted offering Wyndham a lift, but after a while became annoyed with him for his absence. If he wanted a lift, damn him, he should come and get it. He should have been waiting for her, at the ready, bag packed, not put her in the position of having to search for him. A woman in an overall was vacuuming the sitting room when she looked in. The hotel was a restless, uncomfortable place in the morning. Guests were clearly not expected to lounge languidly about in this indecisive manner. They were expected to depart with rod and line and packets of sandwiches provided by the management at crack of dawn and not return until a civilized evening hour.

The helicopter had not yet gone. That surprised her. She could see the men in the cockpit. They seemed deep in technical argument. She went out to check the Mercedes. The cameraman climbed out of the plane and went past her, his face heavy.

"Having trouble?" she asked.

He ignored her.

"Rude bastard." David Kenton had materialized at her side.

"Where did you spring from?" Fiona said.

"I'm just off. I saw you from my bedroom window. I thought I'd say good-bye."

He was clad in his hearty hiker's outfit. He looked weighed down by the burden of rucksack, sleeping bag and other miscellaneous gear.

"Are you stronger than you look?" Fiona inquired.

He grinned, shifted the strap of his rucksack, gave it a final hoist to settle it on his shoulders and held out his hand. "I've come to say good-bye, so good-bye. And good luck."

"I think you're the one who's going to need luck, not me."

"Let's hope so," Kenton said.

She watched his incongruous figure till it

51

disappeared round the bend in the track. When she went back inside, Wyndham was waiting for her in the hall, his packed bag at his feet, all courteous attentiveness.

"I thought I'd let you know I'm ready," he said. "Whenever you are."

The morning had decided to be fine. Clouds moved in high, stately procession across a soft blue sky, casting great patchy shadows onto the dun-colored hills. The black waters of the lochs gleamed and glittered as lightheartedly as any southern ocean and the sparse grasses seemed dried by a southern sun.

The road they took was not a tourist route. There were few cars to wait for at the passing places. Yet Fiona was conscious from time to time of the sound of traffic, a distant hum that seemed to come closer and then recede.

Wyndham appeared aware of it too.

"Stop the car," he said at last.

She drew quietly to the side of the road. "What is it?"

He got out without replying and Fiona did the same. They waited, on either side of the car, in silence, in a growing tension. Suddenly, over a hill to the left, it appeared. Spiraling like a drunken daddy-long-legs, dipping and swaying, sweeping from left to right, then left again and all the time, little by little, advancing.

Fiona gave a laugh of relief. "The helicopter. That explains it. They're searching for backgrounds."

"They're certainly searching for something," Wyndham agreed. He took a pair of binoculars from his bag and examined the helicopter intently. It had ceased its darting motion. It swooped along the valley toward them, then took off suddenly to the left, swinging round the way it had come. In a couple of minutes it had gone, leaving only the echo of its engines.

"Well," Fiona asked as they went on their way, "was it the men from the hotel?"

"Yes," Wyndham said, noncommittally. "It was."

He had proved a socially competent if uninformative companion. He had talked easily and amusingly about fishing, about local eccentrics, about the countryside and even about the qualities of her father's yacht designs. He had avoided the topics of Eliot's death, opera companies and his own job. Yet once she knew he was headed for the west coast there was only one place he could be bound for.

On an island in a quiet bay about a mile or so from the Grant boatyard, there had been set up in recent years a naval research station. Nobody quite knew what the research was, but with the memory of an island whose very soil had been rendered lethal to man and beast as a result of contamination by anthrax during the last war and which was still deadly dangerous to visit after all these years, any new secret research base caused uneasy reactions. On the whole, since it was the province of the navy, it was assumed to be concerned with experimental weapons rather than germ warfare, but apart from rumors of revolutionary antisubmarine devices, the security barrier had been almost totally effective. Few people in the south had ever heard of the place. Lately, however, there had been other rumors, of trouble; different faces had appeared in the local pubs, traffic to and from the island had grown more intense, then practically ceased. At the same time, the base's name and geographical position were published in a radical news-sheet together with a few tentatively probing paragraphs aimed at provoking an official reaction. The bland governmental silence continued but the days of the base's relatively peaceful anonymity seemed ended.

"You're going to Linnay Island?" Fiona asked.

"I suppose that's obvious," Wyndham replied after a moment. "There is no other naval establishment in your area."

She glanced at him. "Temporarily attached, I believe you said. Is it anything to do with the trouble there?"

"What trouble would that be?"

"I've no idea. My mother mentioned something in one of her letters, that's all. That people seemed to think there was. Trouble, I mean."

"I'll let you know when I get there."

"You know you're very mysterious, Commander."

"Not at all. An open book."

"Oh, I realize you can't talk about your work. And I'll accept the deference the police showed you back at the hotel as one uniform fraternizing with another. But there are other things. For instance, what exactly were you doing at the opera rehearsal in London?"

"Ah—" The hesitation was brief but it was enough to make Fiona regret her impulsiveness. In spite of her curiosity and a rather childish desire to score some sort of point off the Commander, to disturb his smooth PR facade just a little, she wished she had left the subject alone.

"It was a public rehearsal, I believe," he said finally. "Friends welcome and all that."

"You have a friend with the company?"

"One of the second violins. A free lance brought in to swell the orchestra. *Rosenkavalier* requires such a large orchestra. But of course you know that." The manner of his reply was offhand. He seemed more interested in something he had found on the dashboard shelf. "Did you know there was a bar of chocolate here?" He picked it up and examined it as if he'd never seen one before. "Is it yours?"

"No. I hadn't noticed it." She was amused. "If you're hungry, why don't you eat it? I'm sure my uncle wouldn't mind."

"Thank you," he said immediately. "I will." He broke off two pieces and offered one to her. She refused it with a shake of the head. He put both pieces in his mouth, folded the paper round the remainder and put it in his pocket.

"Carstairs," he said with his mouth full.

"Who?" The incongruity of the Commander's sweet tooth, which seemed so out of character, had distracted her.

"Carstairs," he explained, "is the name of my friend in the second violins."

"I don't believe it. No one outside Victorian school stories is called Carstairs."

"Alastair Carstairs, a Scot. I would have thought you would know him."

"I don't have very much to do with individual members of the orchestra."

"I am sure they all know you. However, I'm surprised you noticed me. I am not very noticeable and you were very abstracted."

"You have a way of making your presence felt, Commander. But you didn't stay long."

"Regretfully no. I had to get back to work."

"You had better come to Edinburgh to see the final product."

"Perhaps I shall. By the way, I think your costumes will be a great success."

"That police sergeant must have been very talkative," Fiona remarked. "Did he give you any more personal details about me?"

"Don't blame the poor sergeant. When I meet a ravishingly pretty girl I like to find out all about her."

She glanced at him and he returned her gaze with a slightly ironic smile.

"Come on, Commander," Fiona said. "That's a bit too heavy handed for you."

"Do you really think so? By the way, if you're not interested in chocolate, you might be interested in lunch. There's what looks like a pub ahead. Shall we stop and see what they've got?"

"Do you mean to say Mrs. MacNeil hasn't provided you with a nice wee packed lunch?"

"Do you know I'm slowly getting the impression I'm not an entirely welcome passenger in this car."

Fiona relaxed. "I'm sorry. For some reason I'm irritable today. I expect I shall improve."

"I am extremely sorry about the delay yesterday." Wyndham reverted back to his politest naval manner. "But I didn't run into Eliot's car on purpose. I am afraid it was simply your bad luck that you were the next car to come along that road."

"Yes, I know. To make amends would you like to drive the next leg? I'm feeling tired and you probably hate being driven."

"Thank you very much. I appreciate the offer. And now shall we sink our differences in a glass of beer?"

Although Fiona remembered seeing the pub on other journeys along this road, she had never stopped there before. Solid gray stone outside, inside it had a bleak and decayed air. The floors were covered in foot-scuffed linoleum, the bar small and dark, the tables rickety. When the landlord, hawknosed and taciturn, appeared to serve them, Fiona felt the weight of Calvinist disapproval hanging heavy over her.

"Tourists not welcome, I would say," Wyndham murmured. "Locals and fellow poachers only. I wonder if I dare ask for some fresh salmon."

"I think it's simply women who are not welcome," Fiona said. "Especially in trousers."

"Dear me, are we as remote as all that? Let's see what he can offer us."

"I don't think I want anything," Fiona said. "I recognize the pattern. Cheese stolen from the mice, and week-old sliced bread."

"Don't be such a pessimist."

He went and talked to the landlord. Whatever charm he used, Fiona didn't know, but they were rewarded ten minutes later by two plates of cold roast beef, pickles and freshly baked rolls.

"Could you make up two more platefuls like that?"

Looking up, Fiona saw the pilot of the helicopter. Hearing his voice without seeing him, she had been aware, for the first time, of a vaguely Australian tinge to his accent.

"What's happened to the third member of your crew?" Wyndham asked. "Did you drop him out on the way?"

The pilot laughed. "He's looking after the 'copter. We put it down over the hill. Only place to land and this is the only pub we spotted for miles."

He drank down a whisky and ordered two more, leaning with his back against the bar contemplating them.

"Nice car you've got out there."

"Not the best for these road," Fiona said. "Too big."

"Maybe. Of course, our bird is best for the hills. Except the landowners don't like them. Scare the deer. I tell them they could save time and effort using a 'copter to drive the deer to the guns. But they don't approve of that idea. Unsportsmanlike."

He was far more talkative and affable than he had been the previous night. It sat rather oddly on him as if he were out of practice.

"My name's Matt Jackson, by the way."

He had thick tow-colored hair, contrasting strongly with the weather-beaten complexion of his face. He had a heavy jaw and light blue

60

eyes with almost white lashes. He was beginning to run to fat.

Neither Wyndham nor Fiona responded to his overtures by introducing themselves. Instead Wyndham asked if they'd found any suitable locations.

"I can't say we have. Anyway Bob jammed the camera. That's another reason we came down. Thought this place was shut till we saw your car. Some of these pubs open when the hell they feel like it. And shut the same way."

The door opened and one of his colleagues appeared, stooping to avoid the low threshold.

"Any luck, Bob?" Jackson asked.

The other man shrugged.

Jackson handed him a glass of whisky. "Well, put yourself outside that. Then we'll be off. We won't wait for the food. It's later than I thought."

He nodded to Wyndham and Fiona. "See you around. And if you happen to break down in the next hour or so, just wave a rag. We'll see you sooner or later."

The bar seemed a good deal emptier when they had left.

"I didn't hear the helicopter," Fiona said.

"Neither did I," Wyndham said. "They must have put it down quite a way away. Conscientious fellows, aren't they, leaving a guard. They did the same last night. They took it in turns to sleep in the helicopter."

"Well, I suppose it's not the sort of thing you like to lose. How do you know anyway?"

"I was doing some work in my room. I saw them changing the guard."

"No wonder they were so bad-tempered this morning. But I wouldn't have thought they were the kind to give up their creature comforts for the sake of a television company."

"Neither would I," Wyndham said. "Now, changing the subject, would you like to show me the route you want me to take? He moved the empty plates and glasses to another table and produced from his pocket an ordnance survey map. He unfolded it to the right section.

"That's a good deal clearer than my battered one," Fiona said. "It looks brand-new."

"Handsome, isn't it?" Wyndham agreed. "Isn't it yours?"

"No. This is mine." She produced it from her bag. "It's getting a bit tattered, hard to read in the creases, but nothing much changes up here."

"I got this from the car," he said. "I found it in one of the pockets."

"Well, George is a pretty meticulous sort of man, probably changes his maps every year, along with his cars. Put it away, we might get beer on it. Let's use mine."

She spread it out on the table and ran her finger along the twisting line of road.

"Mmm," Wyndham said. "I suppose we should get there by four. Where is your uncle's estate, by the way?"

"It's here." She pointed it out. "I thought you knew the Highlands."

"Not so far north and west as this. I see your uncle's place is only about ten miles from your father's. Are you dropping the car off there first?"

"No, he's sending someone to collect it. It's only ten miles as the crow flies, but there's quite a solid lump of mountain in the way; you have to go round that and then round the head of that small loch before you get there. It's more like thirty or forty miles all told and part of the road not much more than a track."

"Not many roads up here at all, are there?"

"A few more than are shown on my map. Probably George's is a larger scale, if you want to check them."

"No, I think I know where I'm going." He folded up her map and handed it back to her with a smile. "A barren and deserted land. No wonder you went off to London."

"It's beautiful in its own way," Fiona said. "And it's beautiful on the coast. If the navy isn't planning to pollute it." She dropped the car keys into his hand. "Or lay a string of antisubmarine devices just where the fishermen like to go."

"What a lot of wild rumors there must be going about to be sure," Wyndham said. "Do you get many strange craft off your coast?"

"You'll have to ask my father about that. But there's no need, is there? I think you know far more about our coastline and what or who are moving along it than we ever shall."

"How delightful to be presumed so knowledgeable. I'll do my best to preserve your illusions."

Outside he held the keys up. "Which is the door key?"

"That one. But I didn't lock the car. One rarely does up here."

"You never lock the doors of your houses up here either, I suppose. I had an aunt in the country who never locked her doors."

"I know," Fiona said, "you're going to tell me a furniture van drew up one day and carried off the entire contents of the house."

"Well, no, I wasn't. Nobody ever robbed her of as much as a grain of sugar. The wicked south has made you cynical." He tried the door. "More than you realize. You did lock it after all."

Across the heart of the northwest Highlands, the country was scoured to its bones, the ancient gneiss bedrock thrusting through the thinly clinging layer of peat like the knuckles of a fist. It was inescapable, from the smallest outcrops no bigger than a flung stone to the round, humped hills, pared away to their cores by wind and weathering. Water could not drain into a soft earth; it lay and collected and formed bogs of cottonsedge and the myriad streams and lochans that vein the moorland and, near the sea where gentler airs blow, grow thick-reeded and filled with welcoming birds.

No tree grew in that harsh soil but scrub birch and hazel, and the floor of the empty forest was covered in coarse grasses. From the jagged coastline the sea lochs spread long fingers into the land, and the rivers ran down from the inland waters to meet them, full of rich fish, of salmon and sea trout. There the life began, at the coast with the fishing ports and the villages and the crofts and the schools; here a place for camping, there a hotel for tourists. The hinterland was left to the naturalist and the sportsman, to the climber and the wanderer, to those who mended roads and carried post and brought provisions. Few came and few stayed. It was a country of rock and water and silence.

In the late afternoon, Wyndham and Fiona left the high moorland and drove down through plantations of conifer trees to the coast road, following its line that curled like a piece of knotted string round headland and bay. From one turning in the road they could see across blue water to the next promontory. A fishing boat was setting out from an unseen harbor. Then the road twisted back on itself and for a moment the hills they had left came into view. The air was dazzlingly clear. They climbed and turned again and the whole coast was spread before them, wild and beautiful, the sea shimmering and deceptively calm with only the white splashes of distant surf on rocky islets to warn of its hidden temper.

"That's Linnay Island," Fiona said.

Wyndham stopped the car and got out. He took his binoculars from their case. "Where?" he said.

Fiona joined him. She pointed. "The larger of those two islands. On the far left. You'll find there's not much to see. Some buildings, the odd boat. The harbor's round the other side."

"You've been there?" Wyndham asked.

"No, I've looked at it through binoculars as you're doing. Out of curiosity. Only why bother? Your curiosity will be satisfied when you get there."

"I thought I'd see how much could be seen from the mainland."

"You'd get a better view from our house. We're practically opposite the island. All their traffic comes to a quay near the boatyard."

As they got back into the car, she remarked, "So the trouble isn't confined to the island. It involves the mainland too. What's the matter? Someone spying on Linnay and seeing a bit too much?"

Wyndham started the car. "I shall have to be more careful how I behave near you. You're quite a girl for leaping to conclusions, aren't you?"

"Perhaps I should have asked you for identity papers," Fiona remarked lightly. "After this highly suspicious incident, I might conclude you're the one planning to do a little spying."

"There's a fork in the road at the bottom of this hill," Wyndham said. "Which way?"

"Right," Fiona said. "We're nearly home."

Inverlinn, Fiona's town, for its inhabitants called it a town though it was scarcely more than a large village, had consisted originally of one long street of fishermen's cottages following the gentle curve of the sheltering sea loch and known locally as The Strand. Later in its brief time of prosperity as a herring port, a second, grander street was built, parallel to The Strand and connected to it by lanes and alleyways of small houses. In this second street, known as the High Street, were to be found the main shops, the branches of two banks, two small hotels, a tourist craft shop and a café. The new church, built in the nineteenth century, was up the hill by the bridge over the river, with the school nestling beside it. At one end of The Strand was the harbor, deep and large enough to take trawlers, surrounded by sheds and warehouses, the customs house, the offices of the bus company, a garage, a hall for showing films and holding bazaars and dances and other entertainments, two pubs and a fish-and-chip shop. The buildings were set back, forming a square in which people gathered of a summer evening to watch the boats come and go, to wait for buses, to queue for the film, to eat their fish and chips, to gossip and pass the time. It was the heart of the town and through it passed the routes from north and east, the two divergent roads joined into one at the bridge outside the town, the road south going along The Strand, past Grant's boat-yard and away inland.

Wyndham sounded his horn at the children playing by the bridge. He had to sound it again to warn the occupants of a stationary coach half blocking the entrance to the square. He edged the big car past only to find a second coach directly across his path, backing with exasperating slowness into a parking place normally used by fish lorries.

"Busy little place you've got here," he remarked.

"I've never seen it like this before," Fiona said. "Two coaches, and all these people. I didn't realize it had become such a tourist attraction."

"These aren't tourists," Wyndham said.

The passengers of the coaches had descended. They made a straggling mob of seventy to eighty eddying round the square, mostly young men in the student uniform of jeans and anoraks, a few girls of the more earnest sort, their round, healthy faces devoid of makeup. It was a good-humored crowd on the whole. They squatted on the cobbles of the harbor, rucksacks between their feet; they peered in the windows of the chip shop; they constantly formed and reformed small groups. There was laughter and talk and an air of excitement about them. In stiff lines on the pavement the local inhabitants watched them, disapproving and curious. As the Mercedes passed the second coach, Fiona noticed a pile of blankets on one of the seats.

"If I could see any equipment, I'd think

they were a climbing school," she said.

"I think their equipment is over there," Wyndham said.

Fiona looked where he indicated. "Pieces of wood?"

"Now this is more interesting," Wyndham said.

They had come to a third coach, parked a little way along The Strand. Grouped besides it, listening intently to the instructions of what appeared to be their leader, a broad thickset man with red hair, were a tougher set of characters altogether. Some were wearing the hard hats of road workers. They were older, grimmer and did not look in the least bit amusing.

"The tour leader expounding the beauties of the countryside?" Fiona suggested.

"I should think he's the leader anyway," Wyndham agreed.

"The leader of what? What's going on? Oh, I know," she added suddenly. "It's the base, isn't it? It must be. We've run into the trouble all the rumors were about."

"There are a couple of policemen up there," Wyndham said. "Let's ask them what it's all about."

"I know one of them," Fiona said. "We

went to infant school together." She wound her window down and called. "Hallo, Peter!"

The policeman came over and leaned down to talk to them. He had a long, melancholy face and a soft Highland voice. "Fiona, I am very glad to see you. Will you be staying long?"

"About a week. Peter, what's going on? Who are all these people?"

"Well, we gather they are supposed to be a spontaneous local protest against the research station. No doubt they'll collect a few locals when the pubs shut."

"What are they going to do?"

"They are going to gather in the square about ten o'clock tonight and march to the landing stage, singing protest songs. They will then keep silent vigil through the night. They have assured the authorities no violence or illegality will occur. The press are due to arrive anytime now. They were hoping for the television but so far no one has turned up."

"What are they objecting to?" Wyndham asked quietly. "What is the particular theme?"

"I gather there is no one evil they are against," the policeman said. "Just the base in general. They want no wicked warmongers in the bay, that sort of thing," he said to Fiona. "I have seen your father about it. Since they will be near the boatyard he is a little worried about possible damage. There will be quite a few policemen around. We shall stay unobtrusive unless needed. We don't foresee any trouble. They seem quite pleasant lads on the whole."

"I saw what looked like torches," Wyndham said. "Is it to be a torchlight procession?"

"That is so. We are a wee bit worried about that. It would not do for them to be carelessly tossing one of those burning brands about. They could cause damage to life and property with one of those things."

"This is Commander Wyndham," Fiona said. "He's on his way to the base."

"Indeed, sir. Do they know you are coming? I only ask because they have agreed not to send any more boats over until the demonstration is over. They have decided against anything that might look like provocation. They have sent some men over to keep a watch on what goes on. The boat that brought them has just gone back."

"You'd better come to the house," Fiona told Wyndham.

"Thank you," Wyndham said. "Perhaps I can telephone from there."

"By all means. And, Peter, since you'll be so close, why don't you come in for a cup of tea?"

"I may be a little busy. I shall be on duty most of the night. I'll look in when I can."

"Who's behind it?" Fiona asked. "Who are these men?"

"They tell me they are construction workers come to support the just wrath of the students. The students say they have come to support the indignant locals. The students are all on vacation now of course. I don't know what universities they are from. No doubt we shall know a little more by morning."

"Did you know they were coming?"

"Not until this morning." He gave them a gentle smile. "It is quite spontaneous, you understand. Impelled by a sense of outrage, they have gathered together to exercise their democratic right to demonstrate."

"You've learned that very nicely," Fiona said.

"I was always good at the memorizing, if you remember, Fiona. I'll see you later, no doubt. If we can be of any help to you,

74

Commander, let us know." He stood back and saluted as they drove on.

The Grant boatyard was about two miles out of the town. The road, which had been meandering quietly beside the softly wooded shores of the loch, past shallow pebbled beaches and narrow meadows patched with bright green bog grass, suddenly swung away and up to avoid a rocky headland. As they rounded the top of the slope and descended again, the sun struck through the trees, flashing and vanishing, blinding them with its casual, flickering glances. As a result Wyndham nearly missed the turning.

"Here," Fiona said quietly.

He turned off the main road and they drove down through rough fields toward the calm blue waters. The road ended at a T-junction at the loch edge. Before them was a harbor, bounded on one side by the boatyard's complex of buildings. Behind them was a row of stone cottages, the nucleus of the original fishermen's village. One was a general shop, providing stores and marine equipment, Fiona explained. The others were rented to boatyard workers. When her father bought the yard the cottages came with it. Wyndham parked the car and they got out. The town was not visible. The promontory they had driven round hid it from them. It also protected the harbor. And to the south the loch curved round like a cupped hand, its sheltering hills rising steeply from the shore. The bay was more than secluded; it had a hidden, private air, which even the noise and clutter of the yard could not alter.

"There's a deep water channel leading out into the open sea," Fiona said. "That's what attracted my father to it. It meant the yard could keep going with repairs while he built up the design side."

As they stood there, they could see directly ahead the outline of Linnay Island.

"Where is the quay they use for the base?" Wyndham asked.

Fiona pointed down the left arm of the T. "Down there. About a quarter of a mile. The road comes to a dead end there."

"And your house?"

"The other way to the right. Just below the headland. You'll like it. Victorian Scottish Baronial. Used to be some wealthy Glasgow merchant's shooting lodge. Or rather fishing lodge, I suppose. I don't think they did much shooting round here. Then an actor had it in the twenties. Did it up, started a subtropical

76

garden on the lines of Inverewe. It's so sheltered here you can grow quite a lot of unexpected things. But he ran out of money or enthusiasm and abandoned it. But life was quite exotic here for a while, I believe. A reputation was developed for wild parties. The locals grew very shocked. After he left, the place was rented out to various people until my father bought the whole estate for practically a song."

"I'd like to meet your father," Wyndham said.

"Well, let's call in and say hallo on the way to the house. I haven't seen him for months myself."

She led him through the main gate and picking her way with practiced ease amongst chains, ropes, piles of timber, tarpaulined boats, trailers, scrap awaiting collection, drums of oil, coils of wire, empty paint tins, and all the other accumulations of a working yard, guided Wyndham to a low brick building adjacent to the main shed.

"His office is in here," she said, and then stopped. The door of the big shed was open and from it, loud, clear and unmistakable, came the sounds of an almighty row in progress. One of the angry voices was her father's. She couldn't immediately identify the other.

"Well, perhaps this isn't the best time to walk in on him," she said. "He'll be coming up to the house soon."

They returned to the car. As they drove past the yard gates a man came bursting out on a motorbike. He was wearing overalls but no crash helmet. He went into a skidding swerve to avoid them, then roared off along the road to the town, leaving the impression of a ball of condensed fury exploding across the fields.

"Never ride a motorbike in a temper," Wyndham observed mildly. "It's not terribly safe. Do you know him?"

"I've never seen him before," Fiona said.

"I shouldn't think you will again. I would imagine your father has just thrown him off the place."

"He must have had a good reason. He usually sacks people a good deal less noisily and then not very often."

"Now the noise appears to be over, do you want to stop and see your father?"

"No," Fiona decided. "Let's get up to the house. I know you want to ring the base."

The road past the boatyard ended in a wide

stone archway set in crumbling walls. Through this a driveway wound through neglected parkland to the steps of a double-fronted stone house. It sat squarely and confidently on the edge of the promontory, facing a panoramic view of loch and sea, guarded by tall trees, surrounded by thick tangles of wild rhododendron but with its drive weeded and its terrace enlivened by urns of tumbling flowers. A tall woman wearing a tattered sun hat and gardening gloves was digging away with a trowel at a window box outside one of the long bowfronted windows. Fiona called to her.

As she came down the terrace steps to greet them, Fiona was struck as she always was after an absence of any length of time, by her mother's unfailing and completely unself-conscious elegance. It was a gift that never left her no matter what she was doing or what clothes she was wearing, which on this occasion included as well as the working gloves and hat, a patched denim skirt and a faded pink shirt of her husband's. She had retained her willowly figure, but her curling blonde hair was scattered with gray.

She hugged and kissed her daughter. "Sweetheart, I am so glad to see you! I got very nasty feelings about that fog. Your father said you'd had stayed the night somewhere, but I was imagining all sorts of horrors. Anyway I see you've brought George's monster up safe and sound. I don't mean you of course," she smiled at Wyndham. "At least, I hope I don't. You aren't anything to do with my brother-in-law George, are you? No, of course not. Fiona would have told us. You're not an opera singer, are you? I've had nothing but opera singers all day."

"He's on his way to the base." Fiona gave a simplified explanation of the situation, that Wyndham's car was out of action, they had met at the hotel and she had offered him a lift. "He has to ring the island," she said.

"I'm afraid I'm being a great deal of trouble, Mrs. Grant," said Wyndham at his most smooth.

"Not at all, Commander, I'm delighted we can help. Come in and have tea. You can telephone while the kettle's boiling."

They left him by the telephone in the hall and went through into the kitchen. Fiona leaned against the scrubbed wooden table and affectionately watched her mother gather tea-cups together.

"I'm sorry I didn't ring you last night," she

said. "I didn't think I'd mentioned arriving at any particular time. Were you really worried?"

"Of course I was worried," her mother said. "That great car of George's, who wouldn't worry?"

"Still, it was a kind thought of his to ask me—"

"Kind thought, nothing!" her mother interrupted briskly. "It was convenient for him, that's all. Saved him the bother of driving it up and the expense of paying someone to bring it up."

Fiona thoughtfully ate a scone. "I don't know why you and father are so hard on poor old George. He's always quite pleasant to me."

"Poor old George is a mean old bastard and always has been," said Mrs. Grant. "Let's have tea."

Fiona carried the tray into the drawing room. Wyndham was standing by the window. He turned as they entered.

"You have a marvelous view," he said. He was holding a pair of binoculars. Fiona assumed they were his own until he said to her mother: "I hope you don't mind my using these. I found them on the window-sill."

"I keep them there for looking at birds," Mrs. Grant explained.

"Since when have you been interested in birds?" Fiona asked.

"Since your father gave me the binoculars."

"They are very good ones. Barr and Stroud. Powerful." Wyndham put them back in their case. "Does your interest in birds include photographing them, Mrs. Grant?"

"My husband is the photographer, not me. He has a darkroom full of equipment upstairs. And it's not birds he's interested in, but boats. I don't know if you noticed the photographs in the hall?"

"Studies of yachts, yes, I did. Grant designs?"

"Most of them, but not all. He likes to study his competitors. Get any strange yacht sailing into the bay and he'll be off asking permission to photograph it."

"I didn't think he always bothered about the permission," Fiona remarked.

"He must have built up quite a reference library over the years," Wyndham said.

"I suppose he must," Mrs. Grant agreed. She offered him a cup. "Tea, Commander?"

"Did you get through to the base?" Fiona asked.

Wyndham accepted tea and a scone from Mrs. Grant before replying. "Yes. They are sending a boat over for me. But I'll be back later. They rather want me to stay over here tonight. As an observer. With the demonstration going on and so on."

"That wretched demonstration," Mrs. Grant said. "Have you heard about that, Fiona?"

"We saw the coaches in town," Fiona said. "There are quite a few of them. Peter says he'll be over here keeping an eye on the yard."

"It'll only take one drunk with a flaming torch to send the place up like a bonfire. I'm delighted to know you are going to be around too, Commander. Where are you going to stay?"

"I hadn't got around to that," Wyndham said.

"Why not stay here? There's plenty of room."

"I really couldn't impose . . ."

"It's hardly an imposition. If you're going to be out observing most of the night, Commander, you won't be bothering us."

Fiona drove Wyndham down to the quay.

"Your mother is a very charming woman,"

Wyndham said. "But forceful in her way."

Fiona laughed. "Indeed she is."

"I wonder if you've inherited that from her as well."

"As well as what?"

"You know very well what I mean. Her looks. Her beauty."

"I wasn't fishing for compliments, Commander."

"It's very difficult to pay you any."

"Try a little more subtlety next time." She brought the car to a halt. "Here we are and here's your taxi." A motor launch with two sailors on board was just approaching the quay.

"You know I'm very grateful for the help you've given me," Wyndham said. "But I've no intention of accepting your mother's hospitality, so don't be so furious with her for offering it. Are you going to tell her about Eliot's death?"

"I think so. Why not? That hasn't become an official secret, has it?"

"Can you think of any reason why it should?" he asked.

Fiona stared at him. "You're serious, aren't you? You think I might know of a reason why it should."

He reached over to the back seat for his grip. "My questions, like my compliments, are always serious. Good-bye, my dear Miss Grant. Enjoy your holiday."

"Oh, for heaven's sakes," Fiona said. "Come back and have dinner. And stay the night."

"Now that's what I call an offer."

"I don't want the boatyard burned down any more than my mother does."

He smiled and touched her cheek lightly with his hand. "In that case I'll see you later. Don't crash George's car on the way back."

3

MURDO GRANT was home. Fiona saw her father's car in the garage when she drove the Mercedes round the back of the house to put it away. She took her case and overnight bag from the boot and locked the car up. Murdo met her on the terrace, a glass of whisky in his hand.

"You look laden," he said. "Where's the car?"

"I've locked it away." She kissed him. "It's your responsibility now until George claims it."

He put his free arm round her shoulders. "You sound as if you've had enough of it. Put the bags in the hall and come and talk to me. I'll get you a drink."

Fiona dropped the cases inside the open front door and rejoined him.

"You certainly need a holiday," he said. "You look washed out."

"Dear father," Fiona said, "you certainly know how to make a girl feel her best."

Murdo laughed. He was a big man, big in

height and in build, with graying hair and a broad, open face. He looked well, Fiona thought, but there was an air of tension about him. He seemed not exactly worried, but abstracted as if, in spite of his obvious pleasure in seeing her, half of his mind was elsewhere.

"Whisky do you?" he asked. "It's all I've got out here."

"Fine. Where's mother?"

"Doing something about dinner, I imagine."

"Oh, I must tell her. I've invited someone."

"The handsome sailor, no doubt. I've already heard about him. What did Laura say his name was?"

"Wyndham."

"That's it. You needn't bother about it. I gather she was expecting him here to dine anyway."

They lapsed into companionable silence for a moment, sitting on the wide bench outside the drawing room window, the scent of flowers around them and the wide sweep of the bay before them. The colors were changing with the changing light of evening, the water darker, the hills tinged with purple, the whisky in the decanter on the table before them more richly golden, the water in the jug throwing patterns of reflected light onto the painted tray.

Thin streaks of cloud hung motionless over Linnay Island, edged with gold.

On an impulse, Fiona got up and fetched her mother's binoculars from the house.

"What are you looking at?" Murdo asked.

"The Island. I'd forgotten how much you can see from here."

Murdo took the glasses from her and looked through them briefly, then put them down beside him on the bench.

"How is *Rosenkavalier*?" he asked.

Wyndham returned about eight o'clock, just in time to eat. He looked to Fiona even more spruce and decisive as if his meeting with his colleagues on the island had been sufficient to charge him with additional energy and an increased authority. Perhaps that was exactly what had happened. Perhaps he had had to fight a small battle against an entrenched hierarchy to establish his position and his right to use a free hand in dealing with whatever the trouble was. Or perhaps the prospect of the demonstration had thrown the scientists at the base into a mild panic of uncertainty and he had been greeted with open arms. Of course the answer could have been simply that he'd had a hot bath, a few whiskies and changed his shirt.

Whatever was the truth about what was going on on the Island, Fiona felt a little less in the dark. She had asked her father what he had heard about the trouble there and he had told her that the rumor was that the Island was no longer secure. Details of secret processes had apparently been reaching the wrong hands.

"How do they know?" Fiona asked.

"Probably by comparison of technical developments. If someone takes a great leap forward in their instrumentation, for instance, using techniques and knowledge the other side has taken months or years to perfect, then there can be a reasonable suspicion it is not purely the result of an inspired guess. The necessary knowledge has been acquired from somewhere or someone. At one time you were getting quite a lot of that sort of thing in the ordinary business world, from pirating fashion designs to stealing industrial processes. I've had people up here trying to see if I was developing a new revolutionary hull or steering system or whatever. It may still be going on for all I know. They call that industrial sabotage and impose a few fines. However, when it comes to something like weapon development, words like high treason start being used and people see spies in every corner."

"You don't believe there are any spies round here?" Fiona asked.

"I think each side had plenty of other means of learning secrets without employing the cloak-and-dagger men. Observation from a distance by sea or air, tracking tests, satellites, that sort of thing. I should imagine that's the case here. However, I'm perfectly willing to help your Commander Wyndham in any way he likes if he asks me to, and if, that is, he is in charge over this. It's difficult to guess at the position. I suppose if information has got out, then these sort of rumors are inevitable, either deliberately or accidentally planted. Hence the attention centered on the place and the demonstration tonight."

"Do you know exactly what they are doing out on the Island?" Fiona asked.

"No," Murdo said, "and I don't intend asking Commander Wyndham either. However, the moment they seem to be threatening the fishing in these waters, or doing anything destructive to my business, that would be a different matter. I'd be out waving a torch with the demonstrators right away."

"Well, if you're not worried about spies or pollution, what are you worried about?" Fiona said.

Murdo looked at her. "Who says I'm worried about anything?"

"We nearly walked in on you this afternoon," said Fiona. "We retreated tactfully before the noise, and then a man, fortyish, red hair, white face, came tearing out of the yard like a maniac. You could be worried about him?"

Murdo laughed. "Craddock! He was just a damn nuisance. He came looking for work last summer when we were busy and needed men. Said he was a carpenter but his work was pretty indifferent. Used to take off on his own a lot of the time, said he was working on one or other of the boats, but a couple of times he was missing from the yard altogether. I noticed it more out of season when the men are more under my eyes. He had been taking boats out without the owners' permission. Fishing, I suspect, and selling the catch in town. I warned him a couple of times. He tried to con me it was with the owners' agreement. But last night he

91

nearly wrecked a fifty-thousand-pound boat in the fog. I gave him the benefit of the doubt by ringing the owner first, confirmed that permission to take the boat out had certainly not been given. I called Craddock in, gave him a piece of my mind and fired him. He seemed shattered; he began with justifications, followed by excuses, followed by threats. My fault entirely, I should never have taken him on. I wouldn't have done it if we weren't short of workmen up here."

"What sort of threats?" Fiona asked.

"He's irrelevant," Murdo said. "Forget him."

It was Wyndham who, during dinner, told the Grants about Eliot's death. He made quite a drama of the old man, on his way to a fishing holiday, struck down by a heart attack on a lonely road. And he made Fiona into the heroine of the episode, calm, steadfast and helpful. He even mentioned their first encounter at the opera rehearsal, praising the production and the brilliance of Fiona's designs. At first she listened with a quiet amazement, but when he met her appraising glance with a blandly innocent expression, she thought she knew what he was up to. If she had wished to make her parents suspicious of or hostile to him he had cut the ground from under her feet.

"No notice of *Rosenkavalier* in today's paper, I suppose," she asked.

"No," her mother said. "I looked for you. We get the early editions of papers up here," she went on to explain to Wyndham. "Things like reviews of plays are often in a day later than London editions."

"Mother, what did you mean earlier when you said you'd had nothing but opera singers all day?" Fiona asked.

"Boris Askarian," Laura Grant explained succinctly. "Mrs. Niven's been here today cleaning the bathrooms and corridors and she says the phone has never stopped ringing. The first time I was out. When I rang back the number I'd been left, Mr. Askarian was out. He rang again. I was in the garden. When I got to the phone, he'd rung off. And so on."

"Askarian is buying a boat from me," Murdo explained to Wyndham.

"I hope that is what it was about," Fiona said. "Not some catastrophe on the first night."

As if on cue, the telephone began to ring. "I'll take it," Laura said.

They could hear her voice from the hall, rising, exclaiming, laughing.

"That'll be Boris," Fiona observed.

Laura was smiling when she returned. "He says the first night was a triumph. He says he has never sung better. He thought the audience would never stop applauding. He sends kisses and congratulations to you, Fiona, and he's flying up the day after tomorrow. He'll go on from here to Edinburgh. Is that alright with you, Murdo?"

"Of course, why not? I told him to come anytime he liked."

"At least he won't run into the demonstration," Laura said.

After dinner, Wyndham asked Murdo if he could see round his darkroom.

"By all means," Murdo said, "but you won't find any telephoto prints of Linnay Island installations hung up to dry."

Wyndham smiled, "I didn't imagine I would. You have a telephoto lens then?"

"I thought you were going to observe the demonstration?" Fiona said.

"I'm going in half an hour. Would you like to come?"

"Do you want me to drive you?"

"I'm having a navy jeep at my disposal

94

while I'm here. It's being brought here in half an hour. I'd like you to come. You could be my guide to the town."

"That wouldn't take her very long," Laura remarked.

Fiona thought about it. "I'll come."

"Good."

While they waited for the car she helped her mother wash up.

"What does Commander Wyndham want to look round your father's darkroom for?" Laura asked her.

"He thinks he's a spy."

"What nonsense, Fiona!"

"No, it could be true. Look at it from his point of view. If the rumors are right about stolen secrets, who is in a better position to organize things than father? This house is a perfect observation post, you can see everything that's going on in the bay. And there are plenty of fast boats in the yard to get close to the action. How many yachtsmen use this as their base now?"

"I don't know. About ten, I suppose."

"There you are then. They are only here using their boats at weekends and holidays. What's to stop father taking a different one each time he wants a closer look at the Island?

They wouldn't get suspicious of that. And he knows the Island well enough to get ashore in secret if he wanted to."

"With his camera strapped to his chest and his instant spy kit in his back pocket, I suppose. You're being ridiculous, dear."

"It's possible. He sacked a man today for taking boats out without permission, and it took them quite a time to find out it had been happening. Think how much easier for father. Then there are those powerful binoculars of yours, always at the ready, and the telephoto lens and all the other equipment."

"You're not being serious, are you?"

"I'm not, but Wyndham might be."

"What a pity," her mother said. "He's such an attractive man."

The phone rang. This time Laura had a faint look of irritation on her face when she returned.

"That was George," she said. "Ringing to see if you'd arrived safely. He sounded rather put out. Something about your being mixed up with the police. 'Was the car all right?' he asked. Not, you notice, 'Were you all right?' You could have been smashed to pieces in an accident and he would consider it a minor incident as long as his precious car was untouched."

"I suppose I should have rung to reassure him," Fiona said. "I knew the police had been in touch with him."

"Fiddlesticks! I hope they frightened him. Anyway he is coming over himself to collect the Mercedes. Day after tomorrow. You can tell him all your adventures yourself."

"You will have a full house," Fiona said. "I wonder how he'll get on with Boris."

Wyndham and Fiona stood crushed against the bar of the New Inn. It was difficult to see across the room for the smoke and almost impossible to hear for the noise. Wyndham had just bought her the fourth whisky of the evening. She held it in her hand without drinking. The brass edge of the wooden bar pressed against her back and a student struggling past with three pints of beer clutched precariously in his hands trod heavily on her foot.

The New Inn was small, drab and Victorian. If people wanted comfort they went to one of the hotels. They came to the New Inn to drink. The saloon bar had thick brown wallpaper on the upper half of the wall and thick brown paint below. The chairs, what there were of them, were upright, cheap wood, thickly varnished, in the round-bottomed, curved-back style to be found in older church halls. The public bar had benches, painted green to match its walls. Directly in front of Fiona was a two-year-old calendar advertising fish meal. Next to it was a large monochrome print of Daniel in theatrical draperies admonishing a couple of despondent lions in a den about the size of the Wembley Stadium. On the opposite wall hung a companion piece, an exotic, and possibly erotic if one had time to study the writhing forms more closely, depiction of Belshazzar's feast. Both prints were spotted with brown, damp stains and framed in black passe-partout. The resulting ambience did not inspire in one, Fiona reflected, any deep sense of joviality.

Wyndham said in her ear: "What time do the pubs close up here?"

"Half an hour ago," she said. "Perhaps they've got an extension."

"Clever of them to know they'd need it tonight," Wyndham murmured.

From the other bar could be heard occasional snatches of a guitar played with more enthusiasm than skill, voices raised in that defiant chant that the more sociological folk singers affect, and the thudding of leaping feet on the bare boards of the floor. An impromptu ceilidh seemed to have developed.

"I think the demonstrators have forgotten what they're here for," she said.

"They're just getting them nicely warmed up," Wyndham said. "Someone will take the lead and get them moving in a short while. I'm interested to see who it will be."

On the other side of Wyndham a tawny-haired girl in a fisherman's sweater seemed to have decided he was a better bet than the stringy youth she was with and was contriving minute by minute to lean a little closer to him.

"In another moment," Fiona thought, "she's going to accidentally knock his drink all over herself."

They had been in the New Inn about an hour. Before that they had visited both hotels and the rival pub on the other side of the square, but found, as sometimes happens on these occasions, that as if directed by a common voice, the entire drinking population, demonstrators, tourists, locals had all, like lemmings heading for the cliffs, gravitated to the same jumping-off ground.

Four of the construction workers from the third coach of demonstrators, looking even more at close quarters as if they should be dressed in wrestling costumes with names like the Masked Menace and the Mangler stamped on their backs, stormed their way to the bar, incidentally forcing Fiona against Wyndham's chest.

"I'm sorry," she said. It came out more as a gasp than an apology.

"I'm not," Wyndham said. He folded his arms round her waist. "I'll keep you upright," he said.

They regarded each other, eye to eye.

"Are you allowed to drink on duty?" Fiona said.

"For God's sake don't talk like that," he said. "We're a couple of lovers from the caravan site."

"Ah—" Fiona said. "Do you think we're convincing?"

He had left his drink on the bar. The tawny-haired girl leaned past and casually knocked the contents of his glass over her sweater. She gave a little scream of dismay. Wyndham unloosed himself from Fiona and turned toward her, and it was at that moment while his head was turned away that Fiona thought she saw someone she knew. She tugged at Wyndham's arm. He had borrowed a cloth from the barman and was mopping the sweater dry. The girl was laughing delightedly. Fiona put her own untouched drink down and began pushing her way to the connecting door leading to the public bar. When she got inside, the scene was as confused as it had sounded. She couldn't even see the guitarist, while the dancers were disembodied heads occasionally bobbing above the crowd. A bespectacled tourist, the only character she had seen all evening wearing a kilt, tried to seize her hands and drag her into the dance, giving wild Highland cries the while. Fiona disengaged herself with a smile. There was another door beside her. She slipped through it and found herself in the open air.

The silence was like a balm. At first it seemed absolute, then the sound of the sea crept into her ears, shallow waves breaking gently against the shingle beach, the undertow pulling the pebbles back with a faint continuous rattle, soothing and repetitive. It took a moment for her eyes to become accustomed to the dark. The harbor sheds were black, amorphous shapes against a softly gleaming sky. The square seemed empty. The fish-and-chip shop was shut, the hall of entertainment closed and barred. There was a movement behind her. A hand clasped her arm and Wyndham said quietly: "What are you doing?"

"I thought I saw David Kenton."

"Kenton?"

"He was at the hotel last night. A student on a walking holiday. You talked to him, didn't you? After you left me?"

"Was that his name? I didn't know. When did you see him?"

"Just now. Going into the public bar. But I couldn't find him."

"He couldn't have got here so soon," Wyndham said.

"Unless he got a lift."

"I thought he was walking."

"Perhaps he got tired," Fiona said. "How's your girl friend?"

"Damp. Now be quiet, they're coming out." He drew her into the shadows.

"Who gave the signal?" Fiona asked.

"Those four construction men. They suddenly began rounding everyone up like sheepdogs. I was just ahead of them. Look out."

The pub doors burst open, spilling yellow light across the cobbles, and the drinkers flooded out, voluble, excitable, still good-humored but ready to be pushed either way, ready to cheer or break windows, whichever way they were directed. The demonstration was under way at last.

"They are running late, if they were supposed to start off at ten o'clock," Fiona said. "It's long past that."

"An exercise like this isn't much use unless it gets publicity," Wyndham said. "They've been waiting for the media to arrive."

"I haven't seen any cameras," Fiona said. "Anyway, wouldn't they provide their own?"

"Doesn't have the same validity," Wyndham said. "But some of the press must have turned up. That's why they've got them going."

It took some time for the surging, eddying crowd to be marshaled into any kind of orderly ranks. There were cheers when the torches were at last lighted and handed out. They made an impressive sight, lighting up the faces of the students, throwing fantastic shadows across the square, coalescing what had been a disorderly but friendly affair into something far more purposeful. At first Fiona was reminded of the torchlight processions of skiers at winter resorts at Christmastime. Then they began to march forward waving torches held aloft, a new radical song was taken up, the thump and rhythm of the chanting voices matching the beat of the feet on the road, and a more sinister image from old newsreels came into Fiona's mind, of early Nazi youth rallies with just such eager faces, such singing, such comradeship.

"Come along," Wyndham said. "We don't want to be left behind, do we?" And taking Fiona's hand he attached them quietly to the end of the procession.

The two-mile hike along the side of the now darkly mysterious loch sobered up most of the demonstrators. Some dropped out, sitting on the grassy verges, heads drooping, hands clasped round knees. The majority made it, though the songs died out, and the talk. In a silent mass they descended through the fields to the boatyard harbor and found the police waiting for them.

There were only three of them visible. "We shall be unobtrusive," Peter had said. He was one of them. He came forward to meet the leaders and a courteous dialogue ensued in which rules previously agreed upon were confirmed. The police withdrew to a line beside the boatyard entrance and the marchers turned left toward the quay the navy used for Linnay Island.

There were no naval personnel in evidence when they reached the quay. As there was nothing the demonstrators could damage or destroy, a low profile and a complete absence of provocation were the order of the day. The navy's attitude was to let the demonstrators get on with it and good luck to them.

The leaders rallied the group, arms now aching from carrying the torches, chill from the freshening breeze coming in from the bay, vaguely frustrated at the lack of any concrete enemy to shame with their contemptuous slogans. A slight air of anticlimax was settling on them when the noise of an approaching engine enlivened them. It was coming in over the sea, red lights flashing high in the air. The cry was: "Navy helicopter! They've sent a helicopter to look us over!" The excitement was tangible. Their presence had been acknowledged. They cheered and shouted as the helicopter swept low over the quay, circled and came back.

"Hide your faces," came the quick order. "They're taking photographs."

Covered faces and raised fists greeted the next sweep of the whirlybird. Then it was gone, vanishing as quickly as it had come.

Wyndham drew Fiona away from the crowd into the darkness.

"You might as well go home," he said. "Nothing more is going to happen."

"I thought they were going to keep a silent vigil," Fiona said.

"They may hang around till morning but their organizers have got them well in hand. They don't want trouble at your father's boatyard any more than he does. He's not the object of the demo. And your friend Peter will have made it clear that the police are quite ready to handle any trouble. They don't want to clash with the police."

"I thought clashing with the police was what they did like to do."

"Not up here, not in such an isolated position and in the dark."

Fiona looked round the group. "I can't really see that they achieved very much."

"The leaders look quite satisfied to me. They've obviously done what they set out to do."

"Who sent the helicopter over?"

"I don't know," Wyndham said. "But I

mean to find out. What's the matter?"

Fiona had stepped forward, trying to see clearly through the light of the flickering torches.

"That man over there, standing by that post . . ."

"David Kenton?" Wyndham asked.

"No. I think it's the man on the motorbike. The one father sacked. Craddock. Now he's gone. Did you see him?"

"Not clearly enough. Tell your friend Peter on your way past him."

"Do you think if it was Craddock he might try and get into the boatyard?"

"It's a possibility, isn't it?" Wyndham said. "But that's where all the police are, so I don't think you need worry about him. Come on, I'll walk you up to the yard."

"What are you going to do?" Fiona asked.

"I'm still observing," Wyndham said. "That's my job, remember. Have a good night. I'll see you in the morning. I suppose I'll be able to get in?"

"We don't lock our front doors up here," Fiona said. "We're just like your trusting old auntie. Remember?"

Murdo Grant, collar up, shoulders hunched

against the cold, was keeping watch over his boatyard. When he heard that Craddock might be in the area, he decided, against all Fiona's attempts to persuade him to go home to bed, to stay a while longer.

"Peter will see nothing happens," she said.

"The yard's my responsibility, not Peter's," Murdo said. "I'm very glad to have the police around, but it's the demonstration they're here for, not just to guard me. Now go along and keep your mother company. She'll be the one who's worried now, alone in the house."

But when Fiona got home, she found Laura had left a tray of sandwiches and drinks for whoever wanted them and had gone to bed. Fiona went to the kitchen and poured herself a glass of ice-cold milk from the fridge. She took it back to the drawing room and sat on the window seat, drinking the milk and watching the glow in the sky caused by the torches.

She ached all over from the march, from standing around in pubs, from the fatigue of the day's drive. She went and lay down on her bed but found she was too tired to sleep. When she closed her eyes scenes flashed and crashed through her mind from the last few days. Boris waltzing her round his dressing room, Eliot, like an oversize rag doll collapsed over his steering wheel, the helicopter rising up from behind the hill, Wyndham, binoculars to his eyes, staring at Linnay Island.

She got up and put on her warm car coat. She would walk back to the yard and keep her father company. Her bedroom window was open. She went over to shut it and saw a light glimmering below.

Fiona's bedroom was at the back of the house, overlooking the garage. For a moment she saw a figure at the wide double doors, then it moved, blended into deeper shadow and vanished. The light had gone. She raced downstairs and out the back door, seizing a heavy torch on the way. Once outside, she began to move more cautiously. Even so, a twig snapped under her feet, sounding as loud as a pistol shot, and she froze. There was a scuffling sound from the garage, then a scraping noise like metal on cement, and suddenly an engine roared into life. Fiona ran forward along the path. Yellow light blazed in her face, blinding her. She stumbled. Someone grabbed her arms and pulled her sideways into the bushes as a motorbike leaped past, missing her by inches. Its noise, stuttering and panicky, its engine missing, receded into the distance.

The hands holding Fiona relaxed.

"Well, that's that," Wyndham said. "Shall we go and see if he's done any damage?"

Fiona was still holding the torch. She stepped back and shone it into Wyndham's face. "I thought you were staying at the quay?"

He winced. "Put that damn thing down. It's a good thing I wasn't at the quay. What exactly were you doing, apart from getting yourself run over?"

"I saw someone either trying to get in or coming out of the garage. It was Craddock, wasn't it?"

"You worry too much about that car of your uncle's. You should worry a bit more about yourself. You could have been killed, stepping in front of him like that. What were you planning to do? Grab the handlebars and toss him over your shoulder?"

"I didn't expect him to come down here," Fiona said. "It's a path not a drive."

Wyndham sighed. "You're not much good at this sort of thing, are you? Please don't go wandering about after intruders again. I might not be here next time."

"Is there going to be a next time?" Fiona asked.

"Oh, shut up," Wyndham said. He put his arm round her shoulders and guided her along the path to the garage.

The garage looked secure but when Fiona touched the right-hand door it swung gently open. "I know I locked it," she said. "And it hasn't been broken open."

"It's a Yale lock," Wyndham pointed out. "They open those with a piece of perspex. No jemmies needed." They went inside and Fiona switched on the lights. The Mercedes stood next to her mother's old runabout. Both cars looked untouched. She checked their doors and found them locked.

"I must have disturbed him before he could do anything," she said. "I looked out of my window. He must have seen me at the same time I saw him."

Wyndham had been walking round the garage. Now he got down and looked under the cars. "No petrol trails, no fuses, no odd packets strapped to the cars. I think we're all right. As you say, he hadn't time to do any thing. Come on."

They went back outside. "What about the door?" Fiona said.

Wyndham pulled it to. The lock clicked shut. "But you'd better tell your father to get something stronger."

"We've never needed anything stronger," Fiona said.

"Perhaps your father has never made an enemy before."

"I don't like the sound of that," Fiona said.

"Don't worry. Craddock's only a man with a grudge. Once the drink has worn off, he'll think twice about trying anything like this again. I think you scared him to death."

"In that case I did accomplish something. By the way, you didn't say what you were doing, lurking in the bushes."

"I'd been following Craddock. And now I'll go and make sure he's off the premises and let the police and your father know what's happened."

"Will you bring my father back with you?" Fiona asked. "I don't think he should stay out all night."

"I'm afraid I'll have to wait till the demonstration is finished, but I'll tell him you're worried. That'll send him home."

"What is happening down there?" Fiona said.

"Nothing. It's very peaceful. But you never

112

know. There may be a few nutty ones with different ideas about their mission. That's why we have to wait till dawn. When it's over your friend Peter is giving me a lift back to town so I can pick up the jeep. That is, if I can remember where we left it."

"In the lane at the back of the pub," Fiona said.

"So we did. I hope it's still there. I wouldn't like to lose government property on my very first day. It makes such a bad impression. Good night once again. Have the whisky ready for your father."

"Come in and have one yourself," Fiona suggested. "Against the cold."

"You couldn't get me out again. Take care of yourself." And he melted away into the darkness.

Afterward Fiona thought she might at least have thanked him for saving her from injury, and for protecting her and her family by following Craddock when he was supposed to be watching the demonstrators. Or was there another reason for his interest in Craddock? If there was one thing she felt sure of about Wyndham, it was that he was not the most straightforward of men. Everything he did had a purpose.

The rest of the night passed without misadventure. When she finally did get to sleep, aided by more milk, warm this time and with a generous dollop of whisky added by her father, she slept for a solid nine hours and only awoke when her mother arrived rather apologetically with a breakfast tray, explaining that Mrs. Niven was scrubbing the kitchen floor and would shortly be starting on the oven and if she didn't take her breakfast now she'd miss it altogether.

"Has Commander Wyndham had his?" Fiona asked, sitting up in bed.

"Commander Wyndham came in about eight, had a bath and a cup of coffee and went off again. He didn't say where to."

"No, he wouldn't. I hope he thanked you for the bed."

"As far as I can gather, he didn't use the bed," Laura said. "But he thanked me very politely. We had quite a nice wee chat over the coffee cups. I heard all about last night. It seems I slept through some excitement."

"The best thing to do," Fiona said. "I wish I had. Is he coming back tonight?"

"I expect so. I told him to come to dinner if he liked. In fact, I told him he was welcome here anytime, either for a meal or a bed. Well, you did tell me, dear, that he suspected your father of being a spy, and it occurred to me that open hospitality would be one way to disarm his suspicion."

"I don't think he's the sort of man that would make much difference to. But no doubt he'll be glad to have such a comfortable base on the mainland. Has the paper come?"

"It never comes before lunch, don't you remember? And not always then. They've been having trouble with the lads who deliver the papers. They don't mind doing it in the town, but they find this too long a way to cycle, so they tell me."

"The softness of modern youth," said Fiona, getting out of bed. "I'll have a quick bath, then I'll go into town and pick it up and any others I can find. They're usually in the shop by twelve, aren't they?"

"They won't be any the better reviews for seeing them earlier," Laura remarked. "Anyway you know they will be good ones. Boris Askarian said so."

"First-night audiences and music critics don't always see eye to eye. Can I borrow your car?"

"Of course."

"Do you want to come too?"

"No, thank you," Laura said. "I'll give you a list of shopping to do. That will occupy your mind in case of disappointment. By the way, when are you off to Edinburgh?"

"I haven't quite decided. I'll ring Fred up in a couple of days and see what he says. If Boris arrives in a Rolls, I might hitch a lift with him."

"He surely never travels in anything else?" Laura commented.

"I don't think he'd fit into anything else," Fiona said. "He's a very large man."

The town showed all the signs of a massive morning-after. The square looked like a temporary dressing station on the edge of a battlefield. Students lay strewn along the quayside, gray-faced and desolate, wrapped tightly round with blankets like so many woolly chrysalises. Others had retreated to the shelter of the coaches and could be observed sunk in heavy sleep, uncomfortably upright, heads lolling against the rigid seat backs. Those who were awake squatted on the pavement edge, eating chips out of greasy bags, which they dropped wearily into the gutter as they finished, wiping their fingers on their jeans.

They seemed to have been abandoned by their leaders. Fiona had been held up on the road into town by the departure of the third coach. The construction workers, or whoever they really were, having accomplished their task and with stronger heads than their young comrades, were off to the next rallying point, picket line, sit-in, riot, whatever it might be.

"Pathetic, isn't it?" the news agent remarked, gazing at the view through the window. "I don't know what they thought they were up to last night, all that shouting and singing, but you can't help feeling sorry for the poor things this morning."

The bus bringing the papers hadn't yet arrived. He promised to keep for Fiona, as well as her *Times*, a selection of papers that weren't already ordered for other customers and she went off to dispose of her mother's shopping list.

She had parked the car in the lane at the back of the New Inn, where Wyndham had left the jeep the night before. She lugged the full shopping baskets back there and dumped them on the back seat of the car. As she slammed the door shut, she looked up and saw opposite her, leaning against the back entrance of the pub, his rucksack propped beside him, and talking to another student, the figure of David Kenton. He saw her at the same time and waved cheerfully. She went across to him.

"So it was you last night," Fiona remarked in mild triumph, pleased to have her judgment vindicated.

"Was it?" Kenton said. "Where was I?"

"Here, in the New Inn."

Kenton grinned. He looked a good deal perkier than his companion, who stood there registering nail-biting impatience at being held up at the very door of the now open pub.

"Don't tell me you were on the march?" Kenton asked.

"Right behind you," Fiona said. "All the way."

"Fancy that." He turned to his companion. "Then she should join in the rewards, don't you agree?"

The other boy was taller than Kenton, with a bony face and concave chest. His hair was a mass of corkscrew curls and he wore a drooping mustache.

"Look," he said. "Are you coming or not? We'll miss him if we don't watch out."

"Who's going to look after the rest?"

118

Kenton jerked his thumb in the direction of the harbor. "All those sleeping beauties back there?"

"They'll get their share, don't worry. You can't expect them to line up in a queue halfway round the square."

Kenton looked at his watch. "You said another half hour."

"I need a drink."

"See you in half an hour. I want a word with my girl friend."

"O.K. O.K." He pushed open the door leading through to the bars and disappeared inside.

"An old friend of yours?" Fiona asked.

"I met him for the first time last night."

"What are you up to?" she said. "How did you get involved in the demonstration? How did you get here so fast?"

He held a hand up. "One question at a time. Let's go and have coffee somewhere. I'm not ready for a drink yet."

They went to the café in the High Street. There were seats free in the window but Kenton led her to a bench in an alcove at the back.

"You don't want to be seen with me," Fiona said.

"On the contrary, that bright sunlight is too much for me this morning."

He fetched two coffees and sat down next to her. "Did you stay up all night? You don't look as if you did."

"Did that chat with your friend back there mean what I thought it did?" Fiona said. "Are all those demonstrators from rent-a-crowd?"

Kenton laughed. "Well, no, not all of them. I got talking to that chap in the pub last night. He said if I wanted to make a few easy shillings, why didn't I join in, carry a torch. All I had to do was to stay awake all night. As for getting here to the coast so soon, I got lost on the hills, came down to the road to find my bearings and a fish lorry stopped and offered me a lift. You don't say no to a stroke of fortune like that even if it has resulted in cats following me round all day. You live here, don't you? That was your father's boatyard the police were so concerned we shouldn't set alight with our torches."

"What did you do all night?"

"Sang songs, listened to fiery speeches designed to keep us awake, chanted slogans, and then someone reminded us it was supposed to be a silent vigil, after which things got pretty boring. As soon as first light came we were off. Rumor had it the navy might come and stir up some trouble and after a night like that we weren't in any shape for a confrontation, so we limped back here. That last two miles was the worst I've done this trip, I can tell you."

"Are you a believer in the cause?" Fiona asked him.

He gazed back at her with his clear blue eyes. "Well, I'm pro-peace and anti-establishment, pro-conservation and anti-pollution, naturally. Isn't everyone?"

"I think you're a crafty hypocrite," Fiona said. "Shame on you. Sleeping in hotels and hitching lifts. I suppose when you get back you'll tell everyone you walked every inch of the way and slept out every single night."

"Of course. Why are you being so prim?"

"I'm being disillusioned, that's why. I always thought protest marchers were such pure, earnest souls."

"No one who wasn't earnest would have stuck last night. Do you know how cold it gets by your loch on a summer night?" He looked at his watch. "Now I suppose I had better go."

"To get paid off."

"Exactly."

"Who by?" Fiona asked.

He shook his head. "It will be interesting to see, won't it?"

"I'll walk down with you. I've got to go to the news agents to collect some papers."

"We'll go there first. Then you can come and have a drink with me."

"You'll be flushed with money by then, of course."

"Well, the kitty has been getting a bit empty. I've been walking around Scotland a long time, you know."

"I was beginning to think you'd just come up on the overnight train. At least I might have done if you hadn't told me you were a theology student. They can't tell lies, can they?"

"If you saw the state of my feet you'd believe me. Are you getting the papers to see if there's anything about the demonstration?"

"Even I know morning papers won't have a story in that didn't start happening till after eleven," Fiona said. "No, it's a notice of an opera I'm looking for."

Apart from *The Times*, the news agent had kept back for her copies of *The Guardian*, *The Scotsman* and *The Glasgow Herald*. Fiona opened them one after another, standing there in the shop. She was lucky. They all carried reviews of the London first night of *Rosenkavalier*, though the two Scottish papers did little more than note it. They would review it in detail, they stated, when it opened in a few days' time at the Edinburgh Festival. Even so, they praised the production in general terms, while the other two papers devoted several columns to it. Boris had had the triumph he predicted. The lyricism and tenderness of the Princess was balanced against the youthful eagerness of the Octavian. And so on and so on. Fiona skimmed the columns quickly. The orchestra had been superb. The production glowed with both warmth and melancholy . . . the contribution made by the decor . . . splendidly dressed by Fiona Grant. She gazed incredulously at her name. She didn't know that she would have chosen the word splendid to describe what she had tried to achieve, but her name was actually there, in print. She would be accepted as a designer on her own now. And she knew whom she owed it to.

"Dear old Fred," she said aloud.

"Who is Fred?" Kenton asked in some

bewilderment. "What is all this about? Why are you looking so pleased?"

She handed him the folded-over paper. "That's me!"

"What a self-satisfied smile! Which is you?"

"There!" She pointed to her name. Kenton read the whole piece with great attention.

"Good heavens," he said at last. "I'm overwhelmed. So that's what you do. I thought you were one of the idle rich. Congratulations. Now you really must have a drink on me. Can I show this to everyone?"

"No, you can't." She took the paper back from him.

"Pity. I was going to bask in a little reflected glory. My friend the designer. Let's go and get my hard-earned money and see if they're giving us enough for whisky."

They walked through the square to the New Inn. The bodies were stirring now. The driver of one of the coaches had arrived and, after experimentally revving up the engine, had jumped down and was smoking a cigarette with one of the more wide-awake looking students.

"It looks as if they might be off soon," Fiona said. "Are you going with them?"

"They are going back to Glasgow. I've no great desire to go to Glasgow."

"So what will you do now?"

"Oh, I'll be on my way. Wandering Willie, that's me. Shall I go first?"

He led the way into the pub. "I imagine they're in the public bar," he said.

Fiona was following him down the narrow inner passage leading to the door of the bar when it swung open and a man came out. He didn't stop to give way to them and they had to stand back against the wall to let him pass. As he came level with them Fiona found herself face to face with Craddock. She might not immediately have recognized him if he had not stopped himself and stared at her. But then that pallid face with the weasel expression beneath the shock of pale red hair grew threateningly familiar. And he knew who she was, without doubt. A sudden totally unexpected surge of anger shot through her. She pulled herself away from the wall, away from Kenton. She said icily, "What exactly were you doing in my father's garage last night?"

Craddock said nothing. Kenton looked at Fiona in some amazement. She went on with the same deliberation. "If we catch you anywhere near the boatyard or anywhere near the house again, you'll be arrested and charged."

Craddock had recovered from his shock. When he spoke it was with a strong Glasgow accent. "How d'you think you're going to do that? What exactly do you think you can charge me with?"

"Breaking and entering and dangerous driving would do for last night," Fiona said. "I expect my father will be able to think up a good few from your time at the boatyard."

"Never mind your father," Craddock said. "I can deal with your father. And who says I was anywhere near your place last night. Where're your witnesses? Your word against mine, lassie."

"There was another witness," Fiona said. "And if you don't clear out of here and out of the town pretty fast, I won't wait. I'll get the police on to you today."

Craddock's mouth twisted in what Fiona realized could only be described as a sneer. His eyes glittered with fury. She thought he was going to hit her and Kenton thought so too for he began to move between them. Then Craddock backed away, down the corridor to the street door. He paused at the entrance and spat back at her, "Don't think you can threaten me! There's more than one person can go to the police. You can tell that high-and-mighty relative of yours that I know all about the company. All about it! The Grants aren't above the law. None of you!"

He slammed out of the pub and a moment later they heard the echo of his bike exhaust reverberating against the walls of the side alley.

"What the hell was that all about?"

The altercation had roused the drinkers from the public bar. Looking back Fiona saw four or five men grouped round the door. She noticed the curly head of Kenton's acquaintance and beside him another face she knew, whose blunt features and yellow thatch of hair were quite unmistakable.

"Let's get out of here," Kenton said quietly.

Out of the square, Fiona found she was trembling.

"You look as if you need that drink now," Kenton said. "But we'll go to the other pub. You won't be the center of curious attention there."

He waited until they were settled in the slightly more comfortable Ship Inn, hard by the harbor wall, before broaching the subject of Craddock.

"To quote our friends back there," he said, "what the hell was that all about?"

"That was about a man called Craddock," Fiona said, "who worked for my father until yesterday when he fired him for bad workmanship, borrowing boats without permission, and nearly wrecking one altogether. Craddock was furious and threatened him. Last night I caught him breaking into the garage. He got away on his bike and nearly ran me down."

"A very unpleasant character," Kenton said. "Was there another witness or were you bluffing?"

"Commander Wyndham was there. You remember, I gave him a lift here from the hotel."

"Oh, yes, I remember the Commander. Is he staying with you?"

"Yes and no," Fiona said. "My mother keeps inviting him to meals."

Kenton smiled. "I have a mother like that too. What was that about the company? What did Craddock mean by those threats?"

"I've no idea."

"But he worried you."

"He worried me, naturally. Anyone would be worried by that sort of malicious nonsense. But there's nothing to it. There is nothing at all fraudulent or criminal in the way my father runs his company."

"I'm sure there isn't. But he sounded as if he was quite ready to manufacture something. Are you going to tell your father?"

"I don't know. Yes, I suppose I should. In case Craddock tried to make more trouble. A boatyard is so vulnerable."

"I shouldn't worry," Kenton said. "With the business last night, there'll be plenty of navy personnel keeping an eye on things. Tell your Commander Wyndham. He'll detail a couple of tough matelots to warn off any intruders."

Fiona had recovered. In fact she had recovered enough to feel slightly appalled at making a scene in a public house, and in front of people who knew her.

"Did you see who was in the bar?" she said. "Jackson, the pilot of the helicopter which landed at the hotel last night."

"Really?" Kenton said. "I didn't notice him. Are you sure?"

"Yes, he'd come to the door with the other people to see what the row was about. I wonder what he's doing here."

"Searching for backgrounds for some TV program, weren't they?" Kenton said. "I suppose they've been doing a wide sweep as far as the coast."

"You don't think he's anything to do with the demonstration?"

"Remembering what those three were like. I shouldn't think so for a minute. They wouldn't be interested in a long walk and a night spent waving a torch. You didn't see him on the march, did you?"

"No," Fiona admitted. "But it rather looked as if he was with your friend. He was standing next to him. Still, it could have been coincidence."

"From my experience last night," Kenton said, "that boy will talk to anyone who looks as if he might buy him a drink. Which reminds me, would you like another?"

"No, thank you. I ought to get back. I've got some stuff for the freezer in the car and it's probably already dripping through the floor. Thank you for the drink and the moral support."

"You're welcome. And congratulations again. I must try and get to Edinburgh to see your costumes."

"Get in touch with me if you do. I'll try and get you a free ticket."

"Thanks very much. I'll keep you to that."

"There's one thing we've forgotten," Fiona said, "in all the fuss I caused. You didn't collect your money for the demonstration."

"Ah, well," Kenton said. "I think I'll forget about that. Now I think about it, it is rather against my principles to accept money for taking part in a protest march."

"So you'll never know now which of the students was going to pay you."

"I won't, will I?" Kenton grinned. "I'll just have to learn to live with it."

After she had parked the car in the garage and taken out the shopping, Fiona paused to look at the Mercedes. A remark of Wyndham's the previous night came back to her. "No odd packets strapped to the cars." Not strapped outside, she thought, but what about inside. She opened the hood. As far as she could tell, everything looked normal; there didn't appear to be any additional wires and there were certainly no packets. It was the same with the trunk. She got inside the car and searched around the seats back and front, the pockets, compartments, around the dashboard. The only unusual thing she found was a bar of chocolate. It was in exactly the same place as the one Wyndham had found and eaten and was exactly the same kind of chocolate. She could have sworn there had only been one packet there. But if there had, where had this come from and why? Replaced by Wyndham? How? The car had been locked. She hadn't made a mistake about that this time. And she had had the keys from the time they had arrived at the house. The locks hadn't been tampered with and she didn't think Craddock would have been able to open these with a piece of plastic. Anyway Craddock would have only been concerned with damaging the car, not putting bars of chocolate in it. And neither of them would have had time to buy a spare key even if they had found out which number to buy. It had been too late for that by the time she and Wyndham arrived. Either man would have had to go miles to find a place that sold those particular keys and it would have been shut for the night by then. She sighed. She was going into the realms of fantasy imagining anyone going to all those lengths to replace a bar of chocolate. There must have been two there all the time. She got out, relocked the car, pulled the garage doors to, and took her shopping and her newspapers back to the house.

4

WYNDHAM came to dinner that night. Urbane, relaxed, smiling.

"Did you get any sleep?" Fiona asked him.

"Sufficient."

"I've a lot of news for you." She told him about her encounter with Craddock, about meeting Kenton, about Jackson, the helicopter pilot.

"A day crowded with incident," he remarked. "Did he see you?"

"Who?"

"Jackson."

"I don't know. I suppose so. Why?"

"It doesn't matter. I want a word with your father."

Murdo took him to his study at the end of the hall.

"What's so secret?" Fiona said. "Why can't they talk here?"

"Do you think the Commander will want a bed for the night?" Laura wondered.

"Why don't we just ask him to move in?"

134

"Don't be so irritable, dear," Laura said. "Go and paste your cuttings in a scrapbook."

Fiona laughed. "That's a nice way of telling me I'm being childish."

"I'm just as curious as you," Laura said. "I'll winkle it out of your father later. Here you are." She poured out two glasses of sherry. "Take these in and tell them not to be too long drinking them or the lamb will be spoiled."

Laura had insisted on cutting out immediately the reviews of *Rosenkavalier*. "Otherwise papers get thrown away. You forget why you're keeping them and lose the reviews. You must keep them, Fiona. Your first real professional success."

After dinner she showed the cuttings to Wyndham, who made suitably impressed responses. He refused the offer of a bed. "I have to get back to the Island. I still have rather a lot of work to get through today."

"Pursuing your inquiries," Fiona suggested.

"You might call it that, yes."

"Well, we're very glad you're not carrying Murdo away with you," Laura said in a brisk tone. "We were rather afraid your private talk was a euphemism for making an arrest."

135

"You thought your husband might be arrested? What for?"

"Stealing naval secrets, I imagine," Murdo said.

"And is that what you've been doing, Mr. Grant?" Wyndham asked blandly.

"Well, if I have its clear I shan't be doing it much longer. Not with you on the doorstep. By the way, do you want to wait and see the news? I usually watch it at this time—when I can see it. Reception up here is so poor Laura says it's hardly worth having TV except for general elections and declarations of war."

"We're not expecting either of those tonight, are we?" Wyndham said. "No, I'll see it at the base later. Thank you, once again, Mrs. Grant, for the superb meal. Good night."

"Come tomorrow and meet Mr. Askarian," Laura said. "That is, if you can spare the time."

"Not to mention meeting George," Fiona murmured.

"Thank you," Wyndham said. "You're very kind."

His Jeep was parked outside the front door. Fiona walked to it with him. He stopped beside it and said in a different, more serious tone: "You said earlier Craddock threatened to tell the police about the company. Did you mention that to your father?"

"Yes."

"What did he say?"

"He told me to ignore it." She looked at Wyndham's face. "You could have asked him about that yourself. Why didn't you? What did you talk to him about?"

"Details of owners who keep their boats at the yard. Information like that."

"I don't know whether to believe you."

"Ask your father." He paused. "Am I right? Your uncle is coming to collect the Mercedes tomorrow?"

"You'll have the pleasure of meeting him if you come to lunch. Which reminds me. How many bars of chocolate did you find in the car?"

"What an extraordinary question. Why do you ask? Afraid uncle will start counting?"

"Just try and remember."

"All right, I'll try and remember." He gazed at her solemnly as if the number might be inscribed on her forehead.

"Two," he said, after a moment. "There were two."

137

"Thank you," Fiona said. "You've solved a puzzle for me."

"Glad to be of service. When are you off to Edinburgh?"

"Everyone wants to be rid of me. I'm not sure. I'll decide tomorrow when I've seen Boris."

"I can't wait to meet him,"Wyndham said. "Good night."

As Wyndham turned to get in the Jeep, Murdo suddenly called to them from the drawing room window. "Come and see this. Hurry up, it won't be on long."

They ran back to the drawing room where the television, despite a sprinkling of snow effects, was providing a clear enough picture of torches waving beside a faintly visible shoreline, clenched fists menacing the sky and pale anonymous faces mouthing unintelligible insults.

"The helicopter!" Fiona breathed. "They were filming from the navy helicopter."

It had been the last item on the news. After a moment it was replaced by the weather forecast. Murdo switched the television off.

"No naval helicopter was in this area last night," Wyndham said. "And they haven't got one on the Island."

"Where did it come from then?" Laura asked. "A television company?"

"It was a free-lance news agency," Wyndham said. "I presume they picked up the story and sent a team over on spec, then sold the film to the TV companies. Incidentally they managed to get a photograph in various evening papers. I meant to tell you. The nationals will probably pick it up tomorrow."

"So it was a successful venture," Fiona said. "The demonstrators got their publicity after all. You knew they had last night, didn't you? You said after the helicopter had gone that they'd achieved what they wanted."

"The agency was not connected with the demonstrators then?" Murdo said. "It was just a professional job to them?"

"That's what it seems," Wyndham said. "But things are not always what they seem."

"That's why you were interested when I mentioned I'd seen Jackson," Fiona said. "Is he employed by this agency?"

"Who is Jackson?" Laura asked.

"He is the pilot of a helicopter we've encountered a couple of times lately," Fiona said. "He was having a drink with the demonstrators this morning. They were all

139

waiting to be paid for their trouble."

"I don't quite understand," Laura said. "Was he paying them?"

"That's a thought, isn't it?" Wyndham said. "Now I really must go."

Later that evening Fiona asked her father what Wyndham had talked to him about.

"He wanted to know as much as I could tell him about Craddock," Murdo said.

"That's reasonable. Why couldn't he tell me that?"

"Perhaps he likes to keep some aspects of his investigation to himself."

"That sounds very pompous. Does he think I might go and warn someone what he's up to?"

"Perhaps he thinks you might without meaning to."

"It's you he's really suspicious of, Father. You know that, don't you?"

"Don't worry about it," Murdo said. "There's really nothing to worry about."

George was the first of the two luncheon guests to arrive next day. Dressed in shooting tweeds, complete with leather patches on the shoulders, and an old hat that looked as if it should have been studded with fishing flies, he appeared to be busily sustaining his image of the laird at home. But though the tweeds, suitably old, were of excellent quality and cut, George's bony figure could do nothing for them, and his face, which had borne quite a pleasantly open expression the last time Fiona had seen him, was now marked by a strained disapproval. The frown remained even when he stooped to submit to Laura's polite embrace.

"You're looking very well, George," she said.

He nodded. "Where's Murdo?"

"Down at the yard. He'll be back for lunch. Or you could go down to see him if you wish."

"No need. I gather you had trouble with the car, Fiona?"

"Not the car, George. There is nothing wrong with that. I merely became involved as a witness to someone else's accident. And a great nuisance it was too." Despite herself Fiona could hear a self-justifying note in her voice.

Laura, motherlike, sprang to her defense. "You were very lucky to have had Fiona driving the car, George. It is fortunate for you she has such quick reactions. With two

141

cars sprawled across a single track road in thick fog, it was lucky she wasn't killed, let alone saving the Mercedes from damage."

"My dear Laura, I am well aware of what I owe Fiona." He gave them a frosty smile. "May I see the car?"

"Yes, of course, it's in the garage."

"I have brought my mechanic with me." He gestured outside to his chauffeur-driven Land-Rover. "I'd like him to give it a brief overhaul before I drive it back."

Fiona and Laura exchanged glances. Seeing the suppressed exasperation on her mother's face after less than five minutes in George's company, Fiona collected the garage key and removed George as quickly as possible from her presence.

The mechanic backed the Mercedes out of the garage into the yard. He was a small, stocky man with a dourness that matched his employer's. He brought out his tools, a mat to lie on, and starting with the engine, he proceeded to check every component down to the last wire and nut. While he was engaged with the mechanics of the car, George dealt with the interior. With growing fascination, Fiona leaned against the sun-warmed wall and watched the performance. Bent double to examine the carpets, folding and unfolding his long form as he climbed in and out of the back, running a hand round the edge of the seats, opening up ashtrays, feeling in pockets. Fiona began to wonder exactly what he thought she had been doing with his car. When he came up with the bar of chocolate, she couldn't resist an interruption.

"I'm sorry about the other one," she said. "I'll be happy to pay for it."

"Other one?" He turned to gaze at her. She came closer.

"I'm afraid the Commander ate it," she explained, and then as George continued to stare blankly at her, she went on, "You may or may not remember but you left two bars of chocolate there. The Commander was hungry and ate one of them."

"The Commander?" George said.

"Commander Wyndham. You'll meet him at lunch. His car was damaged in the accident and I gave him a lift here." She added, "You've no objection, have you? I didn't intend to take any passengers but these were rather unusual circumstances."

"I've no objection." He put the chocolate back where he had found it. "This Commander Wyndham, did he travel all the way with you?"

"He was going to Linnay Island," Fiona said.

"I see." Continuing his inspection he leaned across the passenger seat and drew the ordnance survey map from the side pocket.

"I didn't use that," Fiona volunteered. "It looked much too new. I had my own."

George grunted. He put the map in his capacious jacket pocket and climbed out of the car. He gazed down at Fiona thoughtfully. "I am sorry you had to suffer inconvenience on my behalf," he said unexpectedly. "The car seems in good enough condition. There's no need for you to stay. I'll wait until my man is finished, then I'll be up to the house. Lunch will be a while yet I suppose."

"About an hour," Fiona said. It was an unusual feeling to be dismissed from her own garage. "We have another guest coming, you know, apart from yourself and the Commander."

"Is it someone I know?"

"Boris Askarian," Fiona said.

"The opera singer? What on earth is he doing up here?" Then comprehension slowly replaced surprise. "Of course, he's coming to see you."

144

"He's buying a boat from father," Fiona said. "Seeing me is incidental."

"I suppose he is on his way to the Festival. Are you traveling with him?"

"I haven't decided yet. George, what were you looking for just now?"

"Looking for?"

"In the car. To put it as plainly as I can, you seemed to be searching the car for something."

He had clearly already dismissed her from his mind as he had from his presence. He refocused his attention on her. He said: "I hadn't realized you were watching. I thought you had gone back to the house," as if that were all the explanation she needed. Then he added casually: "I lost a scarf in Germany. I thought I might have left it in the car." He met her glance with a faintly amused look, as if challenging her to accept his explanation. It didn't seem to matter to him, Fiona thought, whether she did or not. To her the truth seemed most probably linked to the telephone call the police had made to him from the hotel. They had searched the car looking for Eliot's wallet. Perhaps they had asked him to look again when he reclaimed the Mercedes. It amused her, as perhaps it was amusing

George, to realize that as a direct result of bringing the car to Scotland she had become an object of suspicion, to the police, to Wyndham, and now it seemed, to her uncle as well. That was the trouble with doing favors for people, she told herself as she walked back to the house. They always seemed to rebound in some disastrous way.

Boris had arrived. The inevitable Rolls was parked next to George's Land-Rover, and ensconced in the most comfortable chair in the drawing room, whisky glass in hand, Boris was already embarked on the saga of his journey north, his resonant voice, which always seemed slightly too large for domestic use, embellishing a tale of nearly missed flights, recalcitrant taxi drivers and airport bomb scares with as much color and shade as his most dramatic arias. As in any performance, even when his audience consisted solely, as now, of a slightly stunned Laura and the Grant's tremulously dreaming cat, Boris could not give less than his all.

He leaped to his feet when Fiona entered and clasped her in a bear hug.

"My dearest Fiona, how are you? What a success for you! Have you seen the papers? Fred is pale with jealousy."

Fiona disengaged herself. "Green," she said. "You're supposed to go green with jealousy."

"No, he is definitely white, like a ghost, and is continually shouting at people." He looked at Laura. "Your mother knows we are joking, doesn't she? Fred is a little odd, like most artists, Mrs. Grant, but he is devoted to your daughter. As are we all. She's a very talented girl. I have been having a great talk with your mother, Fiona. She is a beautiful and charming woman. How fortunate your father is to have two such women in his household."

"I must leave before I become quite overwhelmed," Laura said dryly. "See if Mr. Askarian would care for another drink, Fiona. Please excuse me," she added to Boris, "I must keep an eye on the lunch."

Fiona poured herself a sherry and refilled Boris's glass.

"All flattery apart," he said, "your mother really is charming. I wish I could stay."

"I thought you were staying tonight."

"I have committed myself to dine with some old friends. I couldn't visit Scotland without seeing them, and then their house is on the way south and I want to be in Edinburgh tomorrow fairly early. I don't know the theater, but I gather it is not ideal. It is going to be a tight fit, particularly for the orchestra. I foresee trouble. You know how bloody-minded musicians can be."

"But they love success, like everyone else," Fiona said. "You've all had such wonderful notices, they're not going to ruin that. They'll want to dazzle Edinburgh, knock everyone sideways, they'll play even better, you'll see."

He shook his head with sudden gloom. "Perhaps."

"How are things going?" Fiona asked.

He shrugged. "I am enjoying it. I am singing very well."

"How is the new Annina?"

"Not bad. She had terrible nerves at the first performance. It affected her voice. But she sang better last night. I gave her some of my special throat spray."

"I hope she was properly grateful."

Boris laughed. "She's not my type, Fiona. By the way, when are you coming to Edinburgh? Do you want to come with me?"

Fiona thought about it and made her decision.

"I wouldn't want to descend on your friends."

"They wouldn't mind. They expect me to travel with a beautiful woman in tow. They are going to be disappointed if I don't."

"I'm not coming just to bolster up your reputation. Besides, leaving here tonight would be a little early for me. I want one more day of holiday before I rejoin Fred's circus."

He shrugged. "A pity, but I accept it." He stood up and crossed to the window. "I can't imagine how you could bear to leave here in the first place. What a lucky man your father is! He knows the way to live. Peace, beauty, a simple, satisfying life."

"I don't think he'd have agreed with you last night," Fiona said. "With a hundred odd torch-waving demonstrators wandering about the place, the boatyard full of police and a crackpot trying to break into the garage."

Boris gazed at her in wonder. "You are joking."

Fiona joined him at the window. "You can ask him yourself. Here he comes. He's the one in the middle. The tall, thin one is my uncle George."

"The man with the Mercedes and the

149

castle," Boris observed. "Who's the other man?"

"Commander Wyndham," Fiona said. "It looks as if he collected my father from the boatyard. That's his Jeep parked by your Rolls. My mother and I had a bet that you'd turn up in a Rolls."

Boris turned to her. "Am I so very predictable?"

"Whether it is you who is predictable or the character you create, I wouldn't know," Fiona said.

"Now that is an odd thing to say," Boris said. "I wonder what you can mean by it."

Fiona herself didn't quite know what she meant by it except perhaps that Boris Askarian, the opera singer, did sometimes seem with his flamboyance, his attractiveness, his charm, almost too good to be true. Like George, with his depiction of an aloof Scottish aristocrat, Boris often seemed to be playing himself like an actor playing a part. Like George again, even his clothes seemed chosen to fit the role. The fashionably casual clothes he was wearing now, for instance, which were just slightly overdone, a little too stagy, with the silk scarf and the gold chain round his wrist. He was wearing either

150

perfume or after-shave, expensive and subtle, his hair curled to exactly the right degree. He was groomed, polished, bursting with vitality and good humor, and there was something in his eyes occasionally which seemed to be mocking it all.

"I mean," Fiona said, "that one couldn't imagine Baron Ochs traveling in anything else."

Boris laughed. "I am afraid he would choose something much more vulgar." He put his arm round her shoulder. "They are having a long talk out there on the terrace. Do you think we should rap on the window?"

"I expect George is cross-examining Commander Wyndham on what exactly did happen to his Mercedes on the way here."

"And how would this commander know that?"

"Because he happened to be there." Fiona told him briefly what had happened.

"Ah, yes," Boris said, "your mother was telling me a little of your adventures. I am afraid I was too interested in recounting mine to pay proper attention. What an alarming experience for you. What does this Commander Wyndham do?"

"No one has quite liked to ask him

directly," Fiona said. "We think he's here to catch spies, but he hasn't actually said so."

"No," Boris said. "I don't suppose he would. So you have spies here?"

"I think that's largely imagination too," Fiona said. "By the way, I haven't congratulated you yet on your success. I think it's wonderful, but I'm not at all surprised."

"Thank you, my dear. Neither am I. I may say it is richly deserved. We have had three performances now and I am getting better with each of them. I shall reach my peak in Edinburgh." He was still gazing out of the window as he spoke, almost absentmindedly.

Fiona laughed. "Oh, Boris."

He turned to look at her. "What is it?"

She said: "I am so very fond of you, but I'm beginning to think you're the most terrible poseur."

He smiled. "Naturally. Aren't we all?"

The opera singer, the Scottish laird, the naval officer, they made an odd trio of guests sitting round the mahogany table in the sunny dining room, eating her mother's excellent food and drinking one of her father's better clarets. Fiona wondered what they thought of each other. Did Boris seem to George the epitome of the fleshy bon viveur, was George being summed up as a puritanical ascetic? As for Wyndham, he was exercising once more his talent for camouflage, merging quietly into the background, saying little, no doubt observing much. Fiona couldn't say why but she had the feeling he was at his most dangerous when he was at his quietest. And that was a ridiculous adjective to use, dangerous. Why should he be dangerous? To whom?

The conversation was at first, naturally enough, about opera. George revealed himself to be more knowledgeable than she would have supposed. Who was playing Sophie, he asked, and when told about the young American soprano who had now sung with the company for two seasons, he immediately remembered her on another occasion at Glyndebourne in *Così fan tutte*. He considered Mozart the greatest test of an artist. He considered her quite accomplished.

"You must come to *Rosenkavalier*," Fiona said.

He nodded. "I fully intend to. I am not overfond of Strauss but I make an exception for *Rosenkavalier*."

"Because it reflects Mozart?" Laura said.

"Hardly musically, my dear, but it captures something of the spirit."

"I've always thought you would prefer Wagner," Murdo remarked. "More suited to your pretensions of grandeur, wouldn't you say?"

"I don't intend to rise to the bait, Murdo," George replied. "Undisciplined chaos based on ridiculous fairy stories is not for me. I like order, in music as in everything else. Order, discipline, purpose. There can be no civilization without a framework of order."

"Unimpeachable sentiments," Murdo said. He winked slyly at Fiona. "Don't you agree, Mr. Askarian?"

"If your brother is saying that *Rosenkavalier* is a product of civilization," Boris replied, "I would certainly agree."

Wyndham, who had remained silent, suddenly put in an unexpected question. "Who is your new Annina?"

"Are you having a new Annina?" Laura asked.

"Don't you remember?" Fiona said. "There was an an accident . . ."

"She committed suicide, Mrs. Grant," Boris said with deliberation. "It was a great tragedy. She was a very foolish young person to behave in such a way."

"It wasn't suicide," Wyndham said. "She was murdered."

How right I was, Fiona thought. He sits there as calmly as can be and casually chucks a bomb like that into the conversation.

"Is that true?" Murdo said.

"How do you know that?" said Boris.

He looked at them with his disarmingly innocent expression. "It was in one of the papers. Or did I hear it on the radio? The post-mortem revealed it. She hadn't taken enough pills to kill herself. She had been suffocated, possibly with a pillow." He smiled apologetically at Laura. "Do forgive me, Mrs. Grant. Hardly the topic for lunch table."

"Unfortunately, Commander," George remarked dryly, "crime is no longer a topic that can be relegated to the police station. It surrounds us, it is a constant intruder into our daily lives. Due to the feebleness of our present society, led by the nose or deluded by lily-livered do-gooders who haven't the faintest idea what they are talking about, betrayed by a succession of weak governments, law and order as such no longer exists. It will not be long before there is a complete breakdown, before it is every man for himself, and harmless householders carry guns as a matter of course to defend themselves."

"My brother," Murdo murmured gently, "is away on his hobbyhorse."

"I would hardly have thought you were one to sneer at me," George replied. "After what I hear went on here last night. Gangs of students roaming the countryside at will, carrying torches, putting the fear of God into the townspeople."

"They were quite well-behaved," Fiona said.

"They might have been on this occasion," George said. "What would you have done if they weren't? How would you have defended your boatyard, then, Murdo, eh?" He gazed at his brother with a certain triumph. "I don't see your local police force standing much chance against an organized riot."

"And what would be your remedy for these ills?" Boris asked him.

"What this country needs, what all Europe needs," George said emphatically, "is strong government. Strengthen the police force, give more teeth to the laws, clamp down on the hooligans, stamp out all this nonsense before it destroys us."

Fiona's father gave a long, gentle sigh. He absorbed himself in refilling Boris's glass. Boris raised it to George. "I quite agree with you, sir," he said.

"Do you really?" asked Fiona.

"Fiona, I would agree with any development that would prevent poor children like Elena Greer being murdered."

"Elena Greer?" Laura queried.

"The young mezzo-soprano who was singing Annina," Fiona explained. "Who on earth would want to kill her? It doesn't make sense."

"Senseless violence," George said. "Isn't that what I've been talking about?"

"More likely a crime of passion," Murdo said. "Not so easy to prevent."

"I think you are probably right," Wyndham said. "She did have a regular visitor. A man who was seen leaving or arriving several times by neighbors. With witnesses and identikit pictures he shouldn't be so hard to find."

"What sort of man?" George asked.

"Not young, over forty, well-dressed."

Boris gave an expressive shrug. "Definitely a crime of passion."

"You seem to know a great deal about

police work," George said to Wyndham. "May one ask why you have come to Linnay Island? Are you a policeman?"

"Fiona says he is here to catch spies," Boris said. "But then Fiona does have an unusual sense of humor."

Wyndham smiled at her. "She is an artist. She has a great gift of imagination."

George persisted. "What are you doing here, Commander?"

"I am temporarily replacing a colleague on leave."

"You really should be a politician," Fiona said. "I don't think I've ever known you give a direct answer to anything."

Laura said: "I don't think you should harass Commander Wyndham, Fiona."

Fiona smiled across the table at him. "Oh, I think the Commander can take care of himself."

"I've heard there is trouble on the island," George said abruptly. "Leakage of secret information. And nothing appears to be done. Why set up secret research bases and then be so criminally casual about security? No one appears to care. It is merely a matter for gossip. My chauffeur told me about it. He heard it discussed in some bar in the town.

And I am sure it is not the only instance. It confirms what I say. We are a country besieged and we are being betrayed by enemies within. And those like me who stand up and say so are laughed at. Observe my brother Murdo's patient, tolerant smile, Commander, and you will understand what I mean. You will understand my frustration."

"You should stand for Parliament," Boris said. "You should enter government. Then your voice will be heard."

"Parliament is as ineffectual as anything else. Power has moved away from it into other hands. I wouldn't waste my time joining a company of time servers whose only ambition is to hang on to their seats and their privileges for as long as possible."

"I hope you're not advocating revolution, George," Murdo said.

"I think we all know George's feelings well enough," Laura said. "Now, who will have some more summer pudding? There is plenty left and a jugful of cream."

She gently maneuvered them into calmer waters.

"Speaking of joining companies," Boris said, "I have been meaning to ask you, Fiona, since you must know the theatrical scene in this country far better than I, if you know anything about the Company of 13."

"I don't believe I've heard of a Company of 13," Fiona said. "Perhaps they are newly established. Have they approached you to sing with them?"

"I don't even know if they are an opera company or in any way connected with music. I heard them mentioned and I was curious to know more about them. I had the idea they were a theatrical company, yet it is a strange name to adopt when stage people are so superstitious."

"Perhaps it is one of the fringe group at the Festival. A university company, perhaps."

"You are right. It is something to do with Scotland. I remember now."

"If you went back to the source of your information, Mr. Askarian," George said, "you could find out all you want to know."

"Well, there is my difficulty," Boris said, "the informant has departed."

"As a general rule, Mr. Askarian," Wyndham said quietly, "isn't it rather risky for a person of your eminence to become involved in this sort of enterprise?"

"He's not involved," Fiona said. "And he doesn't even know what enterprise it is."

Boris looked across at Wyndham. "Sometimes risks are worthwhile, Commander. If we always play safe, we cannot progress. Don't you find that in your work?"

"I believe you mean you took a great risk joining our company," Fiona said.

Boris laughed. "Of course I did. There is no guarantee of success with any production. So many things can go wrong. Temperaments may clash, people find it impossible to work with each other. The producer may not understand the problems of the singers; the singers may hate the conductor; the designs, unless of course they are by Fiona Grant, may be appalling; the soprano may get laryngitis; the bass may get drunk and fall into the orchestra pit; it is endless, endless, the possibilities for disaster. In fact, now I have reminded myself that we have to get used to a new theater in a couple of days with all the problems of moving an entire production from one end of the country to another, I begin to tremble." He held out a hand which appeared to Fiona as steady as a rock. "See, I shake, I tremble. By tomorrow night my voice will be gone."

"I wonder if a glass of my best brandy would help," Murdo said, getting up. "I'll bring some in with the coffee."

"After tonight," Boris explained to Laura, "I shall not drink any alcohol. It is a rule I make for myself when I am performing. Some singers find it makes no difference, others find it positively helpful, it relaxes them, stops the throat becoming tight with tension. Experience teaches us all the right way to nurse our treasure. It is all here." He tapped his throat. "If we lose this, we lose everything, our livelihood, our comfort, our prestige, our fulfillment. No wonder we are so temperamental, so nervous."

"You appear to me," Laura said, "to be the least nervous person I have ever met."

He patted her hand. "It is an act, Mrs. Grant. It is all top show."

"Discipline," George observed. "Discipline and order, that is how it is achieved. You see, Fiona, anyone with a purpose in life must be of my opinion. Mr. Askarian, I look forward with even greater anticipation to your performance."

"Come backstage and see me afterwards," Boris said.

"I should be glad to. However, I may have a number of my guests with me. I wouldn't impose them on you."

"Ah, yes, Fiona has told me about your visitors. How many do you have to stay with you at a time?"

"It varies. Anything from six to a dozen."

"You're not superstitious then," Fiona remarked.

He gazed at her blankly.

"Twelve guests plus you must make thirteen at table," she pointed out.

"Superstitions are for weak minds," George replied.

Before Fiona could think of a suitable riposte the phone in the hall began to ring. Murdo must have been near it, for it stopped almost at once, and a few moments later he appeared at the door.

"It's for you, Commander. Someone from the Island. Fiona, can you give me a hand, I can't get everything on one tray."

As she followed her father to the kitchen, collected a tray of coffee cups and returned with them to the dining room, Fiona caught snatches of Wyndham's conversation: "When? Damn, my fault . . . We shouldn't have waited. . . . Any chance he did it himself . . . ? At once . . ."

He hung up. Turning at the dining room door, Fiona saw him talking to Murdo in the

163

kitchen. When her father finally arrived with the second tray and the brandy, he merely said that Wyndham had been called back to the base and sent his apologies. George and Boris paid little attention. George was launched on his second great passion, the crumbling castle he went to such lengths to maintain.

"You have your own private army, I understand." Boris said when George had finished his brief history of the place. "Like the Dukes of Atholl."

"Hardly an army. A few men from the estate who dress up and put on a show for the guests."

"How long do your guests stay?"

"Anything from one to three nights. That is enough for me, I must admit. A group left this morning. Some more are due tomorrow night. Which is why I was able to come today and why I must get back now." He put down his coffee cup and pushed back his chair. "Excellent meal, my dear Laura. Fiona, perhaps I shall see you in Edinburgh. You are traveling with Mr. Askarian?"

"Unfortunately not," Boris said. "I can't persuade her. She wishes to be idle another day."

"Where are you staying, the North British?"

"I believe so."

George kissed Fiona a little awkwardly on the cheek, avoided another embrace with Laura, said good-bye to Murdo and shook Boris by the hand.

"I hope we shall be in touch, Mr. Askarian. You must come and stay at the castle, at some time when the tiresome visitors are absent."

They escorted him to the front door and watched him drive off in the Mercedes. The mechanic had already left with the Land-Rover. It was a relief to Fiona to see the Mercedes go. Ever since the near miss with Eliot's car on the moorland road, it had been an increasing burden to her. She didn't realize quite how much until it, and George, had gone.

That afternoon, Murdo took Boris sailing. Fiona crewed for them. To the two men it was a practical way of discussing the design of the boat Murdo would build for Boris, the details of the blueprint springing to life in the handling of an actual craft at sea. To Fiona it was pure escape.

There was a good breeze and they soon put

Linnay Island behind them and made their way out into the open sea, and the further they went the more the land revealed itself, folds and ridges and majestic curving sweeps, remote, detached, impressive. A landscape that made no concessions, the softer colors of pasture and woodland on the lower slopes becoming without definition, until only the bare, austere outline of the distant hills remained. The bustle of human life dwindled to unimportance at the foot of that indifferent rock. Like a necklace placed round a throat it had been imposed on the country, and gazing at it across a space of water, there was a feeling that the country might at any time reject it, flinging it like some discarded trinket back into the sea.

It was much choppier when they turned about for home. The wind had veered and their course on the starboard tack brought them quite close in to Linnay. They could see the buildings and harbor installations that were hidden from the shore and figures moving between them. Boris picked up the binoculars and studied the Island. After a few moments he put the glasses down and shrugged when he caught Fiona's glance.

"Curiosity. One has heard so much."

"I didn't think there was a great deal to see."

"No sign of Commander Wyndham?" Murdo said jokingly.

"Take a look." Boris handed him the glasses and took over the helm.

"The watcher is watched," Murdo said. "They are sending a party to warn us off. Or investigate us." Fiona turned to see a fast patrol boat leaving the harbor and heading toward them.

"Something's up," Murdo said. "They've never done that before."

"Perhaps they see through their glasses that you have a stranger aboard," Boris said.

"I've often sailed with clients as close as this past Linnay and they've never sent anyone out before. I've always presumed that as soon as they've identified it as one of my boats, they lose interest in us as potential marauders."

"Perhaps Craddock spoiled that for you," Fiona said. "Using your boats for too many little private fishing trips."

"Perhaps he did," Murdo agreed. "Well, let us continue on our innocent way. I know you don't want to be too late back, Boris, with that drive in front of you. If the navy wants to catch up with us, they can. They've got the speed."

But after a while, as if satisfied with their intentions, the patrol boat turned back, rather like a dog padding back to its kennel after driving intruders from its gates with aggressive barks and leaps.

About ten minutes after they got back, Wyndham rang to apologize to Laura for deserting her lunch party. He wanted to apologize to Boris too, and Laura called him to the phone.

"The navy appears to teach its officers to be almost excessively polite," she observed to Fiona.

Fiona quoted Boris: "It is an act. It is all top show."

Laura laughed. "You've certainly got it in for that young man. But I can't see what advantage he can get from making up to Boris Askarian."

"A good seat at the opera," Murdo suggested.

"Fiona could get him that."

"Perhaps he doesn't dare ask Fiona."

"Opera is one of his passions," Fiona said. "So he has told me."

"There you are then!" Laura exclaimed. "The simple explanation."

"Nothing is simple about Commander Wyndham," Fiona said.

Boris left after tea, kissing both women affectionately, promising to come over once more while the company was in Edinburgh. He departed in a suitable flourish, spraying gravel as he accelerated the Rolls round the bends in the drive, one hand waving a final farewell.

Wyndham did not appear that evening, and Fiona went to bed early, too drowsy from the effects of sea, wind and sun to lie worrying over the hidden motivations behind his actions. She awoke to a breathless summer morning. An early heat haze veiled the far shores of the bay, the trees stood motionless, the air was still and warm.

"I'm going swimming," she told Laura.

"Don't you want any breakfast?"

"Later," she called. She ran down the path that led from the gardens to the loch. It ended in a narrow, rocky inlet, but further along, past the headland where the trees came nearly down to the water, there was a sheltered cove of sand. The tide was going out and she could walk round the promontory to it. She was wearing jeans and a T-shirt over her bikini, a towel slung round her neck. She pulled off her sandals and waded round to the isolated beach.

It took some ten minutes to reach it and she was surprised and momentarily annoyed to find someone already there, a man lying stretched out on the sand. She had made the effort to get there in order to be solitary, to indulge in the luxury of being completely alone. She had almost decided to turn back, when something about the man made her hesitate. The way the small waves nibbled unhindered at his feet; the angle at which his head lay. His stillness.

She began to walk, then run toward him.

He was wearing cotton trousers, a checkered shirt and an anorak. His body was slightly twisted as if he had spun round in the act of falling. His eyes stared up at her out of a drained white face. His mouth hung slackly open, his chin was covered by last night's stubble. A red worm crawled into the hairline of his red hair from the neat dark hole in the center of his forehead.

Fiona sank down on her knees by his side.

When she saw what the exiting bullet had done to the back of his head, a wave of nausea nearly overcame her. She wiped her mouth with her towel and buried her face in it. When she put down the towel and opened her eyes again, she saw a fly walking across the dead man's cheek. Revulsion struck her and she put out her hand to drive it away. Her fingers touched flesh. It was still warm.

She jerked back and as she did so something went past her ear with a sound no louder than a mosquito's whine. In front of her, sand flicked up as if a stone had been thrown. She turned, startled, and the sound came again. From the shelter of the trees, a man dashed toward her, running low. He landed on her in a rugby tackle, rolling her away from the body. She could feel his heart beating against her.

"Craddock," she said. "Someone shot Craddock."

"I know," Wyndham said. "And they're going to shoot us if we don't get the hell out of here."

He grabbed her by the wrist and half dragged, half carried her to the cover of an outcrop of jagged rocks. Scrambling over them, she stumbled and fell, pulling him

171

down with her. He grasped her shoulders, drawing her closer in to the base of the rock, his body protecting her. She turned her head. The sand felt harshly cold against her skin.

"Oh, God," she said.

"It's all right," Wyndham said. "I think we're fairly safe here."

"Who is it?"

"It's someone with a long-range rifle. I was doing a little stalking until you turned up. I saw Craddock arrive. I'd been following him. I was waiting to see who he met. Then, wham, down he goes. I was trying to track the gunman when you suddenly appeared."

"I'm sorry I interrupted you. Why was he trying to kill me? Is he one of those maniacs you read about who suddenly start shooting complete strangers?"

"I don't know that he was aiming at you. I think he might have been trying to make sure Craddock really was dead, in case he was passing on any names to you."

"He must have known he couldn't be alive with that wound."

"He couldn't be absolutely certain. Assassins can get very jittery."

"Why do you say assassin instead of murderer?"

"Because that's what I think he is," Wyndham said.

They had been speaking in rapid, urgent whispers, but now Fiona paused. She said more slowly: "It's political, isn't it? Craddock is—was mixed up with that business at the base. What names might he have given me? What is going on—look, I can't keep calling you Commander any longer, what's your first name?"

"Max, and I'll tell you what I can later. This isn't exactly the place. Let's wait till we're out of here."

"How are we going to get out of here? Won't the gunman be waiting for us?"

"When he saw me, he'll have started wondering how many more of us there are. It must have given him a shock when he saw you come wandering along. Even more so when I appeared. I think he has probably gone, but we'll give it another few minutes. By the way, what are you doing here?"

"I came for what I laughingly thought would be a nice peaceful swim, not to murder anyone. You really do suspect me of something, don't you?"

"I don't know about suspect," Wyndham

173

said. "I've been having some very erotic thoughts about you."

He had managed to disconcert her again, even in this situation. She said: "So that's why you flung me behind this rock. I don't feel the timing is quite right."

"It never is in this sort of game." They were so close he only had to turn his head to find her mouth. "But I can't resist the opportunity." It was a lingering, searching kiss. The response it evoked in her expressed what she had been trying to deny: the attraction that made her so aware of him, even that first time in the theater, even when she most distrusted him.

She spoke, reluctantly, against his lips: "Isn't this dangerous?"

"Very," he murmured. "For me."

"There is a gunman out there somewhere. There's already one dead body he's responsible for lying only yards away from us."

Wyndham sighed. "You're quite right. This is neither the time nor the place. Come on." He stood up cautiously and, satisfied it was safe, pulled Fiona to her feet. "The assassin has fled the scene. We've got to tell the police about Craddock and then I've got to make some decisions about you. Do you think your father could lend us a motorboat? There's someone I want you to see on the Island."

Wyndham's Jeep was parked off the road, hidden by trees. Further on they came across Craddock's motorbike. Wyndham made a note of its position and drove on.

"I wonder how the assassin got here," he said. "He was obviously waiting for Craddock."

"Was the gunman the man he was supposed to meet?"

"Looks like it."

"You mean he was shot by his own side," Fiona said. "Why should they do that?"

Wyndham shrugged. "Talking too much. Causing trouble. Letting his own private spite get in the way of his job. But it may be none of those things. It might have been done as insurance. We're getting too close to the truth for someone's comfort. He seems to be closing the ring and eliminating his agents. We found another body yesterday."

"The phone call you took at lunch?"

He nodded. "Someone else shot with a rifle, exactly like Craddock. Only he was found on a beach on the island. A suspect technician we'd been about to bring in for questioning. And I can't tell you any more than that for the moment."

"You don't really believe my father is involved in this business, do you?" Fiona asked.

"I don't think he would risk killing his own daughter," Wyndham said lightly. "Even if she did get in the way."

"Well, it's a relief to know the family is in the clear."

"I don't know about the family," Wyndham said. "You might have been the person Craddock was waiting to meet. The shots might have been meant for you. To close your mouth as well as Craddock's. You've been involved in some highly suspicious goings-on, you know. If you're innocent, and I'm inclined to believe you are, you have an enormous talent for making dangerous contacts."

"What are you talking about?" Fiona said. "I can't understand what on earth you're talking about." She stared at his now impassive profile, but he refused to say any more.

"I've got to get clearance first," he said. "Phone calls first, explanations later."

"You say you want to take me to the Island," Fiona said. "Is this what you call 'bringing in for questioning'?"

"You don't mind answering a few questions, do you?" He put his hand over hers. "Don't worry, I'll hold your hand. You might even be asked to do the navy a favor."

"Is that what you had in mind on the beach? Getting me in the right frame of mind to do the navy a favor? Or is making love to suspected enemy agents just a routine part of your job?"

"I haven't had the chance of making love to this suspected agent. That's what I'm objecting to." He glanced at her face. He said gently, "You really don't know what this is all about, do you?"

He made the phone calls from the house while Fiona changed and picked up a sweater. It was never warm on the water. Laura had gone shopping. Mrs. Niven had not arrived. Murdo was at the boatyard. Wyndham took the opportunity to speak at some length on the phone. He was still talking when she came downstairs. He glanced up at her, said goodbye and rang off. At least he didn't suspect the house of being bugged, she thought wryly.

"Your father will let us have a boat," he said. "It will be quicker than waiting for a launch to come over from the Island. Shall we go?"

They didn't see Murdo at the yard. He was busy in the main shed, but the boat was ready for them. Fiona waited until they were well out into the bay before asking: "Did you get clearance to tell me?"

He nodded. "But they want me to talk to you formally."

"You mean with someone taking notes? Like a police inquiry?"

"Not as formally as that. But you might be able to help."

"I don't see how."

"You will," Wyndham said.

They didn't speak again on the crossing. But at one point Wyndham took her hand, as she sat beside him, and raised it briefly to his lips in a gesture so tender and protective it quite unnerved her. She could find nothing to say in response to it and in a moment they were coming into Linnay harbor.

The Island seemed in a state of armed alertness. There were guards ready to check Wyndham's identity at the harbor, and a telephone call was made before they were allowed to proceed. A Jeep drove them along a tarmac road between sprawling complexes of large prefabricated huts, each with a guard at its entrance, and up to the door of a more substantial white-washed building that looked as if it might have started life as a shepherd's cottage. There had been a small community on Linnay up to the 1930's, but it had drifted away to the mainland long before the navy took over the Island.

Wyndham led Fiona inside and into a low, light room with a view of the harbor. It was furnished like the room of a slightly austere Oxford don, and the man who rose to greet them from behind his desk had something of an academic air. He was tall and thin, with thinning hair brushed closely back from his narrow, intelligent face. He smiled at Fiona and came across to shake her hand.

"My dear Miss Grant, how very good of you to come and see us. Do sit down. I think you'll find that chair comfortable. Would you like some coffee? I understand you've had no breakfast."

Fiona accepted the coffee. "Thank you—I'm sorry, I don't know your name."

"How very remiss of me. My name is Stanton, Miss Grant. Wallace Stanton." He leaned against the edge of the desk, stirring his coffee. "Your first visit to Linnay, I presume. What do you think of it?"

"You seem to have very tight security," Fiona said. "I'm surprised anything has been stolen from here, let alone anything important."

"I'm afraid the excessive zeal of the security men is rather a case of shutting the stable door after the horse has gone. However—" he paused "—I wasn't quite aware you knew what had gone."

"She doesn't know," Wyndham said. He had gone over to the window and was standing looking down at the harbor. He glanced at Stanton. "Are you going to tell her or am I?"

"I don't believe you know quite what a champion you've had in Commander Wyndham, Miss Grant," Stanton said. "He's been arguing on your behalf right from the beginning."

"The beginning?" Fiona asked. "The beginning of what?"

"Commander Wyndham tells me that the fact that there have been leakages of highly confidential, indeed top secret, information from the base here at Linnay is common

180

gossip in the local pubs. However, the leakages did begin quite a while before the gossip.
And unfortunately for many months before it
was discovered what was happening." He put
his cup down carefully on the tray. Everything he did was with precise, careful movement. "I am not normally a member of the
team here. I have come for the sole purpose of
clearing up this matter and now, with the
help of Commander Wyndham, we are in
sight of a solution. We are coming to the end
of the chain we have been tracing link by
link. And you, Miss Grant, are part of that
chain."

She began to protest. Stanton raised his
hand to stop her. "Wyndham has more or less
persuaded me that you were an innocent part
of that chain, made use of on only one
occasion, but nevertheless you were involved."

Fiona sat back. "Don't you think you had
better tell me the whole story, Mr. Stanton? I
think there have been enough of these vague
accusatory statements."

"I quite agree with you, Miss Grant. I shall
tell you all we have managed to discover. I
shall, as I believe they still say, put you in the
picture. Any espionage operation can be
divided, like Gaul, into three parts: the

acquiring of the information, the transmission of the information, and the payment for the information. We have a basis to work on: we knew where it was coming from and we knew its destination. We worked forward and backward from those two points. We tried to decide how we would act if we were in charge of this operation. We tried to foresee every move, as in a chess problem. Obviously whoever orginally stole the information had to be one of those with access to it, which limited the number of suspects in the base immediately. But how did he get it off the Island? Leave ashore is carefully controlled and all departing personnel routinely searched. However, people off duty do go fishing and walking and, in fine weather, swimming from the beaches on the other side of the Island. And boats do sail past Linnay. It is clear he—and we know definitely who he was, a little too late to question him unfortunately—did establish a fairly foolproof method of passing on his information, and it must clearly have been to someone with a boat and with a good reason for being in a boat near Linnay."

"Craddock," Fiona said. "And his fishing expeditions in borrowed boats."

"Yes," Stanton said. "Craddock. Also, regrettably, beyond questioning."

"And your suspicions of Craddock led you to suspect my father, Craddock's employer?"

"It is only recently we narrowed it down to Craddock. Your father was already under suspicion because of the opportunities offered by his way of life, his boatyard, his house so conveniently placed opposite Linnay. And lately because of his daughter."

Wyndham said impatiently: "Is this elaborate form of narrative really necessary?"

"My dear Max, we don't want to leave Miss Grant at all confused. Let me put it this way, Miss Grant. We had a workable theory as to how the information got to the mainland. We had to trace the next stage of the procedure, and remember this exercise had been going on over a period of months. Wyndham, working from London, set up a net of surveillance on certain possible contacts and discovered an interesting fact. A man well-known to us as a courier had recently developed a passion for fishing and for the Scottish countryside. Every two months or so, in season or out, he would take a night train north to—"

"To Inverlinn," Fiona said. She had a cold

183

sensation in her stomach. She glanced across at Wyndham. He was watching Stanton. He isn't sure he's convinced him, she thought. Stanton still believes I may be guilty. She recognized now the sensation she was feeling. It was fear.

"You're very quick, Miss Grant," Stanton said appreciatively. "Your fellow passenger on the night train to Inverness, the man you dined with, who had the compartment next to yours—"

"Eliot was the courier," she said. She looked again at Wyndham. "You were following him, not me."

"I was following him," he agreed. "I meant, as a matter of routine, to see what happened on these fishing trips of his."

"And when I saw you at the opera house?"

"That was nothing to do with you," he said.

"And I've been under suspicion just because of those chance encounters on the train, sitting at the same table, having a compartment next to his."

"That and the fact that your name was Grant and your father owned a boatyard situated opposite Linnay Island." He paused. "You arranged to meet Eliot somewhere later, didn't you?"

184

She said to Wyndham: "How did you know that?"

He looked at her steadily. "You talked together, waiting for the cars to be unloaded. I thought something must have gone wrong with the arrangement. He looked annoyed."

Fiona said: "He asked me to lunch with him at Lairg."

"And then he died from a heart attack," Stanton said, "before either of you reached Lairg. Now why, Miss Grant, if you knew nothing of the matter, do you think he was so anxious to make contact with you? Why did he book the compartment next to yours? Why did he make sure he dined at your table? We have checked. He did do all of those things. And it was a genuine heart attack which killed him, by the way. He suffered a slight one the night before. If he'd called for a doctor when he felt ill, he'd have been taken off the train at the next station on the line and might have been alive today. But of course he didn't want to call a doctor. He persuaded himself it was indigestion."

"You weren't surprised to find me on that road then?" Fiona said to Wyndham.

"I felt it confirmed that you were his contact," he said evenly. "Then when I dis covered your name it seemed to add to the evidence."

"No wonder the police were so friendly to you at the hotel," she said. "No wonder everyone did everything they could to delay me and keep me there. You were searching Eliot when I first saw you on the road, weren't you? What happened to his missing wallet, by the way?"

Stanton opened a drawer of his desk. He took out a worn leather wallet and placed it exactly in the center of the desk.

"The police found it when they borrowed your keys and searched the Mercedes," Wyndham said. "I hadn't had the chance to take it when you came on the scene. As we thought, it had fallen out of Eliot's jacket when we were getting him into the back of the car."

"However," Stanton said, "Commander Wyndham had already found these." He dropped a ring of keys beside the wallet. "And this one—" he selected a key and held it up "—is the first piece of evidence on your behalf."

"What is it?" Fiona asked.

"A key to the Mercedes. The Commander argues that if it were you, Miss Grant, whom

Eliot had arranged to meet, why should he need a key to your car? You would both drive to some agreed rendezvous, you would produce the goods, he the money, and off you go on your separate ways. A simple exchange. Why complicate matters with keys?"

Fiona sat still and tried to think in a logical way about everything that had been said so far.

"What you are saying," she said at last, "is that Eliot was supposed to meet the car, not me. I was merely the agent for getting the car to Eliot in circumstances that would arouse no suspicion."

"And once you were out of the car," Wyndham said, "all he had to do was unlock the door, take something out, put something in, and drive off. Simplicity itself."

"He thought I would have breakfast at the station hotel," Fiona said slowly. "People continuing their journey usually do. That must have been when he was supposed to make this exchange you speak of. I came back too soon, before the car was unloaded. I was obviously going to wait for it. So he asked me to have lunch at Lairg, where he would have had another chance."

Stanton said: "I think the penny has dropped, Max. Miss Grant is looking suitably stunned. Of course, when Commander Wyndham found out who the car actually belonged to, and that you were merely taking it to Scotland on the owner's behalf, he considered that another proof of your uninvolvement. He also considers I've been too longwinded in my explanation but it is a difficult thing to tell you, Miss Grant, that your highly respected uncle appears to be a spy and a traitor, selling his country's defense secrets for money."

She shook her head. "I don't believe it."

"If he's not guilty, then you are. You might have been knowingly involved with him of course, but having met you I'm inclined to agree with Commander Wyndham that you were an innocent cat's-paw. Not a very nice trick to play on one's niece."

"But—" she struggled to express her thoughts "—you say the stealing of secrets must have been going on for months before it was discovered. I was only involved this once. What happened all the other times? Why was it different this time?"

"I think we shall find that on all the other occasions when Eliot came to Scotland, your uncle was somewhere nearby. They would lunch at the same pub, fish the same river. There would be no spoken contact or acknowledgment. Eliot would choose his moment, effect the exchange from the car and depart. However, this time the inquiry had begun here on the Island. Rumors had already reached the town. This would probably have been the last delivery and the last payment before George Grant closed up the operation. He didn't want to risk going anywhere near Eliot himself. It would never occur to him that we could suspect the car, driven by his niece. Nor would we have, if Eliot hadn't died on the road and Wyndham hadn't found the key."

Fiona said: "When Craddock threatened to tell the police about my relative, he meant George, not my father. Is that right?"

"Yes," Stanton said, "and that got back to George Grant and this morning Craddock was eliminated."

"It couldn't have been George who shot him. He went back to the castle yesterday."

"He could have driven back. In any case, he wouldn't do his own dirty work. It was a special kind of killer behind that gun."

She looked from one to the other of the two

men, both seeming so calm and cold in their assessments. She felt shocked, bewildered, betrayed.

"George is a diehard. He's more than anti-left, he's anti anything even vaguely pink. He always has been. My father calls it his hobby-horse." She turned to Wyndham. "You heard him at lunch yesterday, when he spoke about the demonstration."

"A useful cover," Stanton said, "to be so publicly right wing. We were rather surprised ourselves when we worked out the implications. Of course, we haven't as yet got any evidence against him that would stand up in court. There is no question of an immediate arrest."

"If it really is true, you mean he's going to get away with it: the murders, the spying, everything?"

"Oh, we'll be working away, gathering the evidence, establishing connections, but the two most likely to have talked under a little pressure he's already silenced."

Fiona got up and walked to the window. She looked down at the harbor and then across the bay to the farther shore. The mist had lifted and the sun shimmered on still waters. The hills seemed close enough to touch.

She said: "Did you find anything?" She turned to Wyndham. "The exchange didn't take place, so the goods, as Mr. Stanton calls them, must still have been in the car when we got here. You searched the car, didn't you? When? The first evening you came to the house? Did you find anything?"

"When I said goods, Miss Grant," Stanton said, "I was not using the word in any specifically descriptive sense. There were no documents or anything like that. The information was reduced photographically to a micro-dot."

"Which is why you checked my father's photographic equipment," she said to Wyndham. "It was lucky for your investigations that you were invited to the house so readily."

"Don't blame the Commander," Stanton said. "He was doing his job in the least disturbing way he could."

"He was very tactful, I must say," Fiona said. "But I always did have the feeling that everything he did had an ulterior motive. Even," she said to Wyndham, "eating that bar of chocolate. You wanted the wrapper, I suppose. Was the micro-dot on that?"

"No, it wasn't," he said quietly.

191

"But there was only one bar of chocolate in the car, not two. You replaced it, opening the car with Eliot's key, so that everything would look exactly the same to George. And I told George all about it. So he knows without a shadow of doubt that you're on to him."

"Back to the chess game," Stanton said. "He knows we suspect him, but not whether we've discovered any proof. In fact we've tried to persuade him we haven't, by leaving the evidence."

"You did find the micro-dot then?"

"It was on the map," Wyndham said. "We found another brand-new one, exactly the same, in Eliot's car. All he had to do at Inverlinn station was open the door, substitute one map for the other and leave. The money was placed inside the substituted map."

"How could George be sure I wouldn't look at the map and find the money? After all you took the map into that pub on the road, remember?"

"The money was in a sealed packet. You wouldn't have opened it, you're too well-mannered. You'd have made sure he got it, in fact, reminded him that it was there."

"I think that's probably true. But why did

he search the car so thoroughly when he collected it?"

Stanton said: "Don't forget he didn't know for certain whether the exchange had taken place at Inverness station or not. He had to make absolutely sure that incriminating packet was not in the car. It was only when he got the map back to the castle that he could check whether it was the one with the microdot on it. It was placed on the dot of the 'i' of Linnay Island, by the way. Rather cheeky of them, I thought, but it helped us. It was the first place we looked. One should never be obvious or make jokes in these matters."

"Was that what Craddock was supposed to be doing on the night of the demonstration, searching the car for the money? Did George send him?"

"I am rather of the opinion that Craddock was working on his own. Looking for an opportunity for a little blackmail. Your prompt action prevented it, Miss Grant, and I presume your scene with Craddock in the public house was reported back to your uncle by one of his henchmen who witnessed it."

"You make me feel responsible for Craddock's death," Fiona said. "What henchman? You mean my uncle had spies everywhere?"

193

"In our line we learn never to trust anybody, Miss Grant. It is safer to trust nobody than be betrayed by a friend."

"Not a maxim I would care to live by."

"You are the more fortunate to be able to choose."

There was a brief silence in the room. Then Fiona said, more calmly: "Commander Wyndham mentioned that the navy might ask me to do a favor for them. Can you tell me what that favor might be?"

"Ah . . ." Stanton looked thoughtfully at them. "I hope you two aren't becoming emotionally involved," he said.

"Why should you think that?" Fiona said. She didn't glance at Wyndham.

"One reason I am good at my job," Stanton said, "is because I am sensitive to the subtleties underlying relationships. It would normally be, as you implied but were too polite to state, none of my business. But if it is the one vulnerable factor which, cleverly exploited, might lead to both your deaths and the failure of this undertaking, then it is most certainly my business."

Neither Wyndham nor Fiona responded to him. They remained still, looking at Stanton. He gave a rather dramatic sigh. "Well, I

194

don't have much choice. Let's hope it turns out to be the factor which saves your lives. Are you ready to do it, Miss Grant?"

"I still don't know what you wish me to do. You are bewildering me, Mr. Stanton, with your elliptic phrases."

"I stand corrected. I apologize. I will put it plainly. There are some aspects of your uncle's behaviour we cannot yet understand. Certain contradictions. Things are apparently more complex than they seem. And recently information has come into our hands that needs fuller explanation. Will you help us to get Wyndham inside your uncle's castle? I need to know exactly what is going on there."

"I should have to go to the castle with him," Fiona said.

"I think it is the only way." He paused. "We are," he said gently, "in something of a hurry. Two bodies, you know, in as many days."

"You've implied it would be dangerous," Fiona said. "You've spoken rather glibly of life and death. Why would I risk my life helping you against my own relative, when I am not entirely convinced he is guilty?"

"If he's not guilty," Stanton said, "there's

no risk. If he is, you are no longer safe anywhere. I understand an observer on the beach this morning might have thought you were speaking to Craddock. He might have gained the impression that Craddock had stayed alive long enough to give you vital and dangerous information."

"George wouldn't kill me," Fiona said.

"Do you want to gamble on that? He wouldn't be the one pulling the trigger, remember. Amazing how easy it is to dispose of someone when you don't have to do it yourself. However, I am convinced that a certain blandly naive behavior may be your best defense. Beard him in his den as if nothing in the world has happened, and he may well believe you."

"I could hardly pretend Craddock's murder hadn't happened," Fiona said.

"Naturally not. Very shocking experience for you. You've even talked to the police about it. But nothing to do with your family."

"And supposing I do introduce Commander Wyndham into the castle, with no apparent suspicion on George's part, what happens then?"

"We shall all have to wait and see, won't

we? Leave it to the Commander to direct
you." He turned to Wyndham. "Once in, it
will be up to you, Max, to get Miss Grant
safely out again."

5

LAURA said: "I can see that finding that dreadful man's body must have upset you terribly, darling, but why don't you keep to your original plan and go to Edinburgh tomorrow? If you leave this afternoon, you'll only have to find a place to stay tonight. You can't get to Edinburgh in one hop."

"Max Wyndham has to be there first thing. That's why he's going now. He doesn't mind driving all night. And since he's offered me a lift . . . After all, it means I won't have to drive. I can be a passenger and relax."

Laura was still concerned. "I wish I'd been here when you got back. I think Commander Wyndham was pretty inconsiderate taking you off to Linnay like that. After all, there are police here. You've had to see Peter anyway, so why bring the navy into it?"

"It seems Craddock was involved in that spying business," Fiona said, choosing her words carefully.

"So Peter told me. They wanted to know if

you'd seen anyone or if Craddock had said anything to you."

"That's right," Fiona said.

"They could have asked you that on the phone, or let Max Wyndham do the interviewing."

"I suppose, when it comes to murder . . ."

"I don't know!" Laura moved restlessly from her chair to the window seat. "It seems so unfair. You've worked so hard. You come here for a few days' rest and you walk into this. You look terribly strained, dear. You do need a proper holiday."

"I'll take some time off when the Festival is over," Fiona said. "I'll come home for a long weekend at least."

"We'll see you before that," Laura said. "We are coming to see the production, remember." She turned from the window. "Here's your father at last."

Murdo came into the house, his face grave.

"Have you seen Peter?" he asked Fiona.

"Yes, he's just gone."

"Thank God no one appears to believe I shot Craddock. What with your friend the Commander suspecting me of spying, and then this—I gather you're not being held up by any police formalities, statements and so on."

"I've given Peter a statement."

"Good, good. Well, let's have a drink, for God's sake. I think we all need it."

Nobody was very interested in lunch. Laura made sandwiches and brought them and a pot of coffee into the drawing room. Murdo was of the opinion that Fiona was right to leave as soon as she could. "An opera company in the throes of a new production should seem a haven of peace and quiet after this. It will take your mind off this business, at least. Come back when it's all blown over."

Fiona waited until they were alone to ask him the questions that had been on her mind ever since Wyndham had brought her back from Linnay.

"This right-wing attitude of George's," she said, "the way he rants on about law and order, do you think he puts it on a bit? Could he be exaggerating because he knows it irritates you, for instance?"

"There is no exaggeration," Murdo said. "He has always been the same. He has had a Nietzschean devotion to the philosophy of the strong man practically from the cradle, superman's divine right to rule, casting himself in the role of superman. That's why we never got on as boys. He couldn't understand

why, since I was younger and therefore in-
ferior, I wouldn't submit to his superiority.
He was a nasty child, a bully who always had
to be the boss. And he didn't change as he
grew up. He gravitated naturally towards
dictatorships. If he'd fought in the Spanish
Civil War it would have been for Franco. As for
Hitler, to sum up George's opinion of the
Nazis, he'd say they were a crude bunch of
gangsters but basically they had the right idea.
Democracy in his opinion is a dead duck."

"And it's not put on? It's not an act?"

"That's an odd question. No, it's not an
act. Why?" He studied her face. "Why this
interest in the politics of your uncle George?"

"I can't quite believe he is what he appears
to be."

"You think he's like some old fossil from a
dead age? His ideas are far from dead,
unfortunately for the saner ones among us.
They have an unpleasant habit of resurfacing
every so often like poisonous weeds you can't
quite kill."

"You're very emphatic."

"My relationship with George," Murdo
said, "is an accident of birth. We are
fundamentally opposed and always have
been. There's no law that says you've got to

like someone, merely because he is your brother."

After Wyndham's phone call reporting Craddock's death, the police had called at the boatyard. The senior officer had interviewed Murdo. Peter, as a childhood friend of Fiona's, had waited at the house to talk to her. On her arrival back from Linnay, he had asked her what seemed to Fiona to be most carefully chosen questions. In turn she asked him if he had spoken to anyone on Linnay about Craddock's murder.

"I had quite a long conversation with Commander Wyndham on the telephone," Peter said. "I think you could say we are in accord in our approach to the problem."

"Very diplomatically put. You mean he's told you what's going on?" Fiona said.

"I don't think anyone is quite clear as to that," Peter said.

So there was no one she could confide in, not Peter, not Murdo, not Laura. She couldn't tell her parents where she was going on her way to Edinburgh, nor how dangerous it was, nor how frightened she was about it all, inside. But if what her father said was true, could George really have sustained this cover for all those years, since boyhood? He had been in Spain a lot over the past few years, she remembered now, going on hunting expeditions on the estates of wealthy acquaintances. He had been in Germany too, many times recently, drumming up the tourist trade for the castle. For someone who did not like traveling, he did a good deal of it. Which part of the curious creation Stanton had shown her did these journeys involve: the fascist laird, or the communist spy? No, she believed her father, and on that basis the man behind this spy ring could not be George. The Mercedes was, after all, the only link with him. Someone could have used him as Stanton said she had been used. Making use of his car, without his knowledge, because after all, no one would suspect someone like George Grant.

She became aware that Murdo was speaking to her.

"What happened on Linnay, Fiona?"

"I—" she hesitated.

He took her hand. "It's all right. I can guess. You've been warned to say nothing. Official Secrets Act and all that. But tell me, just between ourselves, did they say anything about me?"

Fiona smiled. She kissed his cheek. "They did suspect you but now they don't."

"Well, that's a relief. We can all get back to normal. We'll see you in Edinburgh and you can enjoy yourself being the beautiful and successful stage designer everyone wants to commission. Laura and I will bask in your reflected glory. When is Wyndham coming for you?"

"In about twenty minutes."

"Then you'd better spend those with your mother. Your hands are very cold. Are you sure you're all right? You're not going to collapse with delayed shock?"

"I'm fine," Fiona said.

"Put all this worrying business behind you," Murdo said. "Enjoy Edinburgh. Enjoy your success."

Wyndham arrived punctually to collect her. He was driving not the Jeep but a dark saloon car.

"Where did you get this?" Fiona asked him.

"On loan from a fellow officer. I thought it would be more comfortable for you."

"And less conspicuous?"

He smiled. "There is that."

They drove through the town and over the bridge past the church and the school. They

204

began the long, curving climb that would finally take them away from the coast, inland to the empty hills.

"How are you feeling?" Wyndham said.

"I'm all right. Where do we make the phone call?"

"There's a box a few miles on. Very rarely used, except for stranded motorists. But it's in working order. I had it checked."

"You know this country as well as I do, probably better. This wasn't your first visit to the base, was it?"

"I was here, briefly, a few months ago, when this matter first blew up."

"So what was all that business with the map? Asking me which road you should take and so on. Ah—" she nodded "—it was to see if I reacted to George's microdotted map."

"There's no fooling you, is there?"

"I don't think George is the one you're after, Max. He couldn't sustain that cover of being the next best thing to a declared fascist all those years. You're not accusing him of running a spy ring all that time, are you?"

"I agree that for most of those years he doesn't appear to have done much more than build up his cover. Until the base was established on Linnay. Then I'd say he more than made up for lost time. At the beginning they made the mistake of believing the island's remoteness to be sufficient security."

"You've seen him, you've heard him talk. I've known him since I was a child. He really does believe all that stuff."

"Even if he does, I don't see it need make all that difference," Wyndham said. "He may find the two ideologies no longer incompatible. Communist states are as totalitarian as fascist ones, after all. Democracy is their common enemy."

"I'd convinced myself," Fiona said. "Now you're getting me frightened all over again."

"Don't worry. You'll be fine. There's the phone box." He pulled up beside it.

They were on the edge of the first barren moorland. The road stretched ahead of them, a narrow ribbon of safety across a gray-green rock-strewn bog. Already they were in shadow from the encroaching hills.

Wyndham switched the engine off. The silence settled around them.

"Well," Fiona said, "I think I'd better rehearse once more what I'm going to say."

Wyndham shook his head. "There's no need. You'll only make yourself nervous."

"Have you got the packet?"

"Yes, it's in my briefcase."

"The original one from Eliot?"

"Yes."

"He'll never believe it," Fiona said.

"Stanton thinks it the only bait he'll swallow. Epecially tonight."

"You agree with Stanton?"

Wyndham nodded.

"Why did you say 'especially tonight'?" Fiona asked him. "What is special about tonight?"

The telephone in the call box began to ring. It had an eerie effect, there in that isolation. Wyndham seemed to expect it. He got out of the car and went to answer it.

Fiona could see him talking. When he came back she said nothing. She waited for him to explain. He seemed at last to come to a decision. He turned to her.

"Before we do anything else," he said. "Before you go into that box and ring your uncle, I've got to talk to you." He seemed for once in their acquaintance to be deadly serious. All lightness and humor gone. "There are certain developments which you must know. Now, first, in spite of your often cogent arguments I think there is no doubt George Grant organized the spy ring. But he didn't do it for any ideological reasons. He did it for money. A great deal of money judging by the amount we found on Eliot. It seems he preferred payment in cash to such refinements as sums paid into Swiss accounts and so on. He was not passing on the secrets he obtained for peanuts, that's certain. And I don't suppose he paid his agents much in spite of the fact they were taking all the risks. When they objected, turned difficult, he got rid of them; vide Craddock. Now the point that interests us is why it was so important to him to get this extra money. He has a large income, but he lives right up to it. He is spending a lot of money and we're not quite sure what on. What can it be that is so important to him that he is willing to risk imprisonment, disgrace, infamy, to achieve it?"

"It's the upkeep of the castle and the estate, isn't it?" Fiona said. "That's what I always understood he needed money for. That's why he started taking tourists in as guests. I know he charges a ridiculously large fee for the privilege."

"But in fact he doesn't take all that many guests throughout the season. He could take more, there is a demand for it. And his normal income is quite sufficient for the maintenance of the castle as well as to keep him in a reasonably lavish style. His many trips abroad, to Spain and Germany for instance."

"So you know about those?"

"We know about the recent ones certainly." He paused. "There is one curious fact we have unearthed. He did use capital from some unknown source about a year ago to buy control of a small company, an agency which television companies, newspapers, film companies and so on use for various jobs. Like filming a demonstration from a helicopter in a remote part of Scotland."

For a moment Fiona couldn't think what he was talking about, what relevance it had. Enough had happened since the torchlight procession to push the students' demonstration to the back of her mind.

"Let me get this clear," she said. "You're saying that George is the owner of that helicopter, the one Jackson pilots, the one that took the film of the demonstration that got so much publicity?"

"Yes," Wyndham said. "That's what I'm saying."

"Well, he can't have known about that

job," Fiona said. "You heard what he thought about that demonstration. He would never have sanctioned giving it publicity."

"You wouldn't think so, would you?" Wyndham said. "That is one point that could do with a little further explanation. There are others. And we are not the only ones to be concerned. His paymasters, the buyers of all those secrets, are not very pleased about George's recent behavior. They are not at all happy about the death of their courier. They find that highly suspicious. The verdict of heart attack does not convince them. They suspect George of double-crossing them, either looking around for a higher bidder or far more dangerous in their eyes, becoming a double agent, feeding them innocuous stuff supplied by us, and giving us names and methods that will help us to close down other operations they may have in hand. The deaths of Craddock and the technician from Linnay seem to confirm this to them. So they want to act first. They may be ready to ditch George. Hand him to us on a plate. The fact that they've been in touch with us indicates that."

"They have been in touch with you?" Fiona said incredulously.

"It happens sometimes. We are all professionals, after all. We get to know our counterparts on the other side. But this, I think, is unusual. The paymaster himself wants to meet me, to discuss matters of mutual interest. That is what that telephone call was about just now, to confirm a previous tentative arrangement. To confirm time and place. I told them I would be at this box within a certain half-hour period. We were both punctual."

"And you know this man, this paymaster?"

"I've known who he is for some time," Wyndham said. "But this is what I want to say, Fiona." He took both her hands in his. He spoke quietly, intently. "I have a strong suspicion of what may be involved. I think this coming meeting may confirm it and the very real danger it could lead us into. In view of this, I want to give you the chance to withdraw from the whole affair. Never mind Stanton and any feelings of duty he may try to arouse in you. It's part of his job to make use of you if he thinks it's going to help him. He doesn't worry about what happens to you. It's my job to take risks. It's not yours. So say the word and I'll ring someone from the box to pick you up and take you straight to Edinburgh.

That will be the end of it. You can take up the threads of your life and carry on."

"And what will you do?" Fiona asked him.

"Get on with my job," Wyndham said.

"I can't withdraw now, you know that," Fiona said. "I'm involved. What was it Stanton said, that I wouldn't be safe anywhere if George was guilty. You're both convinced he is. So my neck is at stake now. So get Eliot's packet of filthy lucre out and let's get on with the phone call. Besides, how much peace of mind do you think I would have in Edinburgh wondering what had happened to you, if you were dead or alive. You see, unlike Mr. Stanton, I do care."

"Oh, dear," Wyndham said. He leaned forward and kissed her. "And we are not supposed to be emotionally involved. Have you got enough change for the telephone?"

"Yes," Fiona said. "And all this self-sacrifice on my part is going to look a little foolish if George doesn't fall for it. What if he asks me to post it?"

"If he does that," Wyndham said, "I shall almost believe in his innocence. But if he does take the bait, don't commit yourself to arriving at any particular time. We have this meeting first."

"What do I do while you're at this meeting?" Fiona asked.

"You're coming too," Wyndham said. He reached for his briefcase on the seat behind, opened it and took out a large packet, sealed with cellophane tape. He handed it to Fiona.

"Will he be able to tell it's been opened?" she said.

"No." He gave her a gentle push. "Go on, get it over with. Don't forget, you're not in the least concerned, one way or another, how George reacts. It couldn't matter to you less."

"What if he's out?" she said.

"We'll try again later."

Fiona got out of the car. A damp heat surrounded her. It was the sort of day the midges loved. Even at this height, there was little movement of air. Inside the telephone box, the air was stale and stifling. She put the package on the shelf and carefully arranged her coins ready for use. She dialed George's private number. There were other numbers for the estate office, the kitchen, the housekeeper and so on. It rang for a long time before anyone answered. She inserted the first of the coins and asked for George.

"Who is calling?" There was a pleasant Highland voice at the other end.

"His niece. I'm in a call box so I would be glad if you could find him quickly. I may run out of change."

"One moment, please."

She held on. She looked at her watch. She pushed open the door for air. In the car Wyndham looked perfectly relaxed, head resting back, eyes closed. A voice spoke in her ear:

"Fiona? Murchison said you are ringing from a call box. Is something the matter? Have you had an accident?"

"No, George, nothing like that. I'm on my way to Edinburgh and I suddenly remembered I had something of yours. I meant to give it to you yesterday but completely forgot. Since I'm not too far from you, I wondered if you'd like me to bring it over. I don't know if it's important or not."

"I thought you weren't going to Edinburgh until tomorrow?"

"I wasn't, but I had an unpleasant experience this morning. An ex-employee of father's was shot in some kind of stupid accident. I found the body. It has rather wiped out my holiday frame of mind so I'm going back to work."

"How very unfortunate. Are the police holding the person responsible?"

"Not yet. He ran away, frightened I suppose by what he had done."

"I see. And you say you have something of mine. I don't recollect leaving anything at the house yesterday. I haven't missed anything."

"It's not something you left yesterday. You left it in the car. I thought it might be some documents to do with your German trip."

There was a pause. When George spoke again, she thought she could detect a difference. The slightest edge of tension in his voice. He said: "Where exactly did you find these . . . documents?"

"They are in a package. I found it on the floor in the back when I got home. My coat had fallen from the back seat onto the floor, hiding it. I noticed it when I picked the coat up."

"Have you opened it?" George said.

"No, but I've got it here. Do you want me to open it now?"

"No, that won't be necessary. I think I know what it is. A packet wrapped in white paper, sealed."

"That's right. There's no name on it or anything to say what it contains. I thought I should let you know I've got it. If it's nothing important I could post it to you from Edinburgh."

"You're not all that far away, you say?"

"Relatively speaking. I'm quite happy to bring it over to you if you want. It's my fault for forgetting to give it to you yesterday."

There was another long pause. Fiona began to worry that she'd have to feed more coins in. Then George spoke again.

"If it's the packet I think it is, it contains notes from my German trip. It would be helpful for me to have them as soon as possible. I hadn't missed them, but I would have been looking for them tomorrow. Since you are kindly making this offer—look, the least I can do is offer you dinner. Where are you staying tonight?"

"We hadn't planned to stay anywhere. We had intended driving through the night."

"We?"

"I'm being given a lift. My own car is in London, of course."

"Yes, yes, quite. Do I know your friend?" Fiona didn't reply. The beeps indicating her money had run out prevented her from having to go into detail about the lift she was being given. She didn't put in any more money and George ended the conversation hastily before they were cut off. "Well,

Fiona, I'm grateful for your offer. I shall see you later. Good-bye."

"Good-bye." Fiona said. She put the phone down and gathered up the remaining coins and the package. She had been holding the receiver so tightly her fingers were clenched and stiff. She went outside and gratefully breathed in the fresher air. Wyndham stirred himself.

"Well?" he said.

"He's taken the bait. He's asked me to take the package to him. Notes from his German trip, he says. He asked me to dinner. That was before he knew I wasn't alone."

"Did you tell him who your companion was?"

"No."

"Good girl." He leaned across and opened her door. "Jump in."

They drove on. For the next few miles they spoke little. At first Fiona felt too tense to talk and Wyndham was concentrating all his attention on the road. After a while she realized he was looking for something, a turning or a building perhaps.

"Where is this meeting?" she asked. "Where are we going?"

He didn't reply directly. "Not long now," he said.

Fiona said: "Do you think George really believed our story? Would he accept as possible that the packet could have fallen out of Eliot's jacket and stayed out of sight? Does he even know we put Eliot's body on the back seat of the car?"

Wyndham glanced at her. "You sound nervous."

"Of course I'm nervous. Would Eliot be carrying that amount of money in his jacket anyway? I don't think George believed a word of it."

Wyndham smiled at her. "Even though you're such a rotten liar I think George would accept the story. The fact that you're such a transparently honest person would help. And it's all quite plausible, you know. We actually found the money tucked inside the map ready for the exchange, but he wouldn't have left it in the car on the journey from London. He'd have had it with him on the train. He'd have it and the map in his jacket at Inverlinn. He was wearing fisherman's tweeds, wasn't he? Lots of capacious pockets. He could still have had it in his pocket on the road. He collapses. You and I rather awkwardly drag him out of

218

his car and heave him on to the back seat of yours. At the hotel, he is manhandled again, out of the car and up to a room. It would be perfectly natural for the money to fall out during all that shoving and pushing. No reason why anyone should notice it. No one was particularly looking for it. When George's men searched the Mercedes on the road, they were looking for his map, not the money."

"You're doing it again," Fiona protested. "The enigmatic comment. Who searched the car on the road? When?"

"When we stopped at the pub for lunch," Wyndham said. "Don't you remember? You were sure you had left the car open but we found it locked. Like most drivers, even though he had found the door open, he automatically locked it when he'd finished his quick search."

"You're talking about Jackson and that other man from the helicopter."

Wyndham nodded. "They'd been keeping an eye on us. When they saw the car parked by the pub, they landed, far enough away not to alert us. Jackson came in to keep us occupied while his friend removed the incriminating map. Either way, if the exchange had taken place or not, George needed to get hold of it. But it wasn't there. I'd taken it into the pub, remember? I imagine that's why your uncle came over as soon as he could get away to collect the car himself, instead of sending someone for it. He must have had a few worrying moments about that map."

"Then those men," Fiona said, "were taking orders directly from George?"

"When the police rang from the hotel to check your story about ownership of the car, he must have got pretty edgy. He sent the helicopter over to see what was going on. To keep an eye on you. To find out if the exchange had taken place as arranged. To get hold of the map if it hadn't, and the money if it had."

Fiona said: "I still haven't grasped it. I still can't take in how someone can be entirely different from the face he presents to the world. When you told me George was the boss of the agency and the helicopter, I was still assuming his cover was genuine. But if I needed any more convincing this would do it. He was involved in the demonstration too. The news the leaders were waiting for that night in the pub was that the helicopter was ready to take the shots."

"That's right," Wyndham said.

"And when Kenton and I saw Jackson in the pub with the students, he was there to pay them. The whole thing was organized and paid for by George."

"It seems highly probable," Wyndham agreed.

"But what for?" Fiona said. "Was he being paid to do that too?"

"That's one of the things I hope we shall soon find out," Wyndham said. "Mind you," he added casually, "all this is deduction based on the single fact that we know George owns the agency. We've no proof of any of it."

"It's a pity David Kenton developed scruples at the last minute about taking money for joining in the demonstration," Fiona said. "If he had gone ahead and had actually been paid by Jackon, there would be the proof you need, wouldn't there?"

"It would certainly have helped," Wyndham said.

"Couldn't you trace some of the students who were there and did get paid?"

"They are hardly likely to admit it."

"Kenton might find you a witness. He wouldn't have to admit he was paid, just that he saw others taking money."

"What a devious creature you're becoming," Wyndham said.

"I wonder how we could find Kenton," Fiona said. "I wonder where he is now."

"Perhaps we shall meet him on the road."

"If he gets tired and starts to hitchhike, perhaps we shall," Fiona said. "But he's supposed to be walking over the hills."

"Rather him than me," Wyndham said. "In this damp heat. The midges will eat him alive."

"Talking of hitchhikers," Fiona said, "there is someone ahead. That's the first person we've seen for miles." She added after a moment, "But it's not Kenton."

"How can you tell at this distance?"

"He's not carrying a rucksack."

"He's carrying something," Wyndham said.

As they drew level with the man, they saw he was wearing a dark city suit. His shoes were thin black town shoes, muddied and damp, and he was carrying, rather incongruously, a yellow plastic bucket. A few yards ahead, a caravan had pulled off the road into one of the semicircular passing places. The car parked beside it had its hood up and its radiator cap off. It was gently steaming.

222

Somewhat to Fiona's surprise, Wyndham swung off the road and into the narrow space left by the other car. He switched the engine off and waited. When the man appeared Wyndham got out, slamming his door shut. Fiona followed. The man paused in the act of pouring brackish burn water from the bucket into the radiator, a hit-and-miss procedure in which a great deal of it was lost.

"You're a long way from the embassy," Wyndham said. "I hope you've told the authorities."

The man gave him a baleful look and put down the bucket.

"Where is he?" Wyndham said. "Inside?"

The man nodded. He said, "Wait," and entered the caravan.

"Who is he?" Fiona whispered.

"Third secretary at the London embassy."

"Is he the one we're supposed to meet? The man who pays George?"

"No. He's here to keep an eye on things. They obviously think it's too delicate a matter to send any lower-grade men along. Otherwise he wouldn't be soiling his shoes fetching water."

The man reappeared and beckoned them to go in. Wyndham turned to Fiona.

"After you," he said.

The curtains had been half drawn across the caravan windows. The interior was gloomy and felt chill after the heat outside. A man was sitting on the bench seat that ran the width of the caravan and at night was transformed into a bed. On a table in front of him was an open bottle of white wine, four glasses, two of them used, a loaf and some cheese. As they came in, he was intent on breaking a crust off the loaf. He balanced a small piece of cheese on top, put it in his mouth and ate it with evident enjoyment. He wiped his mouth delicately with a clean handkerchief and smiled at them.

"My dear Fiona," he said. "What an unexpected pleasure to see you again so soon. And you, Max, efficient as ever, I see. Right on time."

"Hello, Boris," Wyndham said. "There seems a slight lack of efficiency in your outfit, or is the boiling radiator part of your cover?"

"First they send a car hardly powerful enough to pull the caravan, then they forget to refill the water bottles." Boris shrugged. "However, it was organized at short notice and this countryside is not ideally suited to providing unobtrusive, private meeting places." He turned to Fiona. "We have to bring them with us. Why don't you sit down?"

"I think we have shocked Fiona into immobility," Wyndham said. "I didn't give her any warning."

Fiona sat down. She looked carefully at Boris, trying to see what she had missed before. But she had suspected something, hadn't she? Something false.

"All that this—" she gestured toward Boris and Wyndham "—this meeting makes me assume must be true, is it really so?"

Boris said: "Did Max really give you no hint?"

"I don't think I believe it," Fiona said.

He put a large, warm hand over hers. "Of course you don't," he said gently. "I wouldn't be very good at my job if you did. Now Max is different. He is a fellow professional." He poured out a glass of wine and handed it to her. "I know this time of day should be devoted to tea and fruitcake but I'm afraid we have brought none of those civilizing commodities with us. You look as if you could do with something a little stronger than tea anyway."

Fiona took the wine. "Where did you go when you left us last evening?" she asked him. "There were, I presume, no old friends eagerly awaiting you for dinner."

"I flew to London. As a result, this meeting which I had tentatively arranged with Max here was confirmed."

"The phone call you made to Boris after the lunch party, was that what that was all about?" she asked Wyndham.

"I told him about the murder of the suspect technician on Linnay," Wyndham said. "It alarmed him considerably."

"It put the wind up me, you could say," Boris remarked amiably. "It proved to me that, as I suspected, things were getting a little out of hand. And this was before we heard about Craddock. That was very unpleasant for you, Fiona."

She said: "I wish you wouldn't make everything sound so normal. It isn't normal. Here you are, with your enormous talent, your prodigious voice, sitting in this ridiculous caravan in the middle of nowhere talking of murder—what would you have done if I'd said I'd come with you yesterday?"

"I knew you would refuse, or I wouldn't have asked you," Boris said.

"I must be very transparent."

"No more than the rest of us. You saw through me, remember. You told me I was playing a part. I didn't think this revelation would be quite the surprise to you it obviously is."

"Why didn't you warn me?" Fiona said to Wyndham.

"Orders, I would say," Boris observed. "Aren't I right, Max? The wily Stanton, whom God preserve, making doubly sure."

Wyndham nodded. "I was ordered to say nothing to you. I was to spring Boris on you and watch your reaction."

"I hope your report to Stanton will be satisfactory," Fiona said. "Couldn't you have dropped a hint?"

"It wasn't the sort of thing you can very well hint at," Wyndham said. "I'm very sorry. I really am."

"That's all right," Fiona said. "I'm getting used to it already." But there was growing a sad sense of loss, of betrayal. The past few days had been in her the death of a certain kind of innocence. It was probably as well it had gone. Naiveté about the realities of the ruthless world could be dangerous. But it had left behind a perplexing confusion in her mind. She felt as if she had been moving through some grotesque carnival, full of grinning masks. Now all the masks were coming off. Who would be next?

She said: "Can I ask some questions, or isn't there time for that?"

Boris said: "We have both enjoyed your hospitality under false pretenses. I think we owe you a question or two."

"The truth is, Boris," she said, "I find I like you as much as I did ten minutes ago."

He laughed. He sounded genuinely amused. "Why not? I like Max here. In wars it is common to find yourself admiring an enemy and despising an ally. It is perfectly natural. It doesn't alter one's behavior, but it can lead to arrangements of mutual benefit, such as we have met to discuss here."

"You consider yourself as a soldier."

"I am a soldier," Boris said, "and my motive, which I can see is the first question hovering on your lips, is a soldier's motive—patriotism. As it is with Wyndham."

Fiona sighed. "I'm no match for cunning Russians with silvery tongues. Now the one outside. I'd know exactly where I was with him."

"You think charm and a gift for friendship

make me more dangerous than the fellow outside?" Boris said. "That is precisely why he is outside keeping watch and you are talking to me, not him. What were your other questions?"

"How long has Max known you were involved with George?"

"He knew Eliot worked for me. He didn't know about the link with your uncle until Eliot and you led him to him."

"As I told you," Wyndham said quietly, "I had known about Boris's activities for some time. I had never seen him in the flesh. When you saw me at the opera house that afternoon I was there to take a look at him. I may say I was impressed. You are, or were, in a perfect situation, Boris. Entry into any country, any embassy, without question. Ease of contact. A marvelous setup."

"Had you met before the lunch party?" Fiona asked.

"We had been in touch after Eliot's death, yes," Wyndham said.

"I didn't like your use of the past tense in your description of my 'marvelous setup,' " Boris said.

"You've been taking a lot of risks lately," Wyndham said. "Particularly yesterday.

What were you trying to do? Flush him out into the open?"

"The same technique Stanton used with Fiona, I suppose," Boris said. "Looking for reactions. But George must be a good poker player. No reaction."

"I think one of the reactions was Craddock's death. He'd been threatening to tell all he knew about the company and there you were asking questions about it. That was one mouth that had to be stopped."

"The only company I heard Boris asking about was a theatrical one," Fiona said. "The Company of 13, wasn't it, Boris? No one knew anything about it."

"The Company of 13," Wyndham said, "is nothing to do with the theater and three of us sitting at the lunch table had certainly heard of it. Unfortunately George is the only one of the three who knows the whole truth about it, and after Boris's shock tactics it is going to be increasingly dangerous to attempt to find out."

"I've remembered something he said," Fiona said. "He told you to go back to your informant and you said your informant had gone away."

"I said departed," Boris corrected her, "a

word I believe is sometimes used as a synonym for died. My informant was Elena Greer and she is dead because George Grant killed her."

She was alone in the caravan with Wyndham. His colleague had come and called Boris away. Wyndham had had to move to let Boris out of the confined space and he had remained by the open door, watching them, she supposed. She felt drowsy from the lack of air and curiously detached from her surroundings. A safety valve, she thought, a defense mechanism because I don't want to think about what has been said, what has been happening. Delayed shock, as her father had said.

The caravan was not new. One of those hired to families wanting to tour Scotland on the cheap but not trustful enough to the climate to risk a tent. The bright cotton covers of the cushions were wearing thin, there was a handle missing from one of the cupboards, and cracks in the thin veneer of plastic. She turned and pulled aside the curtain from the window behind her. They were in shadow but the late sun struck the slopes of a long, high hill behind them, enriching its bleak flanks with a density of light. It looked like a tawny lion sprawling at ease.

"What is that hill called?" she said. "I should know it."

Wyndham looked round at her. After a moment's hesitation he came and sat beside her.

"It has a long Gaelic name," he said, "which I can never pronounce."

"What are they doing out there?" Fiona said.

"In the car? Talking on the radio."

"They have a radio?"

"Every modern equipment," he said lightly. "Never travel without one. How are you?"

"I'm fine," Fiona said.

He put a hand under her chin and kissed her gently on the mouth.

"What was that for?" Fiona asked.

"To re-establish contact. You've become very withdrawn."

"I don't want to go on with this," she said.

"I know."

"I want to leave you all behind and go back to my nice, safe make-believe world of theater. But that's no longer possible."

"I'm sorry about Boris. I'm sorry I couldn't tell you. But even if I had I don't think you'd have believed it unless you'd talked to him yourself."

She studied his face. When he was off-guard, she thought she could detect the tension and strain beneath the carefully controlled surface. She wanted to touch his face. She wanted him to hold her.

She said: "I'm not exactly making this easy for you, am I?"

"I shall be glad when I can stop apologizing to you every five minutes."

"I wish we could have met under different circumstances."

"Then we'd probably never have met at all. I meant what I said earlier, you know. You don't have to go on with this. He is your uncle, after all. No one could blame you."

"What would you do?" Fiona asked him. "Go to the castle on your own? Say I'd been taken ill? Hand him the packet of money yourself?"

"Once you're there, you'll be no more protected by your relationship with him than I will."

"But you're not going to stop now? If I back out, you'll find another way?"

"Yes, of course. It's a question of doing my job."

"It's not so much a job, is it?" Fiona said. "In these circumstances. It's more a question of doing your duty."

"An unfashionable word to hear from you," Wyndham said, "but I suppose the concept is true."

"Well, it's my duty to help you," Fiona said. "Old-fashioned or not it seems to be the only word that describes what I have to do. All relationships apart." She felt committed and refreshed. "I can accept Boris for what he is. I shan't forget either the system he represents or the artist he is. I shall go on admiring him, but I shan't trust him."

"Stanton would be proud of you," Wyndham said. "But don't get too complicated. Just follow my lead."

There was a murmur of voices outside and Boris re-entered. He was holding a new bottle of wine and a corkscrew. He set them on the table and carefully removed a long green strand of weed from the bottle's damp label.

"It's been cooling in the stream," he explained. "I sent my friend to get it."

"I thought you weren't going to drink any more alcohol after yesterday," Fiona said. "You are still planning to perform?"

Boris looked shocked. "Of course! However, chilled white wine is soothing to the throat, and this is a rather nervous time." He opened the bottle and poured out the wine.

"It's been confirmed," he said to Wyndham. "Two of the men on the list flew to Inverness this morning and were driven to George Grant's castle. The dates she gave us were correct. The meeting is tonight and they should all be there. Elena's list only produced four names. We know now for certain that George Grant is another. If you could get us the rest—"

"Thirteen names, I presume," Fiona interrupted. "You are talking about this Company of 13."

Boris sat down. He rested his elbows on the table, his clasped hands under his chin. "Your uncle has been playing a game on all of us, Fiona. The political pose we all thought to be a cover for his communist sympathies is in fact the genuine one. He doesn't give a damn for East or West. It has become clear he has been making use of us both to help finance what is being increasingly revealed to be an extremely sinister conspiracy. We first heard of it through agents we infiltrated into certain terrorist groups. Rumors about a new source of international finance. We were anxious to know who was sustaining some of these wilder, more vicious gangs. We got nothing definite for a long time. Then there was a stroke of luck. One of our agents, casually referring in a conversation with a contact to the assassination of a leading Middle East politician for which the group had claimed responsibility, was told that it was not one of theirs, it was one of the thirteen's. We pricked up our ears. The number thirteen had come up before in connection with another group but with vaguer implications. Now we could assume a link between them. However, the scraps of intelligence we gathered together built up a picture of an organization very different from the ones we had become accustomed to dealing with. It seemed we had here a new kind of group who were adapting international terrorism to their own ends. The normal run of terrorists have usually no political aim beyond the destruction of the existing system. They see no further ahead than that. But it grew clear that these men, this Company of 13, had for years been making plans and building up resources. Their plan is to create anarchy in order to seize political power. You may think that not such an original concept, but the way in which it appears to be handled is. They are building up private armies, quietly training them, acquiring and storing weapons, waiting patiently for their chance, for the moment when the political situation in their countries is so precarious that a coup d'etat and a strong government, any kind of strong government, will be welcomed by a population wearied of an industrial and social anarchy that is destroying their way of life and leaving them helpless and afraid."

"I would have thought your masters might have welcomed such a development," Fiona said. "Not the seizing of power, perhaps, but the anarchy?"

"We do not approve of anything we cannot control," Boris said. "And they are too inconsistent in their attitudes. In one country they will sell us information. In another they may be infiltrating our own organizations and selling our secrets to our enemies. And the danger is that there may be a nub of truth in their wild schemes. How long does it take to destroy even such a stable society as yours—five, ten years? How far off might civil war be between one section of society and another and how easily could it be controlled if things got out of hand?"

"You think there are members of this conspiracy in the armed forces?" Fiona said.

"That is what we should like to know, wouldn't we, Max? We do know that each member is a leading figure in his own country, some wealthy manufacturers, other financiers, some representatives of a decaying aristocracy, others politicians with a lust for power. The important and dangerous factor is that they are working together, planning together, helping each other. They support strikers with uninvited strong-arm men, foment riots, wherever there is trouble, of whatever political color, you will find them. Agitators are not new but their routine use by these conspirators is far more widespread than any other illegal organization has attempted. And they appear to be making assassination a much used weapon in their arsenal. It has a twofold effect: it creates alarm and confusion and it gets rid of men who may be dangerous to them."

"Have you been able to prove that?" Fiona asked.

"To our satisfaction, yes. We are fairly certain that three recent murders, a politician,

238

a film director and a trade unionist, were directly attributable to them. But we can provide no solid evidence. Nor has Max's organization been any more successful. The only concrete thing to come out of all this is that we have begun to pool our information."

"And you believe George is one of these men?" She glanced at Wyndham.

He gestured toward Boris. "You might as well finish the story," he said.

"Well," Boris said. He drank some wine. "I suppose I am now giving away nothing that you do not know, Max. When your uncle approached us with his offer of information direct from Linnay, we first of all began to find out all we could about him. Among the things we discovered was that he had a mistress whom he visited whenever he was in London. A young singer, a Czech, who had taken the name of Elena Greer. He had first met her at a reception in Edinburgh for a touring opera company. He is fond of opera, but of course you know that. When we knew she was Czech we knew she was vulnerable. She still had relatives at home. Her position here regarding work permits—" He broke off with a shrug. "You may imagine it. She was visited. It was arranged she keep an eye on

George Grant, and let us know about anything unusual. In the meantime the system was set up, the information began to come, the payments to Grant began to be made. Elena Greer let us know Grant's movements, when he went to Spain, when to Germany or Italy. But it wasn't until recently that the breakthrough came about his link with the Company of 13. I had arranged indirectly for her to sing the part of Annina in *Rosenkavalier*—no, I didn't tell you about that, Fiona. It was some small reward to her. When I arrived in London, I went to see her. George was away. He had left some clothes and a briefcase with her for safekeeping. She had been through the briefcase as a matter of routine and she showed me what she had found. Among papers relating to his estate there was a business diary with brief records of appointments, you know the sort of thing. The interesting fact was that two of the names mentioned in that diary were people we already suspected of belonging to the Company of 13. I asked her to start looking for appointments, names, anything, no matter how trivial it might seem. A week later she sent us a list with four names on it and a series of dates, nothing else. But it was important enough to cause her death. He may have found her looking through his papers, she may have asked too pointed a question; we shall never know exactly what happened, but two days later she was dead."

"Poor girl," Fiona said. "No wonder she was always so quiet and subdued. So it was not a crime of passion, after all."

"No, I don't think love was ever involved in the affair. It was more in the way of a convenient arrangement for them both. She was at the beginning of her career. He helped her with money at a difficult time. It suited him, it helped her. Nice and businesslike."

"That would have made her betrayal more shocking to George," Fiona said. "He has a strong sense of business morality. But, of course, Boris, you killed her by involving her."

"It is the fortunes of war," he said. "My back is quite broad enough to bear such responsibilities." He sipped more wine. "My throat is getting tired from all this talking. You continue, Max. By the way, you were taking risks too, at Fiona's lunch party, confronting us with the fact of Elena's murder."

Wyndham said: "I wanted to put a little

pressure on him, get him edgy. Like Boris, Fiona, we had a certain amount of information about this elusive Company of 13. We had some pieces of the puzzle but not enough to make the complete picture. Any name remotely connected with their activities was being investigated. One of those names happened to be Grant. A fairly common name. We selected several men whose history and position might make them candidates and one of those was George. The leakage of information from Linnay seemed at that time to be quite a separate matter. It seemed coincidental that another Grant might be involved, for you see in the early days, we suspected your father of communist sympathies, while it seemed fairly obvious that your uncle was a supporter of fascism. You can imagine how it confused us when it became clear your uncle was running the spy ring. We began to look for the motive behind it. We found out about his association with Elena Greer. In the last few days we discovered he was behind the demonstration, a mild affair but the beginning we are pretty sure of a whole series of such episodes, carefully orchestrated to build up to more and more violent conclusions. We began investigating these tourist visits he presides over with such generous Scottish hospitality. The majority of them appear to be what they seem. We know the tourist agencies which arrange them. But there were three such visits over the past year which he handled entirely himself. We now know that two of those meetings were on dates which appear in Elena Greer's list. The latest date on that list is tonight."

"If they are holding a meeting tonight," Fiona said, "they won't even let us in the castle, surely?"

"You're his niece. He's invited you to dinner. Even when he sees who is accompanying you, he is hardly likely to throw us out without offering us a drink. He is a little contemptuous of our intelligence service. Though he fears we were getting a little too close in the question of the spy ring, remember he ran it successfully for months and still thinks he's got away with it. He may decide we know nothing at all about his connection with the Company of 13, nothing we can prove. He may decide to act as if his visitors are genuine tourists. We shall have to wait and see. But anything I can see, anything I can hear, will be of the utmost importance to us. It really is urgent, Fiona; you see, we have received information that another assassination is planned within the next week. We don't know who and we don't know where, but we believe it is to be in this country. We believe that is what the meeting will be about."

Fiona rubbed a hand over her eyes. She said: "I don't know if I am the person to help you." She looked up. "Don't mistake me. I want to help. But I haven't taken it all in yet. I don't know what George believes or he doesn't. What he thinks my connection is with you. He killed those men to protect himself from being caught as a spy. Does he still think that's why you're after him? For that alone?"

"He is an arrogant man who believes he can run rings round Max here," Boris said. "As he believes he has made fools of us. He is a dangerous man who must be stopped. They must all be stopped, but he is the first one we've got a chance of getting and between us I think we can."

Wyndham looked at his watch. "Time's getting on. You wanted to make a deal, Boris. That's why we're here. What are you offering?"

"We'll give you George Grant, if we can do

it our way. No mention of a spy ring, no treason trial, the Linnay operation closed and forgotten."

"It hasn't been too successful for you, has it?" Wyndham commented. "Do you want us to tell you how much of that stuff they sent you to discount, or have you already found out?"

Boris smiled at Fiona. "Here we have Max playing chess again. He wants us to believe they were planting information for the spy ring to sell us from a very early stage. But no matter, that is not the point at issue. As I said, the operation is closed. You have had some justice, two of the men are dead."

"Then if we don't get Grant on the spying charge, what have you in mind?"

"The *crime passionel*," Boris said. "We get him for Elena's murder. We turn it into the jealous crime of a middle-aged man who found his young mistress was deceiving him. We will provide you with letters every handwriting expert in the country will swear are by his hand. We will provide photographs of them together, a witness to quarrels, and Elena's diary in which she writes down her growing fear of his jealousy. After all, the method of the murder fits in exactly. He suffocated her while she slept; just like Othello."

"And what would you want in return?" Max asked. "Apart from forgetting about Linnay?"

"First, that you continue to share with us any information you may get concerning the Company of 13. Any names you may get tonight for instance. And secondly—" he paused "—that you allow my career to continue without challenge."

"Your singing career, you mean," Max said.

"Of course. I sing at Edinburgh. I come and go as I please."

"I wouldn't come back to this country too often," Max said. "You wouldn't want to put temptation in our way. We're not too happy about spy rings, you know."

"You could never prove anything in court," Boris said.

"Of course not. But we could make things awkward for you. We could damage your career. After all, the rules are when found out you leave the game."

"Or at least play from a different country?"

"Exactly. When could you provide us with this evidence against Grant?"

"Tomorrow. It'll be brought to Edinburgh as soon as we know you agree."

"Get it sent up," Max said. "You'll have the answer tomorrow. By the way, we do have a witness who gave us a clear description of a man she once saw visiting Elena Greer's flat. The only trouble is the man she described was you."

6

THE castle was gray. Early sixteenth-century with Victorian additions, the additions in the Gothic style appearing more ancient than the original until one observed the stained glass, in the manner of Burne-Jones, which embellished the arched windows.

There had been earlier castles on the site, guarding an old route east, a pass between high hills. A confluence of rivers made it a fertile place, an oasis set like a gem in a ring of mountains. These early fortresses, little more than defended towers, had been besieged and stormed and burned and re-built and finally replaced by a more domestic edifice which in spite of the turbulent politics of Mary Stewart's reign was never in danger of direct attack again.

It was approached through parkland, open to the public for picnics and nature observation on certain specific days of the year. There were deer, but those were the wildest animals to be found there. No pride of saddened lions watched listlessly from beneath the trees, no delicate giraffes stilt-walked across the meadow, no zebra or tame elephant surprised the eye. George had not taken to the idea of a safari park in his quest for funds.

It was not a public day. The gates were shut when they arrived. Wyndham sounded the horn and the gatekeeper came out of the lodge to open up for them.

"Hullo, Mr. Macleod," Fiona said. "It's a long time since I've seen you. How are you?"

"Fairly well, fairly well. It is a pleasure to see your, Miss Grant. Your uncle told me to expect you."

"Has everyone else arrived?"

"Not quite all, I understand. I am to wait up to let them in."

"Why not leave the gates open?" Wyndham suggested.

"Oh, no, sir, the gates are always kept shut even for the private parties. Otherwise you might get people coming in at any time."

"A big party this time," Fiona said.

"Big enough. A dozen or so gentlemen, I believe. I'll let them know you're on your way."

He went back into the lodge to telephone. They drove on.

"Nice window dressing," Wyndham said. "He's not going to alarm anyone. A prime example of old retainer even down to the kilt."

"I can't imagine Macleod being part of a private army," Fiona said. "He's been at the lodge as long as I can remember."

"It's not the old ones we have to watch out for," Wyndham said. "It's the new boys. By the way, I noticed that this is the end of the road. It leads to the castle gate and stops. Do you know what happened to the old road that used to run by here? It was still marked on old maps, not on the new."

"It still exists," Fiona said. "It was little more than a track when I last saw it. But you have to go right through the castle grounds to get to it. The rest of it was incorporated in the grounds when they expanded the park early in the century. It's only used by estate workers now."

"I think we'd find it's being used by more people than that. This is a perfect setup for a training base. Those hills make an ideal terrain. Part of George's estate, I presume?"

"Quite a stretch of them," Fiona said.

"An empty deer forest, complete privacy, absolute security. What more could anyone ask. There's probably a camp up there."

"Where they keep the helicopter?"

"Could be."

"There's no doubt about the meeting, is there?" Fiona said. "A dozen gentlemen plus George makes thirteen."

"Quite a full house," Wyndham said.

"And all we've got is a solitary pair," Fiona said.

Wyndham glanced at her. "Do you play much poker?"

"Fred and some boys from the orchestra taught me. I'm hopeless. I always lose."

"Well, we're not going to lose this time," Wyndham said. "The stakes are too high."

"Let's hope you're right," Fiona said. "We're here."

"It looks like the Paris motor show," Wyndham said. "Which of those limousines do you fancy?"

They had emerged into a large open forecourt full of parked cars and centrally placed before the entrance to the castle. It was surrounded by a green verge, and beyond it a formal garden in the Elizabethan style led down to the banks of a narrow river. A rustic bridge had been constructed to cross it and on the other side a summer house, reminiscent in its decorative features of the Albert Memorial, stood like a monument to long Victorian afternoons.

In contrast to the peace and order of this scene, the castle walls rose battlemented and menacing, the modernized facade doing nothing to retrieve the threat of the two round towers that stood on either end of the main block, pinnacled and slit-eyed. At their feet were flower beds full of red geraniums, and trails of dark green ivy clawed their way across the stone.

The gatehouse was original. Inside George waited to greet them, an imposing figure in his Highland dress, the white ruffles of his silk shirt falling across bony wrists as he raised his arms to clasp Fiona in an avuncular embrace. He acknowledged Wyndham's presence with a nod, no expression of surprise or dismay crossing his face.

"Fiona my dear, we had almost given you up. Good evening, Commander, it is very good of you to come out of your way on my account."

"Not at all," Wyndham said. "I'm glad to have the chance to see the castle. I've never happened to be in the district on one of your open days."

"We never open the castle to the public, only the grounds," George said. "But I shall be delighted to show it to you. I'll be happy to give you my special conducted tour. Fiona, did I hear you correctly on the phone? You were planning to drive all night?"

"That's right."

"I won't hear of it. You must stay here, both of you. That is, Commander, if that doesn't interfere with your plans."

"It is very kind of you," Wyndham said. "We would appreciate it." He glanced at Fiona.

"I'd love to stay. If I could just ring Fred, my boss, and let him know what's happening—"

"Of course, of course," George agreed.

"By the way, I mustn't forget the reason for our visit. I have your papers—"

"Not now, if you don't mind," George said. "If you could give them to me a little later. I have left my guests taking drinks, they expect me as part of the tourist package to be with them." He gave them a thin smile. "I have to play my role. Will you join us?"

Fiona looked down at her jeans. "I think I'd better change."

253

"Yes, of course. Do you want to change too, Commander?"

"My tie, perhaps," Wyndham said. Unless you'd like me in my naval uniform?"

"It would add color, wouldn't it? As you please, there's no need. Murchison will show you to your rooms. We are taking drinks in the courtyard, Fiona. Such a pleasant night. Join us when you are ready."

They followed the butler down corridors lined with the antlered skulls of slaughtered deer and up a narrow stone staircase graced with a carved Jacobean bannister.

"You're not putting us in the tower rooms, are you Murchison?" Fiona said.

Murchison paused, his face professionally bland. "No, Miss Grant, but I thought it best to bring you this way, avoiding the gentlemen. It would be a little inconvenient for you to go through the courtyard."

"He's a terrible snob," Fiona commented to Wyndham when Murchison had finally left them, taking the car keys and promising to send their luggage up at once. "He simply couldn't stand the shame of being seen escorting a woman in jeans."

"Don't talk for a moment," Wyndham said. He spoke very softly. "First things first."

He began to walk about the room, looking behind pictures, running his hand along the undersurfaces of the furniture, bringing out a chair and standing on it to check the ceiling light. At last he seemed satisfied.

"This room is clean," he said.

"You thought George had bugged the room?" Fiona asked.

"It was a possibility. It's better to be sure. I'll go and check mine."

Fiona didn't relax until he came back with the same negative answer. It would have seemed such a deliberate trap they had walked into if George had had listening devices placed ready for their arrival.

They were in the Victorian wing of the castle, in adjacent rooms that shared a bathroom, magnificent in marble and mahogany and with a far more impressive view of hill and mountain from its window than the bedrooms themselves. They overlooked the courtyard.

"This is very considerate of George," Wyndham said.

He was leaning against the stone frame of the window embrasure surveying the scene below. Fiona walked over to join him. The inner courtyard of the castle looked very much like a quad in one of the smaller Oxford colleges. Entered from the gatehouse, it was bounded on the other three sides by living quarters, the original L-shaped sixteenth-century buildings completed by the Victorian addition. Facing Fiona and Wyndham was the great hall, a flight of stone steps leading to its massive door. Beneath it were the ancient kitchens and storerooms and beside it the charming family chapel. Opposite the gatehouse, the old lodging house with its rabbit warren of rooms opening one into the other had been converted into guest bedrooms. The Victorian wing contained, as well as further bedrooms and George's private rooms, the large drawing room, library, billiard room, small dining room and modern kitchen. There were additional rooms in the towers. The servants slept in a converted stable block by the garages on the other side of the Victorian wing. An archway, echoing the gatehouse entry, led from the old lodging house into a wide garden encompassed by the castle's still intact retaining walls.

A table stacked with bottles had been set up at the foot of the hall stairs and grouped about the smoothly cut grass of a central lawn were eleven men.

"Ten plus George," Fiona said. "Two more to come. Do you know any of them?"

"Oh yes," Wyndham said softly. "That stocky, bald-headed chap who looks like a butcher, over there on the right, he's a retired army commander. He never got the senior job in NATO he felt he was entitled to. He made a lot of indiscreet speeches, stood for Parliament as an independent, lost his deposit, and then a year ago quietly vanished from the public scene."

"Do you think he's the army link you and Boris mentioned?"

"If they're going to rely on him, they won't get far. I wouldn't have thought he was flexible enough to handle the sort of maneuvers they might get involved in. Still, it's very interesting. He was a tank man originally. I wonder if they've started buying tanks."

Fiona gazed with some incredulity at the fat man in the dinner jacket, who looked, as Wyndham had said, rather like a small tradesman attending a Rotary Club dinner. It was hard to imagine him as a dangerous conspirator.

"Do you know the man he's talking to?"

"No, but I know the one next to him. The

tall fellow with side whiskers. He's a landless Austrian archduke. Easy to see why he's in this. Wants to get the old estates back with a few more thrown in. But that man over there is the most interesting of all." He pointed to an elderly man with a stooped back, leaning on a stick. As they watched, a servant brought a chair from the dining room for him to sit on. He turned to thank the man and Fiona saw his face, pale, drawn parchment like a portrait of a Venetian doge.

"Who is he?" she asked.

"American oil multimillionaire. Our friends in Washington will like to know about him."

It was like watching a play. An elaborate set, a polished group of actors, George, the star performer, holding the eye with his gorgeous plumage as he moved across the emerald carpet of the stage. Clearly an expensive production. For whose benefit? she wondered.

"Max," she said, with increasing disquiet, "doesn't this all seem too easy? First welcomed in with open arms and then all the conspirators paraded before you."

"Yes, well, we've yet to get out again," Wyndham said. "We'll wait and see how easy that is." He had taken a miniature camera from an inside pocket of his jacket and carefully standing just beyond the line of sight from below was engaged in methodically recording every face in the courtyard.

"Do you think it's a trap?"

"Thanks to you, George hasn't had much time to organize a trap. When you rang, you didn't tell him who you were with and in the interval he will have been too busy with his arriving guests to speculate on your companion's identity."

"You think he got a shock when I arrived with you?"

"I think it threw him off-balance for a moment. He was annoyed with himself for not anticipating it. It's an awkward situation for him. How is he going to explain to his distinguished colleagues that his Highland fastness, so remote, so secure, now numbers an English intelligence officer among its inhabitants? He's got to decide what to do, how much to tell, how to find out whether I'm here because of Linnay or because we know about the Company of 13 or because I can't stay away from his niece. He's a man with problems. At the moment he's decided to play it very low-key. He's asked us to stay the night to give himself room for maneuver. He must be sure before he acts."

"So he won't have told anyone about the package I've brought?"

"He'll have reported the business with Eliot all neatly wrapped up. If those fellows down there knew George's niece had been wandering round the countryside with Eliot's packet of money in her handbag, they wouldn't consider it terribly efficient of old George. They're a ruthless bunch. I've a feeling he can't afford the loss of face. On the other hand, I don't see how he can avoid it. Unless, of course, he treats us as normal guests, gives us a good dinner, and sends us on our way rejoicing tomorrow morning."

"George can't bear to lose face," Fiona said. "He'll take the last course."

"Perhaps, but don't get too hopeful about it. He can always have a couple of fellows with rifles waiting for us a few miles out of the gates. Just to be on the safe side."

"You're a real optimist," Fiona said. "Look out, someone's coming."

It was a footman with the luggage. He placed the two cases on a luggage rack beside the door, handed Wyndham the car keys and left. Wyndham bent down and examined his case. "That's a hopeful sign. It hasn't been touched."

"Did you think they'd search our cases?" Fiona asked.

"I gave them the opportunity. It was a calculated risk. If I'd insisted on fetching them myself, that would have given the game away to George."

"What on earth have you got in there?"

"Nothing very much. A small piece of equipment that would have confirmed all George's worst suspicions. I'll show it to you later."

"How can you be sure your case hasn't been opened?"

"I'd marked the lock," Wyndham said. "I'd know if anyone had tampered with it." He smiled at her. "An old trick, Watson, but a useful one. You look worried."

"Suppose they search the rooms while we're at dinner?"

"They'll never have a better chance of going through our things than they had just now. I don't think George will bother about searches. He is far more concerned with my presence than with anything I may have brought with me." He shrugged. "Of course, if I'm wrong, I'm wrong." He looked at

Fiona. "It's going to be all right," he said gently. "Don't worry, you go and get changed."

In the bathroom the mountain light was clear and cool, reflecting from the white marble, the shining brass, the gleaming mirrors. Her face looked pale and translucent in that clean, washed light, her hair damp and tangled from the shower, like a mermaid. She gazed at this unreal reflection of herself. How little her face showed of the experiences of the past few days, how little of what she was feeling now. Perhaps it would be possible for her to deceive them, those actors in the courtyard. Perhaps she could sustain an evening of trivial conversation on the delights of fishing and how many times they had visited Scotland and the wonders of George's castle, just as if they were genuine tourists and she simply the niece of their host. It was going on too long, that was the trouble. It had begun when she came out of the mist to find Eliot's car splayed across her path and it was still going on. But now it was getting worse. The strain and the tension and the fear were coiling up inside her like a tightly wound spring, fear not only for herself, but for Max. Though she could cope with her own fears, she wasn't sure how to deal with this un-expectedly desperate concern for him, the sense of the danger which surrounded him, which, in the coming hours, could so easily entrap and destroy him. She had a sudden vision of Craddock's body, the life blown out of him by that single shot . . .

It was getting late. She was taking too long. She slipped over her head the black silk jersey dress she had taken from her case and eased its narrow straps against her shoulders. It made her look even more ethereal, more ghostly. Defiantly, she made herself up a little more heavily than she needed, then went, barefoot, back into the bedroom to find her evening sandals.

Wyndham was sitting on her bed writing in a small notebook. He looked up.

"My God," he said.

"What's the matter?"

"You're going to take those old boys' minds off their haggis."

Fiona smiled. "Weren't you going to change your tie?"

"Yes, I was, wasn't I?" He put the notebook in his pocket and stood up. Fiona was bending to fasten her sandal. Wyndham came to her and took her hands, gently pulling her upright. They stood facing each other, very close, their hands linked.

"Cold hands," he said.

"It must be getting cold. I'm trembling."

"I don't feel it."

"My heart is trembling."

"Stage fright," Wyndham said. "You'll be all right on the night. Ask Boris."

"Boris never suffers from stage fright."

"But then Boris is never off the stage, is he?"

"Max, what is going to happen?"

"We're going to have a pleasant evening and tomorrow I'll drive you to Edinburgh."

"Do you really believe that?"

"Do you want to have a bet on it?"

They had not heard the knock if there was one, but they heard the door opening. They moved apart as George came in.

"I'm sorry," he said. "I hope I'm not disturbing you. I wasn't sure if you were here."

"We were just coming," Fiona said. "Are we taking too long?"

"I won't be a moment," Wyndham said. He took his case and went into the bathroom, closing the door.

"Please forgive me," George said. "I'm afraid I was disturbing you."

"Not at all."

"I simply thought it might be a good moment for me to collect the package."

"Yes, of course." She took Eliot's package from her case and handed it to him. He took it with a kind of studied indifference.

"It was very kind of you to bring it," he said.

"It's nothing. It is making a pleasant interlude. I'm glad I rang. Otherwise I would have posted it from Edinburgh and missed this evening."

I've known him since childhood, she thought, and I've never really looked him in the face. And yet it is all there in his face, the thin lips, the hooded eyes, the arrogant arch of the neck. Her mother's judgment, made so many years ago and held to stubbornly ever since, was the true one. "George is a bastard," she said plainly and so he was. And like her mother it was impossible for her own judgment to be other than subjective. George had sold God knew how many secrets to the enemy, but it was Elena Greer's subdued and pretty face that Fiona remembered at that moment.

"Commander Wyndham and you—" he hesitated delicately "—are old friends?"

"Not particularly old, but friends, yes," she agreed.

"He is going to Edinburgh on naval business?"

Max would be pleased at this line of questioning, she thought, but did George really think her such a fool? Play up to him then, why not?

"He heard I was going back early to Edinburgh and offered to drive me," she said. "I expect he will stay for the first night."

"I hope to be there too," George said. "A very nice young man."

"Yes, indeed," Fiona said.

"You're looking very elegant, my dear," George said abruptly. "You won't mind being the only woman at dinner?"

"I won't mind. They don't bring their wives with them, on these trips?"

"Sometimes they do," George said, "but I believe for many of them the shooting and fishing make a good excuse to leave their wives at home." He gave her one of his would-be humorous smiles, a smile with closed mouth, like a crack on a plate. "I charge them so very much for the privilege of staying here, it really is too expensive for

266

many of them to bring their wives as well."

"I'm sure you give them good value," Fiona said.

"We try," George said. "We try." He glanced at his watch. "Will you be coming down soon? Dinner will be ready."

"In a few moments," she assured him. "As soon a Commander Wyndham is ready. By the way, George, I should like to ring Edinburgh tonight, if I may. Is there a telephone somewhere I could use?"

"Please," George said, "use the one in my study. At any time. You will be quite private there."

"And what," Wyndham said, emerging from the bathroom after George had left, "could be more innocently open than that offer? Giving us the run of his study. We can be sure there is nothing incriminating there. Can I come with you when you phone?"

"We had better make it after dinner," Fiona said. "We're keeping everyone waiting."

"Polite to the end," Wyndham said with a smile, "even in the company of thirteen villains." He had, she noticed, changed his tie. He looked as smoothly competent as ever. Not a wrinkle in his suit, not a crease in his forehead.

"Eleven villains," Fiona corrected him, "two haven't arrived yet, remember?"

"And your uncle the damnedest smiling villain of them all."

"He thinks we're lovers."

"Good. Perhaps that will put him off the scent. Quite convenient, wasn't it, to be caught practically in each other's arms?"

"You didn't plan it that way, did you?" Fiona asked him.

"I'm not as cold-blooded as that. Mind you, I would have done, if I could have been sure of his entrance. What do they do here at night, after dinner?"

"Is that a change of subject?"

"Do they play bridge or what?"

"Bridge in the library, billiards in the billiards room. But these aren't the usual tourists, are they?"

"They'll postpone their meeting until we've gone," Wyndham said. "At least until we've gone to bed. I just wanted to know where they are likely to be congregating."

The room with its vast wardrobes, its solid, old-fashioned bed, seemed suddenly alien and cold. She shivered.

"Don't leave my side down there, will you? I'm terrified."

He took her hand firmly in his. "Just be yourself, darling," he said. "Just be yourself."

And in the end it was relatively easy. She was playing a part, George's guests were playing a part, but they were practiced at it and easily in command of it, and opera was the subject most readily discussed: her designs, her talent, other famous productions, other famous singers. As the darkness began to gather outside the long windows, turning the flowers gray and the castle walls shadowy with secrets, the piper duly appeared, coinciding with the port, which Fiona as the sole woman present was asked to remain for, and George embarked on his history of the castle without which, contrived or real, none of these dinners was complete.

They dined in the great hall, its white walls patterned with medallions of ancient weapons, arranged by some devoted eighteenth-century antiquary who gathered up the jumble he found in the old armory and stacked in the gatehouse and pinned them up like flowers of death, the petals narrow blades of steel fanned out from the central boss of a highland target.

Muddy portraits of gloomy chiefs gazed down on the candlelit table, none of them George's ancestors. The portrait of his grandfather, who had bought the decaying estate a hundred years ago, hung more suitably in the Victorian drawing room he had built. George, Murdo would remark, like all converts, was more intensely Highland than the Highlander, in inverse proportion to the length of time his family had held land there. Like his grandfather, who had restored the traditions along with the castle, he had adopted their essential stubborn and independent qualities as his own, as if they could be bought with the estate. But his stubbornness was of a kind peculiar to himself, and his independence was rooted in egotism.

As soon as they had entered the hall, Fiona had been separated from Wyndham. She had been asked to sit at one end of the long table, opposite George, becoming with that placing the hostess rather than the guest.

Wyndham, whether by chance or design, was seated between the oil millionaire and a sallow-complexioned man of middle age with the prognathous Hapsburg jaw of a Spanish aristocrat. Toward the end of the meal he monopolized Wyndham, carrying on an interminable monologue in a low, emphatic voice, and when the gathering finally broke up and they all rose and left the hall, Wyndham remained behind her, out of her sight.

It was an unreal sensation to walk across the night-scented courtyard in the company of these men. They seemed to close around her, separate entities coalescing into a group. The undercurrent was there, no matter how civilized, how courteous their manners. The fiction of the tourists, strangers to each other, brought together by chance, wavered and faded under the relaxing influence of the excellent meal and fine wines George had provided. The existence of a joint purpose, a secret and dangerous link binding them together, made itself felt.

She tried to imprint their features on her mind so that she could, if necessary, sketch an identifiable portrait of each one of them once she and Wyndham were away from here. That was her deepest instinct, the constant repetitive urge to run, to get away, to be safe. The gatehouse was barred and chained at night; the lodge gate was locked; beyond the high castle walls was the inhospitable deer forest stretching into emptiness. They were trapped here and the fact that they had come of their own free will did nothing to relieve the panicky feeling of claustrophobia that suddenly assailed her. She looked round for Wyndham. They had come through open French windows into the large drawing room. Coffee had been laid for those who wanted it on a table by the door. A tray of spirits stood beside it.

"You like your coffee black, I remember."

She turned to find Wyndham at her shoulder and immediately the tension began to ease. She took the cup he offered. "How have you been getting on?"

"I've had a very interesting lecture on boar hunting," he said. "I've also been invited to stay in a mansion in Madrid. By the way, have you made your phone call yet?"

"No, I was going to do so in a moment."

"Let's have a stroll first," he murmured, "and see what everyone is doing."

The main reception rooms were connected by double doors left open on these occasions for people to wander to and fro at will. In the library, George and three of his guests were settling down to a rubber of bridge, watched idly from an armchair by the archduke, already into his second post-prandial brandy. He waved to Wyndham. "You won't change your mind? We can easily stir up two of those lazy fellows next door to make up the four."

"Thank you, no," Wyndham said. He leaned against the back of the armchair for a moment watching the game. "You'd regret it. I'm no bridge player."

George's partner glanced up with a smile. "You have better things to do, I'm sure."

"He thinks we have kept my niece away from him for too long," George observed dryly.

"You are not going to take Miss Grant away from us so soon?" said the archduke, "Shame! Miss Grant, stay and talk to me. We can go and sit in that corner over there, away from these boring bridge players, and be very comfortable."

The other men laughed. Wyndham said: "That's a much more dangerous game than bridge. I think you'd be safer with me, Fiona, playing billiards."

Fiona smiled at the archduke. He shrugged regretfully. Wyndham took her hand and led her toward the next room. She was conscious of the eyes of the group behind them, watching them.

In the billiard room, a bald-headed man in braces was preparing to have a game with the general.

"German industrialist," Wyndham murmured to Fiona.

"Yes, I know," she said. "We had a long talk about Bayreuth."

Wyndham rested against the table, chatting amiably to the two men as they chose their cues and set up the balls.

"Well, darling," he said, turning to Fiona, "Shall we leave them to it?"

There was a repetition of the bridge table conversation, slightly less flirtatious and a trifle more heavy-handed. They would enjoy playing before such a charming audience, she would inspire them to brilliance, and so on. But they clearly preferred to be alone and made no serious efforts to detain them as they slipped through the room's other door into the corridor.

"You and George are working overtime at the romantic interpretation of your presence, aren't you?" Fiona said.

"It benefits both of us," Wyndham said. "If he's decided to take that line, we should get away with it. Now let's see; that's all of them accounted for, isn't it? Four in the drawing room, five in the library, two in the billiard room. Does that make eleven?"

"That makes eleven," Fiona agreed.

He took her arm. "All right. Let's make the phone call."

There was a wait of five minutes while they paged Fred through the hotel. Fiona stood beside George's desk, listening to the atmospheric crackle on the line, watching Wyndham. He wandered round the small book-lined room rather like a cat investigating a new home, touching things, pulling out the odd book from the shelves and replacing it, lifting up the heavy brass table lamps from the desk, opening and shutting drawers.

"I thought you said that if George let us into this room it meant there was nothing incriminating here," Fiona said.

"I know," Wyndham said.

"Then what are you looking for?"

"Somewhere to put this." Like a conjurer palming a coin, he opened his hand to reveal a small, round object no bigger than a coat button. Fiona stared at it.

"What's that?"

"I suppose you might call it a listening device. Not the most sophisticated,

275

unfortunately, but all they had to hand. It should be fairly adequate. Better than nothing."

"You're bugging the room?"

"That's the general idea. The question is where is the most effective place to put it. In the other rooms I had no choice."

"When did you bug the other rooms?"

"Just now. The coffee table in the drawing room, the billiard table in the billiard room. I'm not too happy about the library."

"I didn't notice anything," Fiona said.

"You weren't supposed to. Haven't they found your friend yet?"

There was a click and Fred's voice spoke into her ear, impatient, brusque. "Yes?"

"Fred, it's Fiona."

Wyndham leaned across the desk. He said quickly: "Careful what you say."

Fred's tone had moderated: "Fiona! Where are you? Have you had a good holiday?"

"I'm ringing from my uncle's. I'll be in Edinburgh tomorrow night. How are things going?"

"I think we're in for a disaster."

"Surely not. Why?"

"Everything's going too well. The scenery arrived on time. It's all intact and everything

276

fits. The costume trunks did not get lost at Crewe and no one has accidentally ripped any of them to pieces. None of the singers has a cold, the producer has not quarreled with the conductor, and there's a brilliant lighting man at the theater. I think it's very ominous."

"Fred, don't be such a pessimist."

"There is one redeeming feature, I suppose," Fred went on, "one of the second violins fell down the stairs at Waverley Station after a drunken night out. But he didn't even break a leg, only sprained an ankle. By the way, did you see Askarian?"

"He spent yesterday with us, talking boats with my father."

"I wondered. He missed a rehearsal today. Only going over the moves. Someone stood in for him."

"He was staying with friends last night," Fiona said. "He said he'd be in Edinburgh later today."

"I haven't seen him around the hotel."

"Perhaps he went straight to the theater."

"I've just come from there." Fred's voice lightened perceptibly. "Perhaps he's going to be the disaster."

"Fred, shut up. You'll will one of these

disasters to happen one day. Are they rehearsing all tomorrow?"

"And the morning of the performance. If I don't see you at the hotel tomorrow night, I'll see you at the theater. But don't worry, I don't think I'm going to need you. Take your time. By the way, congratulations, the London critics liked your costumes."

"They liked your sets too."

Fred laughed. "We'll have a mutual admiration session when I see you. How are you getting back?"

"I've got a lift with a friend."

"Well, take care. Don't let him drive you off any mountains in all that Highland mist."

"It's beautiful weather up here."

"So it is down here, but you can't trust the Scottish summer. It'll be raining tomorrow. Good-bye, Fiona."

"Good-bye, Fred."

Smiling, she was about to replace the receiver when Wyndham stopped her. He put a finger to his lips and moved quickly to her side. He took the receiver from her and held it so they could both listen. After a moment, Fiona heard a click on the line. Wyndham put the phone down.

"Just to make sure," he said and picked it up

again. Again Fiona heard the faint click. Wyndham replaced the handpiece and looked at her.

"George is taking his precautions," he said. "He's got someone on duty listening in."

"But you don't think he's told the others about you?"

"Not yet. Now I'm going to pick the phone up again. Would you mind holding the bar down so it doesn't register?"

She did as he asked. He produced a small screwdriver from his pocket and, holding the receiver in one hand, deftly undid the mouthpiece.

"Normally," he said conversationally, "we would have sent along a telephone repairman to do this job, and perhaps an electrician to see to some ostensibly faulty wiring and place the bugs. But we haven't had time. We have to rely on my rather amateur efforts."

"Have you placed the bug in this room yet?"

"I did it while you were talking to Fred."

"Where?"

"The less you know the better. There we are." He put back the mouthpiece. "Now there are two of us listening into this phone. You can let go now."

He put his finger on the bar and carefully replaced the receiver. It made no noise.

"Come on," he said. "Let's go for a walk."

They went out through the French windows of the drawing room. Wyndham seemed to want it to be known where they were and what they were doing. The oil millionaire, sunk in a cushioned armchair, watched them pass through a haze of cigar smoke, his black eyes bright as a monkey's in his withered face. They crossed the courtyard and left the castle by the gatehouse.

"When do they usually lock the place up?" Wyndham asked.

She shook her head. "I don't know."

It was a beautiful night, the air warm, and still as death. Sounds carried far. Their footsteps on the gravel seemed to echo endlessly and the scream of some animal on the hillside came unnervingly close.

"Let's hope that's the only kind of hunting going on tonight," Wyndham remarked.

It was not completely dark. As her eyes became accustomed to the gloom, identifiable shapes began to emerge, bushes, trees, the ornate summerhouse across the stream.

Wyndham said softly: "Which way is the old road?"

"You cross the forecourt and follow the continuation of the drive to the left."

His hand, taking hold of hers, felt warm and familiar. Something to cling to in this world of shadows. They followed the curve of the drive in silence.

"It divides here," he said suddenly. "Which way?"

She tried to remember. "One path goes round the back of the castle and ends up in the stable block. The right-hand fork goes on through the park and eventually leads to a gate."

"Is there a wall there? Is the gate set in a wall?"

"Yes, that's right."

"What kind of a gate?"

"An ordinary five-bar gate."

"A wooden farm gate?"

"Yes."

"Is it kept padlocked?"

"I don't know. It's a long time since I've been here. Why do you want to know?"

"I like to know all my options. And once through the gate, you're on the old road?"

"As far as I remember."

He stopped and put an arm round her shoulder.

"Don't say anything," he said. "Just kiss me."

It was a long kiss. She closed her eyes and was lost in it. His body fitted closely against hers. It was as unreal as everything else, this clinging lovers' embrace in darkness and silence. No, not quite silence. But she sensed rather than heard the movement that had alerted Wyndham. He drew a little apart. He called out cheerfully: "Good evening!"

A voice replied: "Good evening, sir."

She turned. She could see the shape of a man approaching them. He was moving very quietly. He came from the direction of the old road. Even when close she could not distinguish his features, but his voice was not that of a local.

"Lovely evening," he remarked politely.

"Yes, indeed," Wyndham replied.

He went past them toward the back of the castle. A dog padded silently at his heels, held tightly on a leash. A large dog that moved like a wolf.

They waited until they could no longer see him.

"Let's get back," Wyndham said.

They walked back toward the gatehouse. He kept his arm, casually now, around her shoulders.

"He was carrying a gun," Fiona said.

"A shotgun. So one could take him for a keeper."

"He isn't though, is he?"

"No, I would say he's part of a regular patrol. There'll be others. I imagine they'll stay round all night."

"Because of the company," Fiona said, "or because of us?"

"I imagine it's routine."

"It makes life more difficult for us, doesn't it? If we wanted to slip away tonight?"

"I don't think we'd be very wise to try that," Wyndham said. "I've a feeling there'd be a great deal of noise. We'd probably be stopped before we reached the lodge gate and then all the advantage we've got would be lost." He paused. "In an emergency, of course, we'd have to run for it."

"I didn't like the look of that dog," Fiona said. "What was it?"

"A Doberman pinscher. I think his master's decided to have another look at us. He's coming back down the drive."

"I can't hear anything."

"Listen."

At last, faintly, she caught the soft sounds that Wyndham had heard. She whispered:

"How is he managing to walk so quietly?"

"Perhaps he's used to stalking. Come on, keep going, we're nearly there."

There was a lamp fixed above the gate-house door. They stopped beneath it. Wyndham glanced out into the darkness.

He said: "He's not far behind us. Shall we give him a repeat performance?"

"You don't think the last one convinced him we had more on our minds than spying?"

"I don't know about him, it certainly convinced me."

"You're enjoying this," Fiona said.

"It's not often I manage to bring a friend along on my expeditions," Wyndham said. He gave her a gentle push. "Let's go inside. We'll deprive our watcher of his vicarious pleasure. Let him go and get his kicks elsewhere."

The great hall was in darkness, but light still streamed across the courtyard from the reception rooms.

"I'm going straight upstairs," Wyndham said. "Go and say goodnight to your uncle and join me there."

"You're not going the way Murchison took us, are you?" Fiona said. "You'll get lost."

284

"I won't get lost. I want to see who else is wandering about."

In the library the bridge party was still in session. George, dummy for that game, had left the table and was pouring himself a whisky when Fiona entered. She told him she had come to say good night. He made a token protest. "So early?"

"We want to get off early tomorrow. And it's been a long day." She suddenly felt it might seem unnatural to George that she hadn't, since she arrived, mentioned Craddock's death. She added: "There was the business of finding that dead man—"

"Yes, yes." He glanced quickly at the bridge players then placing a hand on her arm, drew her out through the open door into the corridor. "We don't want to disturb them," he said "We can speak more privately here."

So he hasn't told them who Max is, she thought. He's hoping they'll accept that he's nothing more than my boy friend. He doesn't want his colleagues to think there has been any trouble over the Linnay operation. Max was right, he's going to let us go to save his face.

"It must have been very upsetting for you," George was saying. "You're quite right. You need your rest."

She said: "I may not see you again before we go."

"We shall be up early too," George said. "I'm taking my guests shooting."

"Well, then—" She paused. "Thank you for this evening. I've enjoyed it."

"Thank you again for bringing the package," George said. "Where is the Commander?"

"He's gone up already," Fiona said.

"Ah, I see— Yes, well, I had better get back. Good night, Fiona."

"Good night, George." His dry lips brushed her cheek.

Wyndham, standing by the window in Fiona's room, was also drinking whisky. A newly opened bottle stood on the dressing table.

"I acquired it on my way up here," he said. "I thought we might need it. It could be a long night."

"Was there anyone wandering about?" Fiona asked him.

"Only the butler, Murchison. He seemed

quite friendly. He got me the whisky. Would you lock the door?"

She turned the key in the lock. "It's not a very strong lock. I don't think it would stop anyone who wanted to get in."

"It will stop people bursting in without warning, like your uncle this evening, and that's all I want. How was your encounter with your uncle, by the way? Uneventful, I hope."

"I mentioned Craddock. He didn't want his friends to hear. He can't have told them he's under suspicion about Linnay. He can't have told them who you really are. I think we're going to get away with it."

"Good. Now let's see if we can find out anything really important. Here, have a drink first."

She accepted the glass he offered her, kicked off her sandals and settled herself on the bed, watching him.

"If I knew what you were talking about, it would help," she said.

He was opening his suitcase and taking something out. He smiled at her. "You haven't forgotten the bugs, have you?" he said. He had produced an instrument rather like a miniature walkie-talkie. "I put a brand-new battery in," he said. "I hope it works."

He cleared the bedside table of its lamp and ashtray and placed the receiver on it. He sat on the bed beside Fiona and began to move knobs and dials. It crackled into life. At first there seemed nothing but atmospherics on it, subdued gurgles and hisses.

"I hope we're not too far away," Wyndham said. "We shouldn't be. We're right over the drawing room."

There came a sound suspiciously like a snort and Wyndham laughed. "I know what that is, that's the oil tycoon. He's fallen asleep in his chair."

"That doesn't sound much like a dangerous conspirator," Fiona commented.

"Let's see if we can get the bridge players."

Suddenly Fiona heard George's voice, faint but clear. "I'm sorry," he was saying. "I've not been playing my best tonight."

Wyndham raised the volume. Another voice came through. "I think we've all had enough for one night. We might as well go to bed. There's nothing we can do until the others arrive."

A new voice was added: "And until your niece and her boy friend have left."

288

"There you are," Fiona whispered. "George hasn't told them about you."

Wyndham nodded. The same voice was still speaking: "That could have been difficult. Why did you let her come?"

"That's the archduke," Wyndham said.

"I had no choice," George said. "She invited herself. It would have looked strange if I'd refused."

"Even with your 'tourists' here?"

"She didn't telephone until she was on the way here. I had no alternative."

"The archduke's no fool," Wyndham said. "He doesn't trust us."

There was a blur of voices, several speaking together, fainter than before, then getting louder.

"I think the two from the billiard room have joined them," Wyndham said.

It was impossible to distinguish clear sentences. There was a clinking sound of glasses and a noise that might have been a chair being pushed back. Someone called good night.

"Damn," Wyndham said. "I think they're going to bed."

Fiona stretched herself out, her head on the pillow. "I don't blame them." They no

289

longer seemed the terrible threat they had earlier. She and Max were going to drive away from the castle in the morning, and all his information, his films and lists of names, would be handed over to Stanton or whoever else was interested and she would be free again. She closed her eyes.

The voice seemed to leap out of the receiver. "Did you get the man I recommended?"

"That's the German who's fond of opera," Fiona said. She sat up, leaning on Wyndham's shoulder.

"Yes." George's answer was faint.

"He's on the other side of the room," Wyndham said. "I think the others have gone."

The German said: "Has he arrived?"

Fiona said: "George will be at the table, getting a drink. He'll bring it over."

After a pause, George spoke again. His voice sounded closer. "He's been here a week. Here you are. I added water. Not too much, I hope."

Wyndham said: "You were right about the drink. You're getting good at this."

The German said: "Thank you, that's fine. Is he in the castle?"

"He's up at the camp. He's been getting a little practice in."

"What's he like?"

"As a marksman excellent. I've not concerned myself with his character."

"Right, we'll use him."

George said: "Shouldn't we wait until the meeting to decide?"

"Yes, of course. But there's no harm in agreeing amongst ourselves. I'm told he's reliable. He's here. And it's too good an opportunity to miss. I don't think we should postpone action or waste time bringing another man in."

"They'll ask why we didn't get the Beirut man," George said.

"His English isn't good enough. Besides, the more successful they are, the more careless they become."

The voices fell silent.

"They're talking about the assassin," Fiona said. "They're planning a murder."

"I hope this thing's recording all right," Wyndham said. "Come on, George, come on, my German friend, drink up, keep talking. I was right about the camp in the hills. We'll have to put a stop to that."

Down in the library, someone yawned and

smothered it with a hand. The German spoke again. There was amusement in his voice. "You know the Edinburgh burghers should thank us, George. They're going to get more free publicity than they ever dreamed of. Start the Festival with a bang. Only I think we should try to arrange the timing so that we hear some of the opera. Askarian sings Ochs very well. I heard him in New York. He matches up to Kipnis."

"I met him yesterday," George said. "He's buying a boat from my brother. He invited me to go backstage. I told him I would have my tourists with me."

"We're surely not all going," the German said. "I don't think that would be wise. Anyway Bertrand is flying back tomorrow for one."

"I shall be there," George said. "Unless the company thinks it unwise."

"No, I think you should be there. You can report on the reaction. I'll be with you. And perhaps one other."

"Then we'd better make it another opera lover," George observed.

"Yes, and we had better make sure we don't sit too close to our man."

"That's all arranged," George said.

"Good. Well, I think I shall follow the

others and go to bed. A splendid evening, George."

"Thank you."

"What time are the others arriving?"

"They'll be here early. We can hold the meeting as soon as my niece has left."

"And her friend," the German said. "The Commander. You're quite sure about him?"

George's voice was as cool and unconcerned as ever. "You saw for yourself. You heard the report on their midnight walk."

The German sighed. "I suppose love strikes down even British naval officers. She's a charming girl. We'll give him the benefit of the doubt. But there have been some leakages about the company. We cannot be too careful."

"They have heard about the Company of 13," George said. "There is no doubt of that. But they have no real information on its members or its purpose. By the time anyone has fitted together even part of the jigsaw, we shall be ready for them."

"We must do better than that," the German said, "we must prevent any pieces of the jigsaw being joined together. Security is one of the points we shall be discussing tomorrow. Good night, my friend."

"Good night." There were some indeterminate sounds. Glass on a table, rustles of movement. Then silence.

Fiona became aware that she was gripping Wyndham's shoulder with both hands. He gently eased himself free and stood up.

"I think we could both do with a drink after that," he said.

"Do you think it's really true?" Fiona said. "They're going to assassinate someone at the first night of *Rosenkavalier?*"

"That's what it added up to," Wyndham said.

"Who?"

"If we knew that, life would be much simpler. Who's coming to the first night, Fiona, any idea?"

She shook her head. "It is the opening performance of the Festival. Everyone will be there."

"Any prime ministers, foreign heads of state, royalty?"

"I don't know. It must be a man, though, mustn't it? They spoke of not sitting too close to 'our man.' "

"That could mean the assassin."

"You mean he'll be one of the audience?"

"It would seem the simplest way to get in."

"What will you do? Cancel the performance?"

"They'd only wait and try and get their victim at another time, when he or she might perhaps have no protection. At least we know what they're planning. We can take general precautions. If we take them by surprise, we might even catch the assassin with the gun on him."

"You mean massive security, everyone searched? On a Gala night? Wouldn't that alert them?"

"It could be discreet. Place our men among the audience."

"The first performance is sold out. You wouldn't get people giving up their seats to a bunch of policemen."

"We'd put them into the front of house staff. Ushers, program sellers, barmen. Add a few to the stagehands."

"Don't forget the orchestra. Didn't you tell me you had a friend in the orchestra?"

"All right," Wyndham said. "What exactly would you do?"

"Cancel the performance. You must. You can't take the chance of someone being killed. And in a crowded auditorium. Think of the panic when the shot goes off."

"If I were the assassin, I would time my shot to the music. During a fortissimo. And if we canceled this performance we would certainly alert them. They would all disperse, cover their tracks."

"Not if you gave an acceptable reason. You could get Boris to develop laryngitis. Everyone would accept that."

"It's too risky. George knows who Boris really is, don't forget. No, this is our chance to tie them all up with murder. Catch the assassin and we can take them. Anyway—" he shrugged "—it won't be up to us. It will be Stanton's decision, Stanton's and others'."

"Yes," Fiona said. "I'm sorry. I'm being unrealistic. It's a shock. I didn't know people discussed murder like that, sitting back in comfortable chairs with a glass of whisky in their hands."

"It's a matter of business to them," Wyndham said. "Like planning a sales campaign. They have no hostile feelings."

"I wonder what their feelings would be about George if they knew how much he's been deceiving them, about the collapse of the Linnay operation, about your real job?"

"I think they would probably hold a meeting about it," Wyndham said. "You look very tired. Why don't you go to bed? There's nothing we can do tonight."

"I don't feel tired," Fiona said. "I think I've got past that. Can we go at the crack of dawn tomorrow? I want to get out of this place."

Wyndham had put down his glass and was packing up his equipment. "We'll go as soon as they unlock the front door."

"What do you think Stanton will do about Boris's offer?" Fiona asked. "To provide evidence George murdered Elena Greer?"

"I think we might now get George without any help from the other side. He's going to find a camp full of armed men a little difficult to explain, for one thing."

"He'll wriggle out of that," Fiona said. "It'll turn out to be a training camp for deprived minorities or something worthy like that. Something like the Outward Bound schools. I don't think you should hesitate. You should take Boris's offer and pin George down for Elena's murder."

"Framing with false evidence is not in the best legal tradition. I won't say we wouldn't do it, but deals like this are frowned on unless we can get from them something we couldn't get any other way."

"I see," Fiona said.

Neither spoke for a while. The silence lengthened between them. Wyndham took off his jacket and loosened his tie. He looked across at Fiona.

"Are we quarreling?" he said.

She smiled. He smiled back. He crossed the short distance of carpet between them. He held out his hands to her and she came gently, inevitably, into his arms.

She said: "You know this is nothing more than physical attraction."

"There's no need to lie," Wyndham said, "for whatever reason. You know it's more, much more than that. I've been terrified all evening in case anything happened to you because of me. I should never have let you come with me. Stanton was right. Emotional involvement is dangerous."

"That's a pompous way of putting it."

"Love, then," Wyndham said. "Love is dangerous, for us."

"Yes," Fiona said. "What are we going to do about it?"

He kissed her neck. "Take the moment that's offered."

"Is this then the right time and the right place?" she said.

"No," Wyndham said. "I don't suppose it is. But does it matter?"

"No," she said. "It doesn't matter."

7

FIONA awoke to find Wyndham, fully dressed, standing by the window, drinking a cup of tea.

"Good morning," he said. "It's going to be another hot day."

"Where did you get the tea?" Fiona said.

"I went down and scrounged it. One of the cleaners made it for me. I also got her to make some toast. The kitchen staff hadn't arrived yet."

"I've been dreaming," Fiona said. "I was backstage at the theater and everything was going wrong." She remembered, "My God, the first night is tomorrow."

Wyndham brought her a cup of tea. He put a plate of toast and marmalade on the night table beside her. "You might as well have your breakfast in bed while you've got the chance. How are you feeling?"

"Drugged," she said.

He smiled. "Eat up and have a shower. It'll wake you up."

"What time is it?"

"About six-thirty."

"Who else did you see downstairs apart from the cleaners?"

"No one."

"I thought George was getting up early to go shooting."

"He may be getting up early but it won't be to go shooting. At least I hope not."

She shook her head. "I'm still not very good at this business, am I? Let's go before he does get up. He'd probably only have to glance at me to see that I know."

While she washed and dressed, Wyndham took the exposed film from his camera and put it in an inside pocket. He took a neat, shiny automatic from his case and stowed that away in another pocket.

"Insurance," he said to Fiona.

"I don't know whether that reassures me or alarms me," she said. She looked out of the open window. The buildings were hazy with mist, the air breathlessly still with all the promise of a summer day. Fiona was back in her jeans and shirt. She picked up her sweater and car coat.

"I'm ready," she said.

It was seven o'clock.

They went downstairs by the back way, the

way Murchison had brought them the night before. They met no one. In the gatehouse, Murchison was in the process of unlocking the door. He seemed surprised to see them.

"Are you leaving, Miss?"

"We're driving to Edinburgh," Fiona explained.

He pulled open the heavy door."Shall I take your luggage to the car, sir?"

"That's all right, Murchison." Wyndham put down the two cases and took out his wallet for the butler's statutory tip.

"Thank you very much, sir. A pleasant journey, sir."

Wyndham picked up the two cases again. There were voices from the courtyard and three men entered the gatehouse: George, the German, and the archduke. Before any of them spoke, Fiona knew it was over. Their run of luck had ended.

"My dear Fiona," George said, "I'm afraid you won't be leaving just yet."

The icy coldness of his voice betrayed his anger.

"Why not?" Fiona said steadily. George's two companions eased forward toward them. Instinctively she moved closer to Wyndham.

"There's little need for me to tell

you that. Treachery by a member of one's own family, let alone abuse of hospitality—"

The archduke cut him short. "Will you come to the drawing room, please, Miss Grant. And you, Commander Wyndham. Keep holding those cases, Commander, if you please. Don't put them down."

That's to stop him reaching his gun, Fiona thought. They're assuming he's carrying a gun. Which means they certainly are. She noticed now that the German had his right hand deep in his pocket.

Wyndham said nothing. He waited, his eyes quiet and watchful.

"I'm going nowhere," Fiona said in a voice as cool as George's, "until you tell me exactly what this is about."

George made a sound that was a mixture of exasperation and contempt. There was fear, she realized, mingled with his indignation. For the first time the security of the Company of 13 was threatened and he was responsible. He was to blame for letting the spies into his citadel. Fortunately for him, only he knew the gamble he had taken, betting with his arrogant sense of superiority that Wyndham was not clever enough to deceive him. Now he had to defend his position in the company, and if that meant sacrificing his niece to prove the ruthlessness of his convictions, he wouldn't hesitate. Max had been wrong when he said her relationship with George would make no difference if they were caught. It did make a difference. It made things worse.

"Last night, Miss Grant," the German said, "after everyone had retired to bed, my friend here—" he indicated the archduke "—came to my room for a nightcap. He was not too happy about the presence of you and Commander Wyndham and the coincidence of your choosing this weekend to visit your uncle, and neither was I. We decided to get up early to make sure you really did leave as you had informed your uncle you intended. Fifteen minutes ago we met in the library. The cleaners were still at work there. One of the ladies, disconcerted perhaps by our appearance, became a little hasty, a little careless. Replacing the cushions of an armchair, she dislodged this from the frame."

With a sinking heart, Fiona looked at the button-shaped object he held in his left hand.

"It was unfortunate for you both that we happened to be there, that we recognized it for what is is."

"I remembered you leaning on that chair last night," the archduke said to Wyndham, "watching the bridge."

"And I remembered the conversation I had with your uncle when the other guests had departed— Ah, I see by your face that you know what I am referring to." He glanced at George. "You see, there is no doubt, George, I am sorry to say. We informed your uncle at once, Miss Grant, and here we are. I must say we didn't expect you to be leaving quite so soon. We were on our way to your rooms. We only came by the gatehouse to tell Murchison to keep the door barred and on no account to allow you to leave. We arrived it seems just in time." He gave a slight smile. "I see you are thinking, if only we had taken another few minutes! But it would have made no difference. We would have stopped you at the lodge. You couldn't have broken through those gates."

How still Max had become, Fiona thought, as if he wanted them to concentrate all their attention on her.

She said: "What do you intend to do?"

The German said: "That is to be decided."

"You'll cancel your plans for tomorrow night?"

"Oh, no, Miss Grant," he said softly, "in preference, we'll cancel you. Shall we go?"

He took a step forward. They all moved closer. From her other side Murchison was approaching. And in that moment of tension, there came a confusion of sounds from beyond the open door. The swirl of wheels on gravel, a horn punched lightly, once, twice, in greeting. It was distraction enough. Wyndham suddenly acted. He swung the cases hard, one after the other. The first caught the archduke in the stomach, winding him; the second hit George a vicious blow across the face. He stumbled back, swearing. Wyndham seized Fiona's arm, and fending off Murchison's ineffectual attempt to block them with a savage shove that sent the butler falling backward against the others, like tumbling skittles in an alley, he pulled her through the gatehouse door and slammed it shut behind them.

He said quickly: "That car's blocking ours. We'll have to take it. Come on."

In the moment before they began to run, Fiona saw the scene in front of them like the frozen frame of a film:

A large green Ford sedan drawn up at the far side of the forecourt, its two front doors open like wings. A man standing by the passenger door, pausing in the act of closing it. Tall, a shock of white hair, a tanned face. The driver, half in, half out of the car, one foot on the ground, edging himself from his seat. A swarthy face, glasses, thinning hair. A French politician. She had seen him on television.

The last two members of the Company of 13.

They glanced across at Wyndham and Fiona, taking them momentarily for a welcoming party. When they started sprinting toward them, the two men's expressions changed to an almost comical bewilderment. The driver got out of the car seconds before Wyndham reached him. The tall passenger stared at Fiona. Behind them the gatehouse door was wrenched open. She heard the German shouting: "Stop them!" She heard a shot and a spurt of gravel leaped up at her feet. The passenger jerked into life and made a grab for her. She dodged under his arm and round the protection of the still open door. A bullet richocheted off the hood, narrowly missing him. While he was still off-balance, she pulled the door toward her, then using all her weight, pushed it back hard against him.

He staggered and fell. She was in the seat, the door shut. She caught a glimpse of the Frenchman sprawled in the gravel. She saw the German running toward the car, gun in hand, Murchison behind him. At the gate-house, George, his face bloody, stood with arm outstretched, revolver in hand, taking cool, deliberate aim at Wyndham. Wyndham flung himself into the driver's seat. He said: "Get your head down." They had moved so fast the Frenchman had had no time to remove the keys from the ignition. Wyndham started the engine.

The car moved slowly at first. As it gathered speed, Wyndham drove it straight at their pursuers, scattering them. He swung round in a screeching circle and turned left out of the forecourt, on the route to the old hill road.

Fiona sat up, pushing her hair out of her eyes. She looked out of the back window. There was, as yet, no one in sight.

"Are you all right?" Wyndham said.

She nodded. "What happens now?"

"They'll be dashing back to phone all their cohorts to cut us off. They'll send some to the lodge and others along the path that meets this one. But we'll beat them to it. Then it'll suddenly dawn on them which way we're going and they'll phone the camp. How soon they intercept us depends on how many miles up in the hills it is. Hang on, here's the turn."

They had reached the point they had got to last night, where the drive forked. Wyndham turned right. "How far to the gate?"

"About half a mile."

They were already climbing, a long, gradual gradient.

"Keep a look out behind," Wyndham said.

"Still clear."

The drive curved round, hiding any signs of pursuit. Wyndham took the bend like a racing driver.

"It's a good surface," he said. "They're using this for more than estate workers."

"There's the gate," Fiona said. She was conscious of her heart racing.

Wyndham reduced speed. He pulled up a few feet before the wooden five-bar gate. On either side of it stretched the stone wall bounding the park, its top encrusted with barbed wire.

"Well, they haven't changed it from a farm gate yet," Wyndham said.

Fiona jumped out and ran to open it. It was

locked firm, with a new length of chain and a strong padlock. She shook it with frustrated anger. From the car, Wyndham beckoned her back. As she climbed back in, she saw the blood on his seat.

"Max!"

"Shut the door!" He backed fast, the tires spitting up stones. "Get down, put your arms over your head. No, wait—" He took a breath. "We'll take the time to put the seat belts on. No point in us smashing through the windscreen. Don't talk. Do it."

She slammed the clasp shut. "Max—"

"It's my leg," Wyndham said. "Through the thigh. Not serious, just messy. Ready?"

"Yes."

"I hope I've given us enough of a run-up. These automatics always start so bloody slowly. Hang on."

He hit the gate at speed, on the left-hand side. There was the sound of breaking glass as the lights went, but the chain snapped and the gate crashed open and they were through, careering wildly up the track of the old road.

Wyndham looked sideways at Fiona and gave her a grin of triumph. "O.K.?"

"I'm fine, what about you?"

310

"I haven't begun to feel the leg yet. What does it look like?"

"As if you're bleeding to death. We ought to put a pressure bandage on it."

"Not yet. We can't stop yet. We've got to find a place to disappear."

"What does that mean?"

"There will be God knows how many cars coming up behind us any minute. And sooner or later there will be men with guns coming down that road ahead of us. We don't want to be in the middle when they meet. We've got to lose the car and ourselves in the next five minutes. Where's the pass this road is supposed to go through?"

"I don't know," Fiona said. "I've never been up here. Quite a way, I believe, five or six miles. The road climbs round the shoulder of that mountain."

"Rough country, isn't it? Good place for a private war. It looks like films of the old Indian North-West Frontier."

They had climbed into a narrow valley, bounded by steeply rising hills. Ahead of them was the craggy outline of a mountain. Fiona could see the thin line of the road crawling across its lower slopes. An empty road. So far. At the end of the valley there was a sharp turn leading immediately to a hairpin bend. Below it the land fell away dramatically. Abruptly, Wyndham stopped the car.

"This will do," he said. "Get out."

"Tell me what you're going to do," Fiona said.

"I'm going to put the car into 'drive,' point its nose at that empty space and let it get on with it."

"How are you going to get out of the way before it reaches the edge?"

"It'll go very slowly, only about five miles an hour."

"You'll get dragged along. Don't forget you've got a bullet hole in your leg. Let me do it."

"Just get out of the car," Max said, "before I start swearing."

Fiona got out. The mist had gone, the sky was an arc of blue, the sun already beginning to gain strength. In the warm silence, she could hear the murmur of insects and the gurgling, liquid sound of a brook. The brilliance of the day seemed to make the rocky heights of the mountain blacker, colder, more threatening. Her glance caught something glittering and it took a moment to realize it was the sun reflecting off the chrome of a motor vehicle. Straining her eyes to look, she could make out three of them moving down the mountain road.

"Max, they're coming," she said.

He said in a rather odd voice: "Come and give me a hand. I can't get out."

She ran round to him. His door was open. He was leaning forward over the wheel, his head on his hands. He sat up and took several deep breaths. His face looked gray and there was sweat on his forehead.

He said: "I think I'm simply stuck to the seat."

"Put your arm round my neck," Fiona said. "I'll hoist you up."

He put his good leg onto the ground, one arm round Fiona's neck and used the other to lever himself up from the seat. She moved backward slowly, dragging him from the car, trying to avoid bumping the wounded leg. Max leaned against the side of the car, breathing quickly.

She said: "You've lost a lot of blood."

"It had begun to congeal. I think we've started it bleeding again. Where are the cars?"

"On the mountain road. I don't know if

they're cars or Jeeps. Three of them."

"We can't waste time," he said. "You'll have to do it."

"Yes."

"You know what to do?"

"Yes," Fiona said.

"Don't go over the cliff with it, for God's sake."

"Let me help you out of the way," she said.

"It's all right. It had just got fixed into one position in the car. I've got to learn to walk with the damn thing." He pushed himself away from the car and limped painfully to the hill side of the road. "All right," he said.

Fiona got into the driving seat, sticky with blood. She backed the car a few feet, then brought it forward again, turning it so that the hood pointed directly at the U-turn of the bend. She stopped the car, letting the engine idle. She put the hand brake on and put the gear into neutral. She got out of the car, leaving the door open. She looked across at Max.

"O.K.," he said. "It's in the right position. Send her over."

She had lost her car coat in the dash from the gatehouse, but her sweater and handbag lay on the floor by the passenger seat. She leaned over to pick them up, tossing them behind her on to the road. There was a small overnight bag and an umbrella on the back seat, and after a moment's thought she threw those out too. She paused and took a deep breath to calm herself. Then she put the gear lever into drive. She reached for the hand brake behind it and very gently began to release it. At first she didn't exercise enough presure, then she thought she was letting it go too fast. The car began to move.

Max yelled: "Jump!"

She leaped back, stumbled, and fell against the open door. With a sudden panic she pushed herself free, sliding away from the wheels. The car rolled majestically forward, just missing her. It reached the edge of the road and took off, hanging in space for a moment like a gigantic bird before it fell, slowly twisting and turning, on to the rocks below.

They heard it crashing and bouncing down the side of the cliff. When Fiona got to the edge and looked over, it was turning over and over, coming to rest at last among the boulders of a dried-up stream bed. As she turned to speak to Max, there was an enormous explosion. When she looked down again, a sheet of fire enveloped the car from end to end.

She looked at Max. "I hope they won't expect us to pay for that."

He managed a grin. "They'll certainly know where we are now. Let's get back round that bend before every binocular in those cars is trained on this spot."

They had about an hour, Max thought, before their pursuers realized they weren't in the burned-out car. It would take that long for them to reach the spot and climb down to the wreck.

"We've got to make the most of it," he said. He spoke urgently, Fiona thought, because he knew, as she did, that he couldn't go much farther without rest.

She had helped him in the slow struggle back to the valley. Every step was agony to him. His trouser leg, dark with dried blood when they began, grew ominously wet as they progressed.

She had given him the umbrella. "I thought it might make a walking stick, if not a splint."

"The leg's not broken," Wyndham said. "That's one relief. Why did you bring the bag?"

"There might be clothes in it," Fiona said, "to make a bandage. I can't tear strips off a petticoat. I'm not wearing one."

"It would be pleasant if there was a bottle of brandy," Wyndham said.

There was no brandy, but there was a bar of chocolate. Wyndham solemnly divided it into two. He put one half in his pocket and handed the other to Fiona. When he did that, she knew what was going to happen.

"I'm not leaving you," she said.

He didn't answer.

"We've got to get to the top of the ridge," he said. "We'll be safe there for a while anyway. You can do your first-aid bit there."

It was a long and arduous climb. The uneven ground and scattered rocks made every step a potential danger. Wyndham couldn't climb it. He had to crawl, pulling himself up foot by foot. When they were nearly there, he called to Fiona to get down.

"Right down," he said. "George is coming."

She lay flat on her stomach, half concealed by a boulder, and looked down the valley. Two cars were coming along the road. A Jeep with three men in it, two of them holding shotguns, and behind, George's Land-Rover.

The chauffeur was driving it. George, a bandage round his head, sat beside him. Two men were in the rear. She couldn't identify them.

"What do you think the rest of the company is doing?" she said.

"They'll have got into their expensive limousines and left," Wyndham said. "This is one mess they're going to leave George to clear up. That will be what the delay has been. They've been having a meeting. And God help him if he doesn't catch us."

The cars disappeared round the corner. Fiona looked up. "We're almost at the top."

Over the ridge there was nothing but moorland, limitless as the sea. There seemed no shelter, no tracks, no landmarks to aim for. There was water, though. Pools of it scattered across the boggy ground, warm and stagnant, but plentiful.

Wyndham was lying on his back, his eyes closed. She sat down beside him and went through the overnight bag. It had belonged to the Frenchman, judging by the hair oil. There was a plastic bag with shaving things, toothbrush, toothpaste and so on. There was a silk dressing gown, silk pyjamas, red

318

Moroccan slippers, handkerchiefs, a clean white shirt.

"Best Sea Island cotton," Fiona read out. "This will do. You don't happen to have a knife on you?"

"Naturally," Wyndham said, without opening his eyes. He put a hand in his trouser pocket and tossed her a penknife, slim and elegant.

"I would have thought you'd have something sturdier like a scout's knife," she remarked, opened the blade.

"It would ruin the line of my suit," Wyndham said. The hand which had thrown her the penknife suddenly closed into a tight fist. He made a sound which wasn't quite a groan.

Fiona tried to keep her voice steady. She was beginning to tremble, from the physical exertion, from apprehension, from anxiety.

"You're lucky. There's a bottle of aspirin in the bag. I'll get you some water in a moment."

She ran the blade of the knife down the seams of the shirt and quickly ripped it into usable pieces. She emptied the plastic bag and filled it with water from one of the pools. When she got back to Wyndham, she thought at first he had fainted. His face was like a mask. Every expression line on it seemed deepened, marked by pain. She understood then what the long haul up the hill had done to him. She couldn't deceive herself that he could go on. He opened his eyes and looked up at her.

"I've got the aspirin here and some water. It's probably not fit to drink."

"I'll risk it." He sat up and swallowed down some of the tablets with a cupped handful of water. "How's the time?"

She looked at her watch. "Getting on. I'm going to clean you up. All right?"

He nodded.

"I'll have to cut the trouser leg to get at the wound," she said.

"Leave me some of it to walk round in," he said. "I don't want to be arrested for indecency."

She took the knife and began to cut away the cloth. The trouser had stuck to his leg with a mixture of dried blood, fresh blood and torn fragments of flesh. She had to keep soaking it with water before she could ease it free. The flesh round the bullet hole when she finally exposed it was swollen and angry.

He didn't speak all the time she was dressing the wound. When she had finished she helped him up and he took a tentative step forward.

"That's all right," he said. "Thank you. With the help of my umbrella walking stick I shall get along fine." He looked at her. "Do you know how to use a compass?"

"Yes. Why?"

"Because I've got a pocket one that's quite reliable." He took it out and handed it to her. "You want to keep going south-east."

"Max—"

"You've got to get to a phone and ring Stanton. Tell him first about the assassination attempt planned for tomorrow, and then if you've got time read him the names we've got of the Company of 13." He tore a page from his notebook and gave it to her with the list he had made up the night before. "Stanton's number is on there. Try and learn it, just in case you lose the paper. Don't worry about money for a call box. If you give the operator that number, they'll put you straight through. If you can't find a public phone box, stop at a village shop or a pub and asked to use their phone. Keep away from isolated houses. You never know. You might find yourself trapped."

"It's Sunday," Fiona said. "Everything is shut."

"Bang on the doors. Make them open up. Get to a road as soon as you can, but follow it from the hill. Don't walk along it."

"They'll send out the helicopter, won't they?"

"If they do, make yourself as inconspicuous as possible. Don't move. Hide your face and hands. Your jeans and shirt will be quite good camouflage. Remember, it's not all that easy to spot one person from the air in a landscape like this. You'll be all right." He added, "I won't burden you with the film; I'll keep that."

"What are you going to do?"

"I shall make my way back in the direction of the castle. They won't be searching that way. I'll find a place to hole up in. If I get a chance, I'll be in touch with Stanton too."

"They'll find you and kill you," Fiona said.

He put his arms round her. She clung to him tightly.

"They won't find me and they won't kill me," Wyndham said. "Don't worry, I shall survive. Just make sure you do. Remember, you've got till tomorrow evening to warn Stanton."

"Surely they won't go through with it now?"

"You don't know them. They're quite confident they'll find us."

"So am I," Fiona said. "That's the trouble."

"Come on." He gave her a smile. "You can do it. Now put everything back in the bag and shove it down the nearest hole."

She did as he said.

"And now you'd better get going," Wyndham said.

"Don't kiss me good-bye, or I won't go."

"All right," he said. "I'll see you in Edinburgh. We'll split a bottle of champagne after the first night."

"Oh, Max—"

"They'll have reached the wreck by now," he said. "They'll be poking around in the remains, wondering where the bodies are. It won't take them long to come to the right conclusion. You must go." He looked at her. "The longer we stand here saying good-bye the more risk we have of being caught."

She took a long look at him, knowing she was doing so in case it was the last time she ever saw him. She bent forward and kissed him on the cheek. She slung her handbag over her shoulder and picked up her sweater.

"Good-bye," said said. "I'll see you in Edinburgh."

When she looked back some five minutes later she could no longer see him. He had gone, merging into the landscape. She was alone, in that desert of rock and marsh and silence.

The car had stopped. First it had driven past as far as the bridge. There was a house by the bridge. They had gone into it. And now returned. Had someone seen her as she crossed the stream farther down? The house had seemed deserted, half hidden in its clump of trees. But she had avoided it anyway. She had learned some sense in the past few days.

The car had driven back and now it had stopped.

Four men got out. From that distance they looked like toy soldiers. Action men with rifles at the ready. No uniforms, though. They hadn't got around to uniforms. Not yet. One of the men raised binoculars to his eyes and began a sweep of the countryside. She dropped back behind the outcrop of rock that sheltered her and let her head rest on her arms. . . .

She risked another glance down at the car. The men were clustered together, looking at something spread out on the hood. A map, probably. The moment they moved away from her, she must move. And if they didn't move away? If they spread out and came up the hill toward her? She lay back and closed her eyes, trying to think, trying to make a plan. But at once the waltz tune was there again, swinging round and round in her tired brain, confusing, bewildering her. Och's waltz. Boris's waltz. She thought of Boris and Max and Stanton, and the unknown target for assassination who might at that moment be considering attendance at the first night of the opera as nothing more than a tedious social duty.

She looked at her watch. Two o'clock. Seven hours since they had made their break from the castle, five hours since she had left Max. She mustn't think about Max. She must think only of her own survival. She was still free, but that was all she could say. And for how long?

Something had distracted the men. They were turning round, looking down the road behind them. The noise reached her a second later.

She buried her face in her hands. This was the closest it had been. This time it could not fail to discover her. She had seen the helicopter twice that morning, but each time it had been no more than a sound in the air and a shape swooping and turning in the distance. This time it was following the line of the road. The noise of its blades grew louder until it filled her head. It seemed to be swinging directly over her. The roaring lessened. When she risked a glance, the helicopter was dropping away behind the ridge above her.

The men below had come to a decision. They were splitting up. No, they were forming a line, separated from each other but all moving forward at the same time. Like beaters flushing out the game for the waiting guns.

Now she had no choice at all. She had to go up. She had to get up over the ridge and hope there was some sort of cover on the other side. She hadn't been seen yet. If she had, they would have come for her in a direct line.

She began to climb diagonally, keeping as low as she could, moving from rock to rock, stopping often to check on the men below. They were coming up the hill at a methodical steady pace, gazing in front of them and to left an right, but by some miracle never upward at any time when she was between shelters. She reached the top and flung herself over it.

The hill sloped down more gently on this side. It fell away in a gradual gradient to a small valley. It was as if the ridge had been some line of demarcation. The country on this side was altogether softer, more welcoming. A stream ran through the valley, bounded by small trees and bushes. A stone bridge crossed it farther down. There was a road.

She began to walk quickly downhill, almost carelessly, almost running. It was illogical to think so, but it looked like the sort of road that would lead to a village. The sort of road country buses would travel linking one isolated hamlet with another. She began to hope. Hope that she was going to succeed. Hope that she could stop the assassination, save Max.

A man rose from the ground at her feet, almost as if he had been lying in wait for her. The shock made her heart leap. It was a moment before she could look at him. He looked a little more tanned than when she had last seen him, but just as boyish, just as cheerful.

"Now this is what I call a lucky coincidence," said David Kenton.

She stared at him. "What are you doing here?"

He smiled. "You don't think Stanton would leave you without any kind of a backup, do you?" he said.

He shook his head at her expression and put a hand on her arm to help her down the last few feet to the road. "Don't let me confuse you any further. You are the one all these armed thugs are combing the countryside for, aren't you?"

She collected her wits. "There are four of them about to come over the top of the hill any moment."

"There were six of them searching this valley. I've been lying low, keeping an eye on them. When I saw a figure coming down the hill I thought for a moment it was another of them, so I went on lying low. Sorry if I startled you. Don't worry, the others have gone. Come on, we haven't got any time to waste. I think the best thing is . . . yes, that's it." He had unfastened his rucksack, which he had dumped on the road beside them, and was rummaging in it. He produced with an air of triumph a bright red thick knit sweater. "I know it's a hot day, but put that on. That should do the trick."

"They'll be able to see me for miles," Fiona protested.

"That's the idea. They're looking for a girl on her own, someone hiding and running. They're not looking for a girl on a walking holiday with a boy friend. Your shoes aren't right, but I haven't a spare pair of walking boots and they'd hardly fit your feet. I've got a cap. Would you like a cap? They're looking for someone bareheaded."

"They're not looking for a girl on her own," Fiona said. "They are looking for a man and a girl. That is unless they've found Max."

He thought about that for a second. "Even so, they wouldn't be expecting to find you both strolling along in the open, with you so conspicuous in red. And they'd never mistake me for Max Wyndham in a hundred years. So get it on and we'll start walking."

She pulled the sweater over her head. It was hot and it was loose, but not too loose.

She pushed the sleeves up above her wrists. She handed Kenton her own sweater, which she had tied round her waist for convenience, and he put it in the rucksack. He refastened the rucksack and swung it onto his back.

"O.K. Let's go," he said.

They were crossing the bridge when the first of the four men came over the brow of the hill. They stopped and leaned on the parapet as if admiring the simple beauty around them, Fiona casually leaning on her elbows with her hands shading her face in case they were being inspected through binoculars. She didn't dare look up. Kenton reported events to her.

"A second chap has joined the first. They're talking together. They're looking down here. Look out, here come the binoculars." He turned his head as if talking casually to her, hiding his own face. "You never know. One of them might have been at the demonstration. If they recognized me they might just get curious." He turned after a minute of slow and agonizing waiting and looked up the hill. "It's all right. They're not coming down. They are waving the other two back. Now they've all vanished. We're in the clear." He paused "What happened at the castle? Where's Max?"

She told him everything that had happened, the list of names Wyndham had gathered, the assassination plot, their escape, Wyndham's injury, his instructions to her.

"Do you know where he will be?" Kenton asked. "Where he might be hiding?"

She shook her head.

He gave her a sympathetic pat. "Don't worry. We'll find him. Now if you feel up to it, shall we get along? I happen to know where we can find a phone."

The relief of knowing that the worst was almost over, that she was no longer alone, and that soon all the responsibility would be handed over to Stanton was nearly Fiona's undoing. She felt suddenly so drained that she could barely find the energy to take even one more step. It was the knowledge that she was the only one who knew, the one person on whom the lives of other people depended, that had sustained her, had driven her on hour after hour. Now she had found help, she could relax, and that she found meant almost total collapse. She swayed and would have fallen but for Kenton's supporting arm.

"Hey!" he said gently. "Take it easy. How

long have those bastards been chasing you?"

"Since about seven this morning."

"Good God! Have you had anything to eat?"

"Half a bar of chocolate."

"Look, sit down, lean against the bridge. We're all right here for a bit. They've searched this valley once. They're not likely to come back." He squatted beside her and opened up the rucksack again. "I've got some sandwiches. Though I'm afraid they're a bit squashed."

"Thank you." She took one and bit into it, but her mouth was so dry the bread nearly choked her. She said: "You don't happen to have anything to drink—"

"I've got a thermos of tea."

She smiled at him. "Bless you." She drank three mugs of the slightly bitter brew and felt a hundred times better. Kenton sat beside her, eating one of the sandwiches. She glanced at his appealing profile.

"I knew from the beginning you were an odd kind of theological student," she said. "Too good to be true. It never occurred to me you might be an agent. So you're one of Stanton's men. Were you working with Max? Is that what you were doing at that hotel when I first met you?"

"Max had phoned through to Stanton about Eliot's death as soon as he got to the hotel. We already knew about Eliot's fishing trips and I'd been sent a week before to do a little fieldwork at pubs where we knew he'd stayed, trying to find out if he'd contacted anyone in particular, that sort of thing. So I was the nearest chap available when this business blew up and I got a message to rendezvous with Max Wyndham at the hotel. I couldn't give him much information that he didn't already have and he told me to make my way to the coast. I rang Stanton to report and he told me to get there as fast as I could and mix in with the students at the demonstration, see what I could find out. I report by phone daily, you see. If I don't ring in, Stanton knows something's up." He grinned. "He may not be able to do anything about it, but at least he knows early on when there's trouble. When I rang this morning, he told me to head for your uncle's castle, keep an eye on developments there, from the outside of course, in case Max could do with an extra hand. I was on my way when I walked into this little lot, looking like an army maneuver."

"Max didn't mention that you might be around," Fiona said.

"He wouldn't know. Stanton decided on it when he had no word from Max last night. I was going to hire or steal a car from the nearest village and beat it up to the ogre's lair when, as I say, I ran into this lot."

"Where is the nearest village?" Fiona asked.

"It's about three miles along this road. There's a village shop which is also a post office and they've got a phone there."

She shook her head. "I don't know it."

"I don't suppose you do. We're off the beaten track here, aren't we? I wouldn't have found it if I hadn't been tramping around these godforsaken beauty spots for the past couple of weeks. I'm now an expert in local topography."

"That's nice to know." Fiona rubbed her aching calf muscles. "My legs are getting stiff."

"Oh, dear." He hoisted himself to his feet and offered her a hand. "We had better be on our way. After your little hike this morning, if you don't keep moving you're likely to seize up altogether."

She pulled herself painfully to her feet. "It's Sunday, you know. The shop will be shut."

"Don't worry, I'll get them to open," Kenton said. "Now, come on, one foot after another, we'll soon be there."

"Once I've spoken to Stanton," Fiona said wearily, "I shan't care if they catch us."

"Speak for yourself," Kenton said. "I've no intention of enacting the part of the stag at bay. Do you want me to talk to Stanton? It will be quicker. I can reach him directly. And I've got to talk to him anyway, see what action he wants me to take."

"All right," Fiona said. "You speak first. If he wants more details of what happened at the castle I'll talk to him."

"I'll tell him first about the assassination plan and then give him the names of the Company of 13 as far as you know them. Max gave you a list, you said."

"Yes, here you are." She handed it to him. "I can't remember the name of the Frenchman whose car we took and I'd never seen the white-haired man with him, but I can draw them for you."

"That's fine. And you've no idea who might be coming to the first night of the opera who is important enough to be worth shooting?"

"No. The press officer would know. But if

it was someone of international importance wouldn't the police already know? Don't those sort of people always have bodyguards on public occasions?"

"Bodyguards have rarely stopped a really determined assassin," Kenton said, "as the history of the past two decades has shown. But forewarned is forearmed. Don't worry, we'll stop this one. You didn't get a name or any description of this chap they're hiring to do the job?"

"No, just that he was staying at the camp. Is there a chance Stanton might catch him there?"

Kenton shrugged. "If he's someone who's known, perhaps. But I doubt it. I also doubt if he's still at the camp. He's got his appointment in Edinburgh tomorrow night, remember?"

"If they don't catch me and Max, they might decide it's too risky and abandon it."

"Well, then, we'll have to make sure they don't catch you, won't we?" Kenton said.

When they finally reached it, the village, a glorified hamlet consisting of two small rows of cottages, the village shop and a garage with one petrol pump, looked as dead and deserted as if struck by the plague. There was no sign of any inhabitants and the garage, a decayed-looking building with holes in its corrugated iron roof and paint peeling from its double doors, was undoubtedly closed; whether or not it ever opened was a matter for speculation. The silence surrounding Fiona and Kenton as they stood looking about them was absolute.

"Scottish Sundays," Kenton observed, "are a serious business."

He tried the door of the shop. It was locked and the blinds drawn down over door and windows made it impossible to look inside.

"I think the whole place has closed for August," Fiona said, "the way the French do." She pulled off the red sweater. "I can't stand it a moment longer," she explained. "I'll die of heat exhaustion."

There was a small gate and an asphalt path leading presumably to the back of the shop.

"You wait here," Kenton said. "I'll go and see if I can rouse anyone."

Fiona felt conspicuous when he had gone, the sole living creature in an empty planet, and followed him a little way along the path until she was sure she was out of sight of anyone driving through the village or observing it with binoculars from a height. She leaned against the side wall of the shop, waiting for Kenton to return and trying not to think about Max. Her tiredness enveloped her. She was half asleep on her feet when Kenton reappeared. She caught a glimpse behind him of a middle-aged woman, iron gray hair crimped into waves, face red and curious; then the apparition vanished. Kenton took her by the elbow and steered her back to the shop door. He seemed pleased.

"She's going to open up," he said. "I told her I'd heard an S.O.S. on the radio asking me to ring a hospital in Edinburgh where my father was seriously ill. They hadn't been able to get in touch with me because I was on a walking holiday with my fiancée. All right?"

"Yes, indeed," Fiona said admiringly. "I've heard those messages broadcast."

The blind on the shop door flew up and the woman's face peered through at them.

"The only thing is," Kenton said, "you must keep her occupied while I'm phoning. She'll listen in otherwise."

Bolts were pulled back and the door was opened, the woman standing back to let them enter.

"The phone's back there," she said. "Have you enough change for long-distance?"

"I shall reverse the charges," Kenton said. He said to Fiona: "I shan't be long, darling."

The woman's glance flicked to Fiona's bare ring finger and back to her face. She looked at her doubtfully. Fiona decided against smiling at her. She said: "This is very kind of you, opening up the shop for us."

"I've not opened the shop," the woman said, "just the telephone."

"That's what I meant," Fiona said. "It's very kind of you."

"We are supposed to make the telephone available in an emergency," the woman said. "Only in an emergency, mind you." She was standing with arms tightly folded across her narrow chest as if protecting herself from imminent assault.

"Oh, this is certainly an emergency!" Fiona said. She spoke in such heartfelt tones that the most suspicious mind could not have doubted her. The woman's manner eased slightly. She offered Fiona a chair.

The shop interior was quite large but its floor space so taken up with counters, frozen food cabinets and sacks of potatoes, onions and other assorted vegetables that there seemed hardly room to move. At the very back of the shop was the post office counter, complete with grille, and beside it the glass cubicle of the public telephone. Kenton was standing inside it with his back to them. Fiona could hear the occasional murmur of his voice but could distinguish nothing that he was saying.

The woman brought forward a wooden upright chair for Fiona. She herself leaned against one of the food cabinets, watching her. Her curiosity, fortunately, seemed entirely fixed on Fiona. Fiona asked her about bus services.

"Twice a week," she said. "Tuesdays and Saturdays."

"Nothing on Sundays?" Fiona asked. "Nothing today?"

She shook her head. She seemed slightly shocked at the idea.

"We have to get to Edinburgh, you see," Fiona explained. "As soon as possible. Perhaps there's a car we could hire. Perhaps the garage—"

She broke off. She had turned her head to look at the garage as she spoke. A Land-Rover was just drawing up outside it. Two men got out. They were both carrying guns.

She looked desperately at Kenton, but he still had his back to them. She turned her head away from the road. She wanted to run and hide behind the counter, but had to remain where she was. Now she couldn't even see what the men were doing. If they came into the shop, she was doomed.

The woman went to the door and pulled down the blind. She shot the top bolt home. "Can't have everyone coming in," she said. "If they see us they'll think the shop's open."

She glanced at Kenton. "I hope he's got through all right. Of course, they always make you wait, hospitals. You can be left waiting for minutes on end. It'll be hard for you to get to Edinburgh. There are no cars for hire in the village. Mr. Watson never opens the garage here except when he needs the extra space for repairs. People ring him when they want petrol and he comes and opens up the pump. He's got a bigger garage ten miles away. His old father used to run this one, but it never paid. He might have a car you could hire at the other garage. You'd have to ring him at his home, though. Catch him before the evening service. Do you want the number?"

Fiona was about to say that she did when Kenton appeared.

"How is your father?" the woman asked.

"We have to get to Edinburgh as soon as we can," he said.

"I was telling your young lady about Mr. Watson's garage—" the woman began.

Kenton interrupted her. "That's right. Watson's. Your telephone operator was most helpful. She gave me Mr. Watson's number. He can let us have a car. The only trouble is we have to get to his village. It's about eight miles from here," he said."

"Ten," the woman said.

"Couldn't he collect us?" Fiona asked.

"Apparently that's not possible," Kenton said. "He's doing us a favor. I couldn't insist."

"Why don't you ask those men to give you a lift?" the woman said.

"What men?" Kenton lifted the blind and looked outside. He turned and met Fiona's gaze. He nodded.

"What a good idea," he said to the woman. "Well, we mustn't disturb you any longer. We do appreciate your kindness."

"That's all right," she said. "I'll lock up behind you."

Kenton shouldered his rucksack. He opened the door for Fiona. She felt as apprehensive as if he'd opened the door of a lion's cage for her. They stepped out into the road. Behind them the shop door clicked shut and the bolts were fastened home.

"It's all right," Kenton said. "I saw the men. They're going up a hill path behind the garage. We've plenty of time."

"Plenty of time for what?" Fiona said despairingly.

"To steal their Land-Rover," Kenton said. George's thugs, if the two men were George's and not local countrymen out for an afternoon's shooting, were trusting souls indeed. The Land-Rover was unlocked and the keys were in the ignition. They got in it and drove off. It was as simple as that.

"Did you speak to Stanton?" Fiona asked.

"Of course."

"What did he say? What's he going to do? Did you tell him about Max?"

"He said he was full of admiration for you. He said he thought you'd done a wonderful job. He said don't worry, he'll deal with everything. He wants me to get you to Edinburgh and stay with you until the first night is over. He said he doesn't want anything to happen to you."

"But nothing will happen now," Fiona

said. "Stanton's been told. The secret is out."

"Ah, yes," Kenton said. "But the Company of 13 don't know that, do they? As far as they are concerned, you are still the most dangerous threat they have."

Fiona sighed. "I wish you hadn't said that."

"Better to face facts," Kenton said. "Don't worry. I'll look after you. Those are my instructions. Look after Miss Grant. You do exactly as I say and no harm will come to you."

"I wish you'd had time to grow a beard or something," Fiona said. "You look too young to look after me."

Kenton laughed. "I'm young," he said, "but I'm very vicious. Believe me."

The hired car was waiting for them. It was parked in the road in front of an isolated gray stone villa with a carefully nurtured front garden and a striped awning protecting the front door from the paint-blistering effects of the summer sun. Considering the usual Scottish summers, a house owned by an optimist, Fiona concluded. Kenton left her in the Land-Rover and, taking out his wallet, disappeared round the back of the house. He returned a few minutes later holding an insurance certificate and a bunch of keys.

"And what do you intend to do with the Land-Rover?" Fiona inquired.

"Hop out," he said. "I'll take it up the road a bit and run it into a ditch."

Fiona got out. "This will be the second perfectly good car I've helped to smash up today."

Kenton grinned. "Better the car than us, dear lady." He tossed her the keys of the hired car. "Make yourself comfortable. I shan't be a moment."

Ironically enough, it was another Ford automatic. Fiona settled herself in the front passenger seat. She leaned her head back and closed her eyes. The greatest unappreciated luxury, she thought, was to be able to get off your feet and sit down when you wanted to. The greatest difficulty was to stay awake when everything in you ached for sleep.

"Excuse me . . ." A soft Highland voice was speaking in her ear. She opened her eyes. The window beside her was open and standing beside it was a woman of about forty. Her fair hair was well cut. She was wearing an expensive silk shirt dress, and her expression was one of apologetic concern.

"I am so sorry to disturb you," she said, "but I wonder if you could move your car.

It's blocking the entrance to our garage. I can't get my car out."

Fiona jerked wide awake. "I'm so sorry." She moved across into the driver's seat, after two false starts found the correct key and started the engine. The Ford had been left with the nose of its hood halfway across an open gateway leading to the villa's double garage. Since the woman's husband was the one who had parked the car in that position, there was really no need for Fiona to apologize but she did so once again after she had backed the car out of the way.

"I'm sorry about that, Mrs. Watson," she called. "Is that all right for you now?"

The woman seemed surprised Fiona knew her name. She gave her a slightly uncertain smile, nodded and walked back up the drive. A few moments later, she emerged in a Jaguar and roared away up the lane.

"Who was that?" Kenton asked, arriving back on foot.

"Mrs. Watson. I had to move the car out of her way. Have you disposed of the Land-Rover?"

"Yes, that's nicely out of the way." He looked at her, still seated in the driver's seat. "Do you want to drive?"

346

"No thank you," she said hastily and moved back into the passenger seat.

Kenton got in and started the engine.

"Do you know where we are?" Fiona asked. "I'm hopelessly lost."

"We are quite a long way from Edinburgh. We shan't get there tonight."

"As long as we get a long way from here." As she said it, she knew she didn't want to go. She wanted to go back to the castle and find Max. She had had to leave him to get help. Now help had been found and she wanted to get back to him. She knew whereabouts he might be. They would never find him without her. If he had to spend a night on the open hillside he could die of exposure.

Kenton was unimpressed by her reasoning when she tried to explain this to him.

"Max told you to go to Edinburgh," he said. "Stanton told you to go to Edinburgh. Your job and the opera are in Edinburgh. I have been ordered to take you to Edinburgh and that is where we are going. So why don't you try and get some sleep and let me get on with it."

She subsided into silence but she didn't sleep. She watched the road go by and ached, not for sleep, but at the thought that every

347

mile they went was taking her farther and farther away from Max. After half an hour they joined a road she knew and she realized how far they had to travel.

About nine o'clock, Kenton pulled in at a hotel.

"I think it's time we made a stop, don't you?" he said.

"Can you ring Stanton from here?" she said. "Can you find out what's happening?"

"Stanton won't be there," Kenton said. "You'll have to be patient. From now on he'll be getting in touch with us, not the other way round. It's more important that he gets on with it, isn't it, than that he keeps you informed?"

"Yes," she said. "Yes, of course."

"I'll see if we can get anything to eat here," he said and disappeared inside.

When he came back he said: "The dining room's closed but they can give us coffee and sandwiches, or whisky and sandwiches if you prefer."

Fiona got out of the car. "I'll have both," she said. Every muscle seemed to have stiffened up. She felt like a creaking board. "Perhaps we ought to try and stay here," she said. "You must be very tired."

"I asked the receptionist," Kenton said. "They've no single rooms left. In fact they have only one room left, a double. So I took it. I hope you don't mind." He looked very young and abashed when he said that and Fiona smiled.

"As long as it's got two separate beds in it," she said, "I shan't give a damn."

"I could sleep in the car," he said.

"Don't be silly," Fiona said.

They had the whisky, coffee and sandwiches sent up to the room. They were both relieved to see it had twin beds. Fiona had a glass of whisky and one sandwich and then felt too tired to eat any more. Kenton wolfed the rest of the plateful and then went down to the bar to keep out of her way and to see if there was anything of interest on the television news. Fiona ran a bath and soaked herself in it, ridding herself of some of the fear and stress of the day along with its grime. Clean sheets and a soft mattress had never seemed so desirable before. She slipped into bed and was asleep as soon as her head touched the pillow. It was like drifting out into a warm sea.

8

THEY arrived in Edinburgh at two o'clock and made directly for the theater. The streets were jammed with traffic, the pavements crowded, the shops full. There were flags on Princes Street and the gardens were ablaze with flowers. A wind from the sea ruffled flags and trees and tossed the white clouds into airy pyramids, constantly dissolving and reforming their shapes, creating a sense of movement and excitement.

They got lost in the one-way system and had to ask the way.

"It's so much easier to walk round this place than drive round it," Fiona said. "The hotel is simple to find. Perhaps we should go there first."

"You said there would be no one there," Kenton said. "You said they would all be at the theater."

"There might be a message at the hotel," she said. "For you. Perhaps for me. About Max."

"No," he said. He was quite decisive

about it. "There won't be a message yet."

Fiona sighed. "All right. Let's go on. We're going the right way now. I recognize where we are."

They found a place to park near the theater and locked the car.

"How's the car getting back to Watson's garage?" Fiona said. "Are you going to drive it back?"

"Someone will," Kenton said. He seemed taut and edgy. There was a strung-up quality about him that had been absent before. The time for joking is over, Fiona thought, even for him. Or perhaps he's just annoyed at being tied to me, playing bodyguard, when he'd rather be free to go hunting the assassin.

As they approached the stage door, Kenton stopped. He turned to face her.

"Look," he said. "One word of warning. Don't say anything to anyone about the possibility of there being trouble tonight. As far as you are concerned everything is normal. Behave as usual. We don't want any rumors flying around, or a panic starting."

"The producer will have been told, at least, won't he? And the manager of the theater?"

He shrugged. "Stanton has his own way of

doing things. You will probably notice nothing out of the ordinary tonight. Either they will pick the man up before he can act, or the attempt will be abandoned. I think once they know you've got to Edinburgh, they'll give up. Too risky."

"How will they know I've reached Edinburgh?" Fiona asked.

"Someone will be watching," Kenton said.

She shivered. She felt that she and Kenton were so isolated. They were at the center of events and yet cut off from them. She wondered what had happened at the castle. Had George been arrested? Had his men been disarmed, the camp closed down? Had they found Max? Had they found him alive? Had any action been taken at all?

She said: "Won't the assassin already know that it's all over, that the Company of 13 is being broken up, its members arrested?"

"He may be like us," Kenton said, "out of communication with his boss. In which case the only thing that might put him off is seeing you."

"Then let's make sure I'm seen," Fiona said. She paused. "The fact that you knew there would be no message for us, that you're not expecting to get one—that means you know Stanton will be concentrating on the assassination attempt. You think he will have done nothing yet, about the castle and the Company or about Max."

"Those sort of affairs requiring a lot of men take time to organize. He'll have his priorities. He only got your information yesterday afternoon, remember?"

"He's had twenty-four hours," Fiona said.

But Stanton was ruthless, like George. He would get his priorities right and Max would not number among them. And there was nothing she could do about it. I'll talk to Boris, she thought. There is no reason why I should not tell him what is happening. He already knows half of it.

But Boris was not there. He had left the theater about half an hour before, the stage doorkeeper informed them, and was not expected to return until the time of the performance. He inquired who Fiona was and looked her name up in a list. She wondered if this was the first sign of Stanton's preparations, but then it was every stage doorkeeper's job to keep track of who came and went in his theater, who belonged to the company and who did not. She noticed that Kenton made a point of telling the man his name and making sure that he would know him again.

There were few people backstage. The last rehearsal call had been at ten, the doorkeeper told her, and had ended ten minutes ago. There was to be a final check on the lighting at four, but the orchestra and most of the singers had gone. Not everyone, however. She found Fred in the greenroom having a cup of coffee with the stage manager. He greeted her with great good humor.

"My dear girl, here you are at last. Is this the boy friend?"

She introduced Kenton.

"Have you a ticket for tonight?" Fred asked him.

"I'm afraid not."

"You must see what you can do for him, Fiona. Though we're sold out, I hear. No paper tickets tonight."

"Perhaps no one would object if I came backstage with Fiona," Kenton said diffidently. "Saw a little from the wings?"

The stage manager frowned.

"I don't know if they'd let you stand in the wings," Fred said. "Too much traffic. Still, you'd certainly hear everything backstage. And that's what it's all about, isn't it? Fiona, you just missed Boris. I had a long talk with him. He tells me your father has a wonderful place up there in the wilds. He was hoping to see you before the performance if you arrived in time."

"Where is he?"

"Back at the hotel, I presume. By the way, I took the precaution of telling them this morning that you definitely wanted your room. The city is so crowded, rooms are like gold dust. You'd better book in soon or you'll lose it."

"I'll go right away. Fred, do you know who is coming tonight? Anyone of importance?"

"They'll all be important, according to themselves. All the local bigwigs will be coming, the Festival officials and guests, any actors, dancers, musicians who aren't performing tonight, music critics, hundreds of avid opera lovers—"

"But you don't know any political figures coming, no foreign statesmen, no royalty?"

"Not that I know of." He smiled at the stage manager. "I would say, with the cast we've got, the most illustrious and famous people in the theater tonight will be on the stage."

"Things are going well then?" Kenton said.

"Superbly. Even I am beginning to think nothing can go wrong." He pulled a face and immediately tapped the wood of his chair. "I shouldn't have said that. Bad luck. But try and come tonight, Mr. Kenton. It will be an evening to remember."

As they were leaving, Fred suddenly asked: "Why the questions about the audience tonight, Fiona? Were you hoping to sell some news to the press?"

"I'm a great autograph hunter," she said with a smile. "Didn't you know that, Fred? By the way, do you want me for anything?"

"Kind of you to ask. What can designers do now? It's out of our hands."

It certainly was, Fiona thought. Right out of their hands. She turned to Kenton. "Let's get to the hotel."

In the lounge of the North British Hotel, they found Boris taking tea. He manipulated teacups with great daintiness for so large a man. He was eating scones dripping with butter when they arrived.

"My dear Fiona!" He struggled to his feet, hampered by his closeness to the table, mopping melted butter from his chin. "Where's Max?"

"It's a long story," Fiona said.

"Ah . . ." He gave Kenton a shrewd glance. He pulled out chairs for them. "Can you talk?"

They sat down. Kenton looked round at their neighbors. The pleasant room was full. Tea time was a popular occasion.

"The more disreputable-looking customers are members of the orchestra," Boris said. "The place is swamped with them. The tourists haven't a hope."

"Rehearsals have gone very well, Fred tells us," Fiona said.

"Yes. It is going exactly as I have planned. I shall reach my peak tonight. You mustn't miss it, Mr. Kenton. It will be a performance of *Rosenkavalier* that will be talked about for years."

"So I keep being told," Kenton said.

"Who is this boy, Fiona?" Boris said. "Why is he smiling?"

"He is one of Stanton's men," Fiona said. "I've no idea why he is smiling."

"What happened to Max?"

"We nearly got away," Fiona said. "He was shot. He made me leave him. I don't know what has happened to him."

Boris put a large hand over hers and pressed it comfortingly. "I thought you

357

looked a little distrait. How did you get away?"

"David here got me to Edinburgh."

"Well done, Mr. Kenton. Did you get any more names, Fiona?"

"Yes. Have you still got the list Max gave me, David? Will you give it to Mr. Askarian?"

"Not without Stanton's permission," Kenton said.

Boris raised his hands expressively. "Dear me. Never mind. It is always the same with underlings. I'll get it from Stanton. Did you find out about the assassination plot?"

"It is tonight," Fiona said. "At the opera." She was conscious of Kenton's almost rigid disapproval. "Mr. Askarian and Max," she said, "have made a deal."

"They are going to try for someone at the first night of *Rosenkavalier?*" Boris said. "Who, for God's sake? Who is coming worth the shooting?"

"Well that," Fiona said, "is something no one knows, or is admitting."

"Does Stanton know about this?" Boris said.

"Yes."

Boris smiled. "Then we can relax. In fact,

it will add a little spice to my performance. I shall be singing with one eye on the conductor and one eye out for the assassin."

"I should think that would ruin your performance," Fiona said. "Have you got the documents you and Max discussed?"

"What documents?" Kenton said.

"He's too inquisitive, Fiona," Boris said. "Send him away."

"Have you got them?"

"Yes, but to take a leaf out of Mr. Kenton's book, I'll only hand them over to Max. And without indulging in false optimism, Fiona, I am sure Max will survive. He's come through worse situations than this. He's a great survivor."

"Thank you, Boris," Fiona said. "You're a very kind man. Now I must go and claim my room before they give it away."

"If you have any trouble," Boris said, "come to me. I have two very nice beds in my room. It's a shame to leave one unused."

"I'm surprised it still is," Fiona said. "By the way, what did you do with the caravan? You didn't tow that all the way to Edinburgh, did you?"

Boris laughed. "No. We left it for someone else to pick up. There are advantages at times in playing the autocrat, off as well as onstage."

The hotel had kept Fiona's room, in spite of pressures to let it.

"I'm afraid if you hadn't arrived by six," the receptionist explained courteously, "we should have had to let it go."

Fiona expressed her thanks. A young porter took her key and looked expectantly round for her luggage.

"It's coming later," she said.

Kenton came up with her. It was he who tipped the porter and took the key from him. He put it down on the dressing table.

"You shouldn't have told Askarian so much," he said. "You know who he is, don't you?"

"There is a pact, I understand," Fiona said, "between the two opposing sides in order to deal with the Company of 13. It seemed odd to me too, but I believe it works to everyone's advantage."

"Stanton's a fool if he thinks that."

"Do you really think so?" Fiona said. "That Stanton's a fool?"

Kenton shrugged. "I suppose not." He walked to the window and back again, restless as a cat. "You must forgive me. I'm not used

360

to this inaction. I'm like you. I can't bear to be cut off from news."

"Is there no way we can get in touch with Stanton?"

"No. I have a rendezvous for later, after the performance."

"I would have thought they would have enlisted your help at the theater."

"I believe Stanton thinks I am helping, in protecting you," he said a little stiffly.

"Yes, well, I know how much I owe to you," Fiona said. "When I see Stanton I shall tell him."

He looked at his watch. In a kind of reflex action Fiona glanced at hers. Five o'clock. He gave her a sudden grin.

"I'm ravenous," he said. "Do you think we could get something to eat?"

Room service sent up a full Scottish tea: scones, breads, cakes, jams. Kenton ate with a schoolboy appetite but it did not seem to calm him. Fiona was reminded of an actor's pre-performance nerves. He looked more than once at his watch and finally seemed to come to a decision.

"I'm going to ring Stanton's office. He won't be there but I might get something out of them."

"Are you ringing from here?" Fiona asked.

"I'll go downstairs and use the public telephone." He paused at the door. "Stay put, won't you? Don't leave the room."

His restlessness had infected her. Waiting for him, she walked aimlessly about the room. He was gone twenty minutes. As soon as he comes back, she thought, I'm going to the theater. It's pointless to stay here.

She opened the door to his knock and let him in.

"I didn't speak to Stanton," he said, "but there was a message about you. He doesn't want you to go to the theater. He wants you to stay here in your room at the hotel until he contacts you."

"Did he say why?"

He shook his head. "He'll have his reasons."

"Was there nothing about Max?"

"I'm sorry. But things are clearly moving." He turned to go.

"You're not staying?" She gave him a wry smile. "To protect me?"

He turned back. He put a hand on her wrist. He said seriously: "If you stay here you'll be safe. Nothing will happen to you.

Get a meal, drinks, sent up, watch the television. It will all be over before you know it. Whatever happens I'll come back here and tell you. That's a promise. Wait here for me."

"We've been told it's going to be such a wonderful performance," she said. "It will be a pity to miss it." She smiled at his expression. "I'm sorry. I didn't mean it. I'll stay."

"Thank you. Don't forget," he added, "there may not be a performance at all."

She felt, when he had gone, oddly deserted. Banished back to the waiting room again. She remembered the time she had spent waiting in the fishing hotel after Eliot's death, the sense she had had of being used or manipulated. She was hardly being used in this situation. The position was quite opposite. She was now a slightly awkward encumbrance. She had no part to play. She was simply being put out of the way in a corner, like a piece of left luggage. Keep until called for.

She caught sight of herself in a mirror. Burned brown by the sun, her eyes looking larger by contrast, still wearing the shirt and jeans she had put on yesterday morning at the castle, she was hardly a figure for a cosmopolitan first night at the opera. She had tried to clean the jeans last night, but they still bore the stain of Max's blood from the seat of the car she had sent over the cliff, and both they and the shirt were marked by the terrain she had covered during that long and terrifying day. If she had gone to the theater she could have borrowed something from Wardrobe. It was too late to go out to the shops even if she hadn't promised to stay in her room. Half-past six. An hour till curtain up. Boris might not have left for the theater yet. She wanted to tell him what had happened. Why she was not going to be there. She wanted to wish him luck. She went to the telephone and asked for his room.

There was no reply. She replaced the receiver and after a moment's reflection rang the reception desk. Had Mr. Askarian left? Mr. Askarian, she was told, had just that moment left his key at the desk.

"Ask him to wait." She grabbed the key of her room and ran for the lift. She made no conscious decision, she acted purely on impulse, and it was impulse that led her, when she discovered that Boris had gone before her message could be given to him, whisked away in a cab to the theater, to follow his path out of the hotel and into the street. She crossed to the other side of Princes Street and began walking along the line of shops.

She rationalized her action to herself. In Festival week some shops might stay open later. She might be able to buy another shirt and jeans, or perhaps a dress. At the very least she could get a toothbrush and cream for her face. But in reality she knew she was walking to keep her mind from what might be happening at the theater, and because she could not stand the thought of three or four hours more trapped in her hotel room. Above all, she was walking to exorcise those haunting images of Max that never left her; Max alone on the moor, dying from shock and loss of blood and exposure; Max hunted down and shot dead like an animal by those faceless men with guns.

She had few fears for her own safety in leaving the hotel. In spite of Kenton's insistence that she stay in her room, she could not believe there could be any danger to her here. It was the theater they wanted her to avoid. She was prepared to obey them in that. She would simply walk a little and then go back. But even then, in all logic, she could not see what threat there could be to her at the theater. She was not the one George and his friends had planned to kill. Perhaps Stanton thought the sight of her might make the assassin change his mind. Perhaps he wanted to catch him in the act and so get more solid evidence against the Company of 13. He was cold-blooded enough to risk that.

All the shops were closed or closing. It was nearly seven o'clock. She was too late to buy anything and in any case she realized she would not have been able to do so. She had rushed from her room carrying only her door key. Her bag had been left locked inside. She had no money, no card or checkbook with her.

Seven o'clock. The audience arriving, the excitement building up. The singers dressing, making up, going through whatever rituals helped them through this last half hour. She wanted to be there. Whatever might happen, she wanted to be there.

She sighed and stopped, looking around her. The glowing evening light was changing the city before her eyes. The castle seemed to float on its rock above her. Princes Street itself, slashed like a knife-thrust through the heart of Edinburgh, shimmered with color and movement. The bleak granite of the old town was softened, its harsh edges blurred. It was an evening for walking and looking, but instead she turned back. She would keep her promise. No doubt, as Kenton had said, there were good reasons for it.

From the north side of the street, side roads led away into the Georgian terraces and crescents of the new town. In one of these side streets, nearly opposite the hotel, Kenton had left the car. Fiona had to wait to cross the top of it, and as she did so, she looked casually along it. The car was still there. More surprisingly so was Kenton. She had been under the impression when he left her that he was going directly to the theater. He was standing on the pavement by the open car door, talking to someone. His body masked the figure from Fiona's view. Who could it be? One of Stanton's men? Stanton himself? She began walking quickly toward them. Whoever it was, Kenton's delay meant she had a second chance. She wasn't even going to discuss it with him. She was going to make him take her with him.

Kenton moved. He bent down and placed something on the back seat of the car. She could see he was smiling. He shook hands with his companion and got into the car. The other man slammed the door shut. He gave a mock salute as Kenton drove away. He turned toward her. He was smiling too. Fiona stood frozen with disbelief. The other man was Jackson, the yellow-haired pilot of the helicopter.

Fiona acted then entirely from instinct. She was too stunned for rational thought. She turned and walked rapidly back to Princes Street. She didn't run. Running draws attention to you. People were strolling, gazing in shop windows. She tried to merge with them. She didn't dare look behind her. She crossed the road with a crowd of others. She slipped into the hotel. She made for the sanctuary of her room. She locked the door and sat on the bed. Her heart was pounding as if she had run a race.

She forced herself to be calm. She took deep breaths. She relaxed the tense muscles of her neck and shoulders. She had to think coldly and clearly. She had to understand the implications of what she had seen. She had to decide the right action to take.

David Kenton and the helicopter pilot. Now that she thought of it, when she had seen one, the other had never been far away. At the fishing hotel, after Eliot's death, Kenton had arrived first, then the helicopter. He and Jackson had both been in the town at the time of the demonstration. Was that why David had suddenly turned back that morning at the New Inn when he was going to collect his payment for taking part in the demonstration? Because he hadn't realized it was Jackson who was making the payments and he didn't want to risk Fiona seeing how well they knew each other? And on the hill yesterday, her almost miraculous escape from her pursuers; suppose she had been seen, suppose they knew she was on the hill? They let headquarters know and headquarters sent the helicopter with David on board, David whom they knew she trusted, and dropped him on the other side of the hill. Then the four men with guns drove her over the hilltop and into his waiting arms.

She had wondered how they could have missed her; she had thought it was luck, nothing but luck. No wonder the Land-Rover had been left unattended outside the post office with the keys in the ignition. It had all been arranged, as had the car left outside the stone villa. The woman had looked at her oddly when she called her Mrs. Watson. That was because she wasn't Mrs. Watson; there had been no car hired from Watson's garage; that was just a name snatched by Kenton from the post office woman's casual remark to make events seem more credible. He hadn't gone to the house; he had gone round the back of the house and then walked straight back simply to convince her. He had had the keys and the insurance paper all along. The whole thing had been a gigantic charade. Everything Kenton did was a charade. The helicopter had dropped him off at the fishing inn after Eliot's death to play the part of the student hiker, to find out how much Max and Stanton knew, how much had been lost. He had been sent to the demonstration for the same reason or perhaps to find out what Craddock was up to. And now this, the longest and most elaborate deception of them all.

Why? Why had she been brought to Edinburgh? What was the purpose of it? She remembered David Kenton talking to the stage doorkeeper, making sure he would know him again, would let him into the theater again without question. She remembered him asking if he could come backstage, watch the opera from the wings. And as she remembered it all became clear. Her sole purpose in the operation had been to get Kenton unquestioned access to the theater backstage. After this afternoon, he could come and go there as he wished. He could safely choose anyplace he liked to set up the assassination. Max had thought the assassin would be in the audience. It had never occurred to either of them that he would be backstage.

For the implications could not be avoided. Kenton was the assassin. "I am young," he had told Fiona, "but I'm very vicious," and he had been speaking no less than the truth. He was at the camp, George had said; he had been there a week, getting some practice. The practice had consisted of murdering the technician on Linnay, of shooting Craddock. His restless behavior in the hotel that had reminded her of an actor's stage nerves had been exactly that. He had been nervous until he had, by a pre-arranged phone call, made contact with Jackson. It was Jackson who had brought him the gun he would use in the assassination. Once he had got that, how relaxed he had been, how smiling and relaxed at the car, for everything had been going exactly as planned. He believed Fiona had

371

been frightened into staying in her room, to await God knew what fate after the killing at the opera had been accomplished. His only moment of worry had been when she had insisted on telling Boris what was planned. But Boris had been content to leave it to Stanton. And Stanton knew nothing.

That was the worst fact Fiona had to face. There had been no call to Stanton from that country post office. No warning had been passed to him, no list of names of the Company of 13 read out to him. She was only thankful she hadn't been able to tell David Kenton where Max might be hiding. If she had, he would be dead by now.

There would be no police marksmen waiting to intercept the assassin, no ring of police round the theater, no secret-service stagehands or front-of-house staff. Nothing at all would have been done to prevent the assassination. Nobody in Edinburgh knew about it but herself. And Boris.

She had given the paper with Stanton's number on it to David. But Max had told her to remember it. Could she remember it? Once she thought David Kenton had made the vital phone call, she had relaxed. She had let her mind relax. She went to the dressing table and took a piece of hotel notepaper. She sat staring at it, concentrating all her mind on remembering the look of the paper Max had given her. She could see the numbers. She could read them off in her mind. She took a pen and wrote them down on the notepaper. Stanton could get things moving faster than she could. He would be there, waiting for a call from them. But if for some reason she couldn't reach him, if she had got the numbers wrong, then she would ring the Edinburgh police and tell them there was a bomb in the theater. Anything to get the police on the spot, to get the theater cleared.

She went to pick up the telephone. There was a loud insistent knocking on her door. She was immediately wary, suspicious. She went up to the door. She called through it, asking who was there and what they wanted. A Scottish voice answered. There was an urgent message from Mr. Askarian. He had asked that it should be given her without delay. Read it to her, Fiona said. That wasn't possible. It was sealed and marked confidential. Fiona unlocked the door and opened it barely an inch to take in the message. An inch was enough. The door was pushed violently against her. She stumbled backward and Jackson slipped into the room.

He slammed the door shut again and stood with his back to it, grinning at her.

"How'd you like the Scots accent?" he said. "Good, eh? Good enough to fool you anyway. Did you really think Askarian would send you a message?"

"He might have done," she said coolly. "He might have found out who Kenton is and have sent to warn me."

"Ah!" Jackson said. "I wasn't sure you'd seen us together. I saw you in the street after Dave had driven off. But you might have missed us. Now you've made it certain."

"What took you so long getting here?" Fiona said.

"Oh, I've been here as long as you. I followed you here. Then I made a phone call. I needed to know exactly what to do about you."

"And what did my uncle tell you?" Fiona asked.

Jackson took a revolver out of his jacket pocket. It was considerably larger than the one Max had been carrying. It looked very lethal. He saw Fiona's expression and made a deprecatory gesture with his hand.

374

"Don't worry. I'm not using this on you. Not yet. Not if you behave."

"We're waiting here for Kenton, is that it?"

Jackson came forward. "Why don't you sit down? There won't be long to wait."

Fiona sat down on one of the two beds. She looked at her watch. Seven-thirty. She had been back here barely fifteen minutes. At the theater the curtain would be going up.

She said: "You'll have to wait a good deal longer than you think if you expect David Kenton to come back. You weren't the only one doing a little telephoning these past ten minutes."

Jackson shook his head. He grinned at her. He was patronizing, almost friendly. "That won't work. I checked. No calls made from this room all evening."

"I'm surprised they had time to check that for you," Fiona said. "Are you sure they did?"

"Are you trying to cause me trouble? I'm quite sure. And to make certain you don't get any bright ideas about picking up the receiver and yelling help—" The telephone stood on the bedside table. He bent down and ripped the wires out from the wall. "There!" He looked at her triumphantly. "You led us a dance, you know. I was the one who spotted you at last."

"Were you the one who thought up the idea of having David rescue me?" she asked.

"No. That was Dave's own idea. He said you could be very useful to him so the business got the go-ahead. Worked like a charm, didn't it? The boy's got such a nice open face. Anyone would trust him."

"I presume he's a lot older than he looks," Fiona said.

"Not a lot older," Jackson said. "You're talkative, aren't you?"

"What's his real nationality?"

"Now look, girl, don't try and pump me. I'm just here to keep an eye on you. If you hadn't come wandering out of the hotel and spotted us, I'd be on my way out of town by now. What made you come out anyway? Dave said you'd stay in your room."

"I got bored," Fiona said.

Jackson laughed. He sat down on the bed opposite her. He put the gun down and lit a cigarette. He offered one to Fiona.

"I don't smoke."

"Wise girl. Live longer that way."

"I don't know why you're all so worried about me," Fiona said. "Shouldn't you be more concerned about Max Wyndham. You haven't caught him, have you?"

"He's dead, isn't he?"

Fiona's heart gave a painful leap. Then she realized it was a question.

"Your uncle swore he'd shot him," Jackson went on. "When we saw you alone he was sure of it. He said you wouldn't have left Wyndham if he was still alive. Right?"

"Yes," Fiona said quietly. "You're right." He hadn't had time to discuss Max with Kenton. Let him go on thinking Max was dead. She didn't allow herself to think that by now it could well be true. She hugged to herself the knowledge that they hadn't found him, dead or alive.

"So you see," Jackson said, "it's all wrapped up. You're the only one who might have been a worry to us and here I am looking after you."

"Boris Askarian knows about the assassination plan," Fiona said. "I told him, in front of David Kenton. I shouldn't wait around too long looking after me. Askarian will have taken independent action. You could be trapped here, sitting in this room with me."

Jackson looked at her with admiration. "You're a tryer, aren't you? Playing the old psychological warfare with me. If Askarian knew anything, he wouldn't go within a mile of that theater. And he's there all right; I saw him arrive before I went to meet Dave. He'll be going onstage, opening up that big voice of his, thrilling all the ladies. And then it will all be over and he'll no longer be any trouble, to us or to anyone else."

Fiona stared at him. "What do you mean?"

"Didn't you guess? He's the one. Didn't you really know? What a way to go. He ought to thank us. Shot in the middle of a note, on a Gala night, in front of an enthusiastic audience. Who could top that?" He repeated. "Didn't you really know?"

And, of course, now that it had been said, it was obvious. All the clues had been there if she'd had the sense to read them. There was no one of real political importance coming to the first night. Hadn't Fred said that the most illustrious people in the theater would be those on the stage? And which of those was as internationally famous as Boris? Whose assassination at the height of his powers would cause as much shock or make such an impact as his? His background would only add to the complications, making accusation and counteraccusation from East and West, from left and right, almost inevitable. Political extremists of all the colors in the spectrum would be suspected and many of them would claim responsibility just to get the publicity. To the public it would be another reason to back the forces of law and order, and if Kenton got away with it, it would be another failure to put at the door of conventional police forces, another step on the way to acceptance of unorthodox claimants to the guardianship of the law, such as, when it finally emerged from its self-imposed anonymity, the Company of 13.

Boris was dangerous to the Company. He was out to get them. He was even cooperating with opponents like Stanton to get them. By killing him they would achieve several goals at once: the continued undermining of confidence in established authority; on a lower, more secret level, the creation of distrust between different sides; and above all the destruction of a personal enemy.

Those must have been the reasons George Grant gave to his colleagues in the Company of 13 when he put forward Boris's name as their next victim. But he would have had more urgent private reasons to press for this assassination. Boris had been his paymaster in the Linnay affair. Boris knew his secrets and there was little doubt he had kept evidence of George's treason. Perhaps George even guessed that Boris was ready to betray him. For George to survive, Boris had to go. It would have been clear-cut, black and white to George. There would have been no hesitation as to purpose, only matters of method and timing to be considered.

They had been told, Fiona realized, as she and Max had listened in to George's conversation with the German that night. The German had even suggested that the timing be delayed so that he could enjoy Boris's singing one last time. It had never occurred to her that one might sincerely admire an artist's voice while planning to silence it forever.

She said to Jackson: "When's he going to do it?"

He looked at his watch. "Let me see. About forty minutes into the first act, he said. If it started promptly at seven-thirty, that would make it about ten past eight. It's twenty to eight now. Half an hour to wait."

"Why that timing?" she said. "Why so exact?"

"He said by that time everyone in the

audience should be relaxed, absorbed, watching nothing but the stage—if it's as good as everyone says it's going to be, that is. And backstage, they'll be too busy or too intent on their own affairs to notice a quiet, well-behaved fellow like him. He's had a recording of *Rosenkavalier* up at the camp. Been playing it all the time. Says he found the perfect moment. Stage full of people, lots of movement, people singing at the same time, then the character Boris Askarian is playing bangs a table loud as hell. Wham!" He suddenly struck his open palm with his clenched right fist. He grinned at Fiona. "That's it. Perfect cover for a shot. Askarian collapses. Everyone rushes round. They think at first he's ill, fainted, had a heart attack, you name it. Dave drops the gun out of sight in a quiet corner, walks out of the stage door and there you are. If anyone questions him, he'll say he's fetching a doctor. But nobody will. Nobody does in those first few minutes."

"You sound as if you've had experience of this before," Fiona said.

He shrugged. "You could say I know what I'm talking about."

And it would work, Fiona thought. By the

time people realized Boris had not collapsed from illness, but had been shot, Kenton would have escaped. How many minutes from the wings to the stage door? Enough. He could do it. He was going to do it.

She glanced at her watch. Quarter to eight. She had to get out of here. She had to get to the theater. She had to stop him herself. By the time she had rung the police, convinced them it wasn't a hoax, got them to take action, it would be too late. And how was she going to get away? She had no weapon, nothing. She glanced round the room. As if reading her mind, Jackson picked up the gun again. He sat there, cradling it, smiling at her.

"Have you been working with my uncle for long?" she asked.

"Long enough. Couple of years."

"Why? Why are you doing it?"

"You mean what's in it for me? Money, some fun, a sense of achievement."

"You're Australian, aren't you?"

"You could call me a returned immigrant. Parents took me out there when I was a kid. Came back to see the old country and stayed. Helping to put it to rights. Too many

382

commies running things. Got to make a stand somewhere."

"You approve of the killings? The one tonight?"

"Can't make an omelette without breaking eggs. We're not the only ones. It's going on all round you. You want to open your eyes, sweetheart."

"What's going to happen to me when Kenton gets back?"

"Dave won't be coming back here. Your uncle is coming for you."

"George is in Edinburgh?"

"He's at the theater, fourth row front stalls. He wasn't going to miss this." He looked at her. "You'll relax now, won't you. Now you know it's Uncle George coming for you."

"At least I can talk to him," Fiona said. "I'm his niece. He's not going to harm me."

"If you say so." He looked at his watch again. "Ten to. Not long to wait. Pity they're not televising it. We could have seen exactly what happened."

"Can I get my handbag?" Fiona said. "I want something out of it. It's over there."

"I'll get it." He stood up, went across to the dressing table. "Make sure you haven't got a gun or a brick in it." He picked it up, looked inside, brought it over to her. She had edged herself a little closer to the bedside table. As he handed the bag to her, she let it slip. It fell on the carpet by his feet. He was off-guard, unsuspecting. The waiting time was nearly over and she had been no trouble. He bent down to pick up the handbag. Fiona took hold of the telephone with both hands and hit him as hard as she could with it on the back of the head. She hit him so hard the plastic of the phone cracked. He fell forward against the bed.

She thought at first she had killed him. Then he gave a moan and began feeling round with his hands on the carpet. She realized he was feeling for his gun. In another moment he would be struggling to hands and knees. In another moment it would be too late. She pulled her handbag out from beneath his prone body, climbed round him and ran for the door.

She had to wait for the lift, and out in the street in front of hotel she had to wait for a cab. She made herself stay calm. Telephoning would take too much time. A car was the only way to get to the theater. She thought of flagging one down, any one, making up a story of some believable emergency. She looked at her watch. She was going to be too late. She stepped forward, determined to stop the next car. The head porter tapped her on the shoulder. "Here you are, miss!" She'd already tipped him to get her a cab. She thanked him, jumped in. The porter shut the door.

She told the driver a pretty thin story, but she told it with such desperation he believed her. She was one of the singers in the opera. She'd been trapped in a lift at the hotel and they'd only just managed to release her. She had fifteen minutes to get onstage. She needed five of those to dress and make up.

"You'll need more than five minutes for that," he said, entering into the spirit of it. He went down Princes Street like a rocket, he cut corners, he jumped lights, he got her to the theater in seven minutes.

"Send me a free ticket," he said with a grin when she thanked him. She gave him a five pound note instead.

The clock at the stage door read five past eight.

"Hallo, Miss Grant," said the stage door-keeper. "You look in a hurry."

"Will you ring the police?" she said as

quietly as she could. "Will you tell them there is a man with a gun in the theater and we need them straightaway?"

"Is that true?" he said. "Did Mr. Stewart ask you to tell me?"

Mr. Stewart was the stage manager.

"Yes," Fiona said. "Mr. Stewart said would you ring straightaway. Have you seen my friend, Mr. Kenton, tonight?"

"He came in about half an hour ago. I've not seen him since."

"Did they start on time?" she asked.

"More or less," he said. "About five minutes late, I'd say."

"Thank God," said Fiona.

In the corridor by the greenroom she ran into Fred.

"What's the hell's the matter with you?" he said. "You look like a ghost."

"Have you seen Kenton?"

"Your boy friend? No?"

"He's not my boy friend. I can't go into it, but he's been paid to kill Boris. He'll be in the wings."

Fred took her by the shoulders and looked her in the face. "To make sure you're not under the influence of drugs or drink," he said. "Your not. Come on."

386

From the backstage loudspeakers the tenor's mock Italian aria soared sweetly:

"Di rigori armato il seno,
Contro amore mi ribellai . . ."

It seemed nothing but steps and corridors and bends and turns and steps again. Fred paused by an open door and dashed inside. He came back waving something.

"What on earth's that?"

"Prop sword. I was looking for a gun, but there isn't time."

"How much farther?"

"Keep quiet. We're practically onstage."

Now she didn't need the loudspeakers to hear the singers. Ebullient, enjoying himself, Boris was throwing himself into his part. The Baron was arguing with the attorney about his marriage settlement. In a moment the tenor, as a professional singer hoping to entertain the Marschallin, would begin again. The Baron in anger would crash his fist down on the table . . .

There were several people standing in the wings. She could see Boris now quite clearly, seated at a table center stage, his attorney in front of him. The Marschallin at her dressing table was out of her vision. To the right of the Baron were gathered his servants. There were others at the back of the stage she couldn't see without moving nearer. The singer with his accompanying flutist was well forward. He took up an elaborately formal stance. The flutist raised his flute to his lips.

She couldn't see Kenton. God, suppose he had gone round, suppose he was in the wings on the other side? No, he couldn't have seen Boris so clearly from there. The Marschallin would have blocked his view. He'd been here half an hour. He'd had time to choose the best position.

There were several stagehands in the wings, and Stewart the stage manager. No Kenton, no tousled boyish figure. the tenor began to sing:

"Ma si caro è'l mio tormento
Dolce è si la piaga mia . . ."

One of the stage hands was moving quietly into the shadows. Dark hair, anorak, jeans. Why did he need an anorak in this heat? His hand was inside the jacket, drawing something out.

She came to life. She yelled, "Fred, there!"

388

The stagehand swung round. She saw Kenton's face beneath the wig. She saw the gun in his hand. She saw Fred flinging his highly unfit body across the space, butting Kenton full in the stomach. They collapsed together on the floor. As, onstage, Baron Ochs slammed his fist down on the table the gun went off harmlessly into the air.

It took the combined efforts of the other three stagehands, Stewart and Fred to drag Kenton into the nearest dressing room. One of the men went and found some rope and they tied him to a chair. He sat with his head down, his face expressionless. He had said nothing since they caught him. He had not looked at Fiona once.

"My God!" Stewart kept saying. "To think I was standing next to him. I was right next to him all the time."

He had brought Kenton's gun back. He put it carefully on the makeup table.

"We haven't disturbed the performance at all. The Italian singer and the flutist have come off. They said they didn't notice anything. However, everyone backstage knows something's up. Stand outside and keep people out," he told one of the men. He told another to fetch the police.

"They should be here soon," Fiona said. "I asked the stage doorkeeper to ring them."

"They're here already," Stewart said. "They've been here ten minutes."

Fiona stared at him. "Why? Who sent for them?"

"No one did, they just arrived. They were very discreet. They said they'd had information there might be some nut with a rifle in the audience. They didn't say he was going to shoot the singers. They were checking the auditorium. I think they had in mind someone at the back of the circle with a high-powered rifle, not someone wandering backstage with a gun."

"Who's the man in charge?" Fiona said. "Where is he?"

"Last time I saw him he was outside the stalls bar."

"Can you find him? Can you take me to him?"

"Sure." Stewart looked uncertainly at Kenton.

"It's all right," Fred said rather grandly. "I'll keep an eye on him."

"You deserve a medal, Fred," Fiona said.

"I know," Fred said. "I know."

"When the police come to collect him, will you tell them I left a half-stunned friend of Kenton's in my room at the hotel. I doubt if he's still there, but he might be."

Stewart took Fiona quietly through the pass door and into the auditorium. The theater was packed. There were people standing at the back of the stalls, and down the sides were a few latecomers, who arriving after curtain up, had been asked to wait until the end of the first act before taking their seats.

The first person Fiona saw was George. He was, as Jackson had told her, seated in the center of the fourth row of the stalls, flanked by two empty seats. A dedicated music lover might have chosen to sit further back, to achieve a better balance between orchestra and voices. For someone who wanted to watch an enemy die, he was very well placed.

His face looked stony and implacable. The head bandage had gone and he wore now merely a large plaster over the wound Max had given him. Onstage Boris was handing the Marschallin the silver rose in a leather case.

"Und da ist nun die silberne Rose!"

George must know Kenton has failed,

Fiona thought. He must know it's all over. His colleagues had already deserted him. Neither the German nor whoever was the other opera lover in the Company of 13 scheduled to attend had taken their seats beside him. Then she noticed, as if on a signal, two men in dark suits beginning to make their way along the row toward him, one from either side. George turned his head and looked at them, first one, then the other. He looked back at the stage. Footmen were opening the double doors of the Marschallin's bedroom. The Baron was about to depart. Boris was making an elaborate bow. In a moment he would have left the stage. Fiona looked at George's face and knew exactly what he was going to do. And this time there was nothing she could do to stop it. She was too far away. The two men were too far away. And they hadn't seen the revolver he had taken from his jacket. George was a good shot. He wouldn't miss.

She turned desperately to Stewart. But Stewart was murmuring quietly to one of the men in the side aisle, no doubt asking where his chief was. If she shouted a warning, Fiona thought, she wouldn't be heard above the music. Even if she were heard, it wouldn't stop George. She looked back. He was rising, taking aim.

Someone had taken Stewart's place beside her. She saw him from the corner of her eye. A tall man in a dark suit. He had raised his left forearm and was resting his right wrist on it, using it to steady his hand. As Fiona turned to him, he took careful aim and shot George Grant through the right shoulder.

There was no sound. The gun had a silencer on it. No one noticed. It had happened in shadow and the audience was intent on the stage. George sank gently down into his seat. The two men reached him. In the flurry of departures on the stage, they unobtrusively removed him, half lifting him, half carrying, as if he had merely fainted and was being taken out to recover.

The man who had shot him had already replaced his gun. He took Fiona by the arm and drew her through swing doors into the lighted corridor.

"Well," Wyndham said, "as Wellington said after Waterloo, that was a damned close-run thing."

It was two o'clock in the morning. The three of them were in Boris's room at the hotel,

Fiona, Wyndham and Boris. Boris had just ordered another bottle of champagne. He was only now beginning to unwind after the performance. There was no doubt of the success of *Rosenkavalier*, nor of Boris's own personal success. There had been a standing ovation for him and for all the cast. The first night party was officially over, but offshoots were continuing all over Edinburgh, all over the hotel.

Wyndham was lying, eyes half shut, on one of the beds. He looked very pale. Fiona thought she knew exactly how he felt: elated, exhausted, relieved. She was sitting curled up in an armchair. Boris paced about the room, coming to rest occasionally to refill their glasses. It was the first chance he had had of hearing the full story of the evening.

"To have your life saved twice in as many minutes," he said, "is more than an extravagant piece of good fortune, it shows the clear hand of fate. I cannot ignore it. I shall retire. I shall go out of public life tonight exactly as if I had been killed. I shall go out on a moment of triumph."

"Don't be so bloody Russian," Wyndham said.

Boris paused beside him. "How is the leg now?"

"Painful when I think about it," Wyndham said. "I'm rapidly anesthetizing it with alcohol. I walked on it too much tonight."

After she had left him on the moors, he had walked, Fiona had discovered, or rather dragged himself right back to the castle grounds. It had taken him most of the day. Going on the theory that no one looks for an escaped prisoner in the prison, he had then taken refuge in the Victorian summerhouse opposite the gatehouse. He had wedged the door shut with a bamboo chair, wrapped himself in a moth-eaten horse blanket he found there, and slept till morning. He awoke to find the castle practically deserted. All the expensive cars had gone. The Company of 13 had dispersed like blown leaves before the wind. The car in which he had driven Fiona to the castle remained where he had parked it. He had got into it in the dawn light and slowly and painfully driven it down to the lodge. He had sounded the horn as if he had every right to be there And Macleod had come out and opened the gate.

"He had been given no instructions to stop me, I suppose," he said. "In the furor the day before, if he'd been told anything, it would have been to let no one through. It was another day, everyone had gone, George included. So he opened the gate."

"What if he hadn't opened the gate?" Boris asked.

"I think I would have persuaded him," Wyndham remarked with a smile.

He had stopped at the nearest telephone box and rung Stanton. Stanton had sent a helicopter to fetch him. He had made his report, had his leg seen to, and then before coming to Edinburgh had insisted on going out with a helicopter to search for Fiona.

"I was very much concerned when I found you hadn't rung through to Stanton," he said.

"English understatement, I presume," Boris said to Fiona. "What happened at the camp?"

"It's been closed down. They got most of the men. They've been handed over to the police. They also picked up several of the Company of 13 at the airport. I'm not quite sure what they can charge them with. Criminal conspiracy, perhaps. They'll probably have to let them go, but their future operations will be limited. They won't risk much now that their names are known."

"Are you going to give me their names?" Boris said.

"Ask Stanton," Wyndham said.

Boris smiled. "You think because you saved my life, you can go back on our deal."

Wyndham sipped champagne. "There is no deal," he said. "George Grant had a heart attack in the ambulance on the way to hospital. He's dead."

Fiona looked at him. "You didn't tell me."

"No," Wyndham said. "I was wondering how you'd react to the knowledge I'd killed him."

"You didn't kill him," Fiona said. "Though most people would have said he'd deserved it even if you had. But I'm glad you feel that way."

"What way?" Boris said. "It wasn't your fault you missed the heart, Max. In the circumstances, even I might have missed."

"She means she's glad I've not yet become like Kenton, or you, Boris," Wyndham said. "Or Stanton."

"He wasn't aiming to kill him, you see, Boris," Fiona said. "Only to stop him."

"These finely differentiated ethical gradations are too subtle for me," Boris said.

"Where is Stanton, by in the way? Is he in Edinburgh?"

"Sitting at the center of his web," Wyndham said. "Spinning to catch flies."

"You won't be needing these now." Boris took out a large sealed envelope. "The documents concerning Grant and Elena Greer. His death closes a lot of files. Linnay, for instance?"

Wyndham smiled. "It may be so. Though when some other departments hear of the trouble we took to save your neck tonight, there are going to be a few raised eyebrows." He raised an eyebrow himself. "Perhaps we can turn you? How about becoming a double agent, Boris? After all, isn't there some old Russian proverb that after you've saved a man's life, he belongs to you?"

Boris laughed. "That sounds more Chinese than Russian to me, dear boy. Don't spoil the celebration with tedious thoughts of business."

"I'm going to bed," Wyndham said. "It's been a long day."

"You're on a bed! Where are you going? Where are you staying?"

Wyndham swung his legs off the bed and stood up. "Not in your room, Askarian. Our reputations would never recover."

"Where is he staying, Fiona?"

"None of your business," Fiona said.

"That's what I like to hear," Wyndham said. "Tell him where he gets off." He linked his arm in hers. "Shall we hobble along together? Good night, Boris. I'll come and hear you sing tomorrow night. Make up my mind if it was worth it."

"Good night, Boris," Fiona said.

He bent down and kissed her firmly on the mouth.

"Thank you," he said simply.

Outside Fiona's room, Wyndham leaned against the wall and watched her as she found the key and unlocked the door.

"Jackson is all right, by the way," he said. "Concussion, that's all. The damage to his male pride is probably going to be more difficult for him to overcome."

Fiona sighed. "First thing in the morning," she said, "I must go out and buy some clothes."

"I like you just the way you are," Wyndham said. "Dirty, sweaty and bloody."

"Thank you very much," she said. "If you'd said basic and earthy, I might have been quite flattered."

He put his arms round her and held her close.

"I thought I'd never see you again," he said.

"So did I," Fiona said.

"I've nothing to offer you. This isn't the sort of game in which to have a wife."

"It doesn't matter."

"It does matter. I love you."

"I'm content with that," Fiona said.

"Things will change," he said. "After all, we've already got a great deal more than we had last night. We're both alive. We've got a certain tomorrow."

"Yes," Fiona said. "We've got tomorrow."

They stood together in the long empty hotel corridor, reluctant to move, reluctant to break away.

After a while, Wyndham opened the door and they went inside.

THE END

GUIDE
TO THE COLOUR CODING
OF
ULVERSCROFT BOOKS

Many of our readers have written to us expressing their appreciation for the way in which our colour coding has assisted them in selecting the Ulverscroft books of their choice. To remind everyone of our colour coding—this is as follows:

BLACK COVERS
Mysteries

★

BLUE COVERS
Romances

★

RED COVERS
Adventure Suspense and General Fiction

★

ORANGE COVERS
Westerns

★

GREEN COVERS
Non-Fiction

ROMANCE TITLES
in the
Ulverscroft Large Print Series

THE SHADOWS
OF THE CROWN TITLES
in the
Ulverscroft Large Print Series

The Trial of Charles I   *C. V. Wedgwood*
Royal Flush   *Margaret Irwin*
The Sceptre and the Rose   *Doris Leslie*
Mary II: Queen of England   *Hester Chapman*
That Enchantress   *Doris Leslie*
The Princess of Celle   *Jean Plaidy*
Caroline the Queen   *Jean Plaidy*
The Third George   *Jean Plaidy*
The Great Corinthian   *Doris Leslie*
Victoria in the Wings   *Jean Plaidy*
The Captive of Kensington Palace
    Jean Plaidy
The Queen and Lord 'M'   *Jean Plaidy*
The Queen's Husband   *Jean Plaidy*
The Widow of Windsor   *Jean Plaidy*
Bertie and Alix   *Graham and Heather Fisher*
The Duke of Windsor   *Ursula Bloom*